MEMPHIS MOVIE

COREY MESLER

MEMPHIS MOVIE

SOFT SKULL PRESS | AN IMPRINT OF COUNTERPOINT | BERKELEY

Library of Congress Cataloging-in-Publication Data

Mesler, Corey.
Memphis movie : a novel / Corey Mesler.
   pages ; cm
   ISBN 978-1-59376-614-6 (softcover)
1. Motion picture producers and directors—Tennessee—Memphis—Fiction. 2. Motion pictures—Tennessee—Memphis—Fiction. I. Title.
PS3613.E789M46 2015
813'.6—dc23
                                    2014048925
Cover art by Jeane Umbreit
Interior design by Elyse Strongin, Neuwirth & Associates, Inc.

SOFT SKULL PRESS
An imprint of COUNTERPOINT
2560 Ninth Street, Suite 318
Berkeley, CA 94710
www.counterpointpress.com

Printed in the United States of America
Distributed by Publishers Group West

10 9 8 7 6 5 4 3 2 1

for Cheryl, Toby and Chloe
and for Craig Brewer, Ira Sachs, and Linn Sitler
and
Willie, David, and Ed
and
BLACK LODGE VIDEO

The events and characters in this photoplay are fictitious and any resemblance to persons living or dead is coincidental.

ERIC WARBERG FILMOGRAPHY

Shlomo Stern, Boy Mystic (1981) (student film)
The Hen Man (1983) (writer only)
Situations Defined as Normal (1983) (Assistant Director)
Strangers in Love (1985)
Titanic Opera (1990) (not released)
After You I Almost Disappeared (1994)
Sunset Striptease (1995)
When I See Beverly (1997)
Dog Soup (1998)
The "Hill" Trilogy:
  Huck and Hominy (1999)
  Cracker Hobgoblin (2000)
  Diddy-Wah-Diddy (2002)
She and He in a Swivet (2003)
Spondulicks (British title: *What, Ducks?*) (2005)
Memphis Movie (working title) (2007 . . . in progress)

CAST

THE DIRECTOR: Eric Warberg
THE WRITER: Sandy Shoars
THE ACTORS: Dan Yumont, Hope Davis (as herself), Ike Bana,
  Suze Everingham, Deni Kohut, Kimberly Winks (a local), Sue
  (Lying Sue) Pine
STILL PHOTOGRAPHER: Ricky Lime
CINEMATOGRAPHER: Rica Sash
A.D.: Reuben Wickring
SET DECORATOR: Kay Tell

LOCALS: Dudu Orr, Ray Verbely, Bandy Lyle Most, Mimsy
    Borogoves, Sean Meezen
THE DRIVER: Hassle Cooley
A LOCATION SCOUT: Jimbo Cole
A MOVIE CRITIC: Luke Apenail
A LOCAL WRITER: Camel Jeremy Eros
A SPRITE: Lorax
A BORDER COLLIE: Fido
VARIOUS GHOSTS

"You can't banish the world by decree if it's in you. Is that it, Joseph?"

"How can you? You have gone to its schools and seen its movies, listened to its radios, read its magazines. What if you declare you are alienated, you say you reject the Hollywood dream, the soap opera, the cheap thriller? The very denial implicates you."

—SAUL BELLOW, from *Dangling Man*

We live two lives—one with our eyes open and one with them closed. Eyes open are for perceiving the exterior universe. Eyes shut are for exploring the inner cosmos. I spend all day with my eyes shut bumping into people and things.

—FEDERICO FELLINI

It meant nothing that Hollywood was filled with great musicians, poets and philosophers. It was also filled with spiritualists, religious nuts and swindlers. It devoured everyone, and whoever was unable to save himself in time, would lose his identity, whether he thought so himself or not.

—ERICH MARIA REMARQUE

Are ghosts dreadful because they bring toward us from the future some component . . . of our own deaths? Are they partially defectively, our own dead selves, thrust back, in recoil from the mirrorface at the end, to haunt us?

—THOMAS PYNCHON

REEL ONE: ARRIVAL

Art attracts us only by what it reveals of our most secret self.

—Jean-Luc Godard

1.

Q: So you've come back to Memphis to make a movie.

A: Yes. Is that it? Is that all you want to know?

Q: Ha, no. Why Memphis? Why now?

A: Well, Donald, I'll tell you. Memphis is ground zero for me, that is, emotionally. It is, obviously, where I came from, but it is also where my heart goes when I am in need of solace, reparation, succor.

Q: I see. Plus your last movie in Hollywood tanked.

A: Yes. Yes, it did.

Q: What happened? You were being hailed as the next—

A: Don't say it.

Q: Tarantino.

A: Shit. Yeah, I know. I got that, the next Tarantino. It's like being the next Dylan, you know? Like they called Springsteen that when he started. And, first, he had to live that down. First, he had to kill that spiritual father before he could become whatever it is he was to become.

Q: Would you say you're the Springsteen of movies?

A: Huh. But, Tarantino, you know, at first I thought Tarantino wanted to be Robert Altman—now it's clear he always wanted to be St. Spielberg. It's the same gee-whiz, eternal-child, look-at-me, everything-is-nostalgic shtick. It makes one want to throw up one's pabulum.

Q: You had a falling out.

A: No, no, I've never met the man. The whole Tarantino tag began and ended with movie critics. I think it was *Premiere* who first threw that one out there.

Q: Would you say this has been a long gap between films, a longer than usual—

A: You know, Donald, after 9/11 I found it very hard to work. Forget whether the world was waiting anxiously for another film from me. But 9/11 just blew me out of the water, creatively. I imagine other artists found themselves in similar straits—why create? The attack was the last artistic statement in a way. A negation statement. It made null future art. Or so I felt at the time. Then, someone said something to me that kicked me back into gear.

Q: That if you don't make this movie the terrorists have won?

A: No. No, not that. That was tired the second time I heard it. If you don't shop the terrorists have won. If you don't buy this car the terrorists have won. If you don't eat steak, if you don't go to the laundromat—anyway—

Q: So what was said to you?

A: A friend of mine, a writer, who was working in Prague at the time, said, Eric, buck up, you little bastard.

Q: That's it.

A: Well, I admit, as pith it lacks a certain elegance. Still, as a kick in the ass it was sufficient.

Q: Ok. So, the last movie—

A: You can call it by name. I'm not ashamed of it.

Q: *Spondulicks.*

A: A title only its progenitor could love.

Q: What does it mean?

A: Didn't you read the crabby press? Money, it means money. A subject in Hollywood more taboo than incest or child molestation.

Q: You think you opened some sores—

A: Yes, that's one way of putting it. Hollywood, even more so than Las Vegas, is a city built on greed, on making money. Say all you want about Dream Factories and such. The dollar rules. And, the irony is, that there is more money in Hollywood than in the mob's secret stashes. Pocket money out there is measured in the thousands. Tens of thousands.

Q: And your movie—

A: Besides being disrespectful to the dream, it was disrespectful of the banks. Of the deep pockets.

Q: Chris, in the movie, the character played by Peter Riegert, he seems a product of Hollywood rather than a man who dreams independently.

A: Yes, I think so. Chris, with eye on the prize, thought that if he made one more movie, one more stab at contemporary angst, he would hit it big. He was seduced by the city, by the idea that a movie could both be provocative and profitable.

Q: And his end is tragic, don't you think?

A: Tragic and inevitable.

Q: Inevitably tragic.

A: Right.

Q: So how much of Chris is you?

A: Ah, that question. I'd say about 26 percent.

Q: Ha. So, it's a question that bedevils you, one you have grown weary of.

A: Well, a friend of mine sent me a T-shirt that read, I AM NOT CHRIS.

Q: Uh-huh.

A: So, yeah, you know. I am not Chris. But I am, too. I am that piece of the dream.

Q: Do you see your end as tragic?

A: Well, I hope I haven't reached the end.

Q: No, no, I meant, in Hollywood. Do you—

A: Think I'm washed up in Hollywood? For today. You know it's also a city where a comeback is pre-programmed and expected. They count you out only to wish you to rise again someday, renewed, reinvented, the Phoenix from the flameout.

Q: Hm.

A: You know, Donald. The thing is that most filmmakers have to do the Hollywood thing once or they don't feel validated. But, really, the reality is that today, with digital, with co-ops, with every state offering film companies incentives to work there, it's all so diverse, spread out, dispersed.

Q: Do you see that as a healthy thing?

A: Well, as an independent I have to. I would be a fool not to celebrate it.

Q: Because it benefits you.

A: Yes.

Q: So, at the height of your Hollywood fame, you made . . .

A: Titanic Opera.

Q: Wha—I don't have that in my notes. Titanic Opera?

A: Well, it's become a personal in-joke.

Q: How so?

A: Well, I made this film, this epic, three and a half hours. It was gonna be my—my—

Q: *Heaven's Gate.*

A:

Q: Sorry.

A: My magnum opus. It was great, I mean really great. The cast was superb: Jon Voigt, Gene Hackman, Ellen Green, Halle Berry, Faith Glory, Blue Positive. And the photography— my God, Haskell Wexler, some of his best late work—and a sprawling, multigenerational tale, loosely based on Nabokov's *Ada*, but set in the San Fernando Valley.

Q: It sounds incredible. What happened to it?

A: It disappeared. Poof. Cut down so small, bit by bit, both sides, studio and artistic, though I was left out and given no reason, snipping, snipping, so that eventually it was shown for the first and last time between features on IFC. About four and a half minutes, I think was the final run time.

Q: Incredible.

A: Yes, I think it's some kind of record.

Q: Hm.

A: Yes.

Q: Ok, so, the new film. Let's talk about that.

A: Of course.

Q: What is its working title?

A: Curiology.

Q: What is that?

A: It means picture writing. So, an obvious pun.

Q: Do you think that will be the final title?

A: No, I learned my lesson with *Spondulicks*. We have also discussed *Potemkin Village*.

Q: Tell me why, what does that mean? An Eisenstein reference—

A: It's a city that appears as an impressive showy facade designed to mask undesirable facts.

Q: A city with dark secrets.

A: Yes, dark city secrets down its dark streets.

Q: Is this another Hollywood metaphor?

A: No, not this time.

Q: Then—

A: Well, running the risk of ruffling feathers, it's Memphis that is the dark end of the street.

Q: That's Dan Penn, our homeboy.

A: Of course.

Q: So you think that title will stick?

A: Don't know. The working title is, simply, *Memphis Movie*. Sandy wanted it to be called *S Is for Symbolism*.

Q: That's Sandy Shoars, your wife and collaborator.

A: We're not married, but, yes. My collaborator and paramour. She has written every one of my movies.

Q: And received an Independent Spirit Award for *After You I Almost Disappeared*.

A: A nomination.

Q: She didn't win?

A: No, that was the year *Sleeping in a Box* won everything.

Q: Oh, right.

A: Sandy's new script, that is, for this movie set in Memphis, is the best thing she's ever done.

Q: That's very exciting.

A: Yes, it is. It is how we get the actors we want, the power of her words. Actors relish good scripts, as they should.

Q: Hope Davis.

A: Exactly. My first choice for all my movies, but this is the first time we'll be working together. She's the right stuff.

Q: And lovely.

A: Yes.

Q: Elena Musick, Ike Bana, Suze Everingham. It's quite a cast.

A: Yes, we're very lucky.

Q: Trinka Dukes, Deni Kohut.

A: Yes.

Q: And this is the first time you'll be working with Dan Yumont.

A: Yes, it is.

Q: His reputation precedes him. How do you think he'll be to work with?

A: I don't anticipate any problems.

Q: Yet, upon his arrival in Memphis for preliminary meetings he was arrested at the airport.

A: A misunderstanding.

Q: They found a box cutter and a roach clip in his pockets.

A: He explained that.

Q: Ok.

A: Dan is a complex man, a thinking man's actor. He is this generation's De Niro.

Q: Some papers have compared him to Sean Penn—

A: Or this generation's Sean Penn, an actor of the first water—

Q: Sean Penn, of the Madonna era, I was going to say. The spitting at paparazzi, the antagonism with the press.

A: The press . . . well, best I keep myself to myself. Let's talk about the new movie—the soundtrack—

Q: And the soundtrack, you—

A: Will be all Stax.

Q: Stax—whatever—the whole Stax canon?

A: Yes.

Q: One would have thought you'd come to Memphis and use Memphis music. Is it too predictable, do you think?

A: One doesn't use unpredictability just to be unpredictable. Maybe I'll switch to a klezmer band, that suit you?

Q: Ok.

A: Donald, don't print that. I'll come off as an asshole. I love Memphis music. You know, my other films are peppered with it. Scott Bomar helped with *Sunset Striptease*. That's his deconstructed version of "Eight Miles High" at the end. There's the "Big Star" song in *Cracker Hobgoblin*. I used "Your Eyes May Shine" as the opening theme for *Huck and Hominy*. Uh, John Kilzer and Rob Jungklas in *She and He in a Swivet*. And in *After You I Almost Disappeared* that's Reverend Al covering "Big Ass Truck." How's that for Memphis mojo?

Q: I guess I didn't realize—

A: Right.

Q: Hm.

A: Amy LaVere.

Q: What about her?

A: I just wanted to say her name because I have a crush on her. Anyway. The music—

Q: Memphis is there—

A: In every film, yes. I have been, over the years, going home again and again. And now—

Q: You're literally here.

A: Yes.

Q: Let's talk about the movie.

A: Fair enough.

Q: You said in a recent interview that you were coming back to Memphis to make your next film because its themes were Southern. What did you mean by that?

A: Well, again, I don't want to give too much away. But the story concerns a man who comes up against the racism in his own family and has to make a choice between the people he came from and what his future may possibly hold, which includes a beautiful woman from New York. That's Hope Davis. She represents for him what he's never had, what he's dreamed of.

Q: The Southern angle being the racism—

A: No, no, now, don't go off on a toot. Racism isn't exclusive to the South. But for the character that Dan plays, this kind of racism, deeply ingrained in his family history, is like an anchor holding him back.

Q: I see. *Monster's Ball*—

A: Crossed with *The Reivers*. I can see the campaign already.

Q: The Hope Davis character. Is she based on anyone?

A: Anyone out there—in the real world?

Q: Yes.

A: No.

Q: Yet, she—

A: I see where you're going.

Q: Well, the tabloids were full of stories about you and Ms. Davis. That you were seen nightclubbing—

A: Is that really a verb?

Q: For our purposes.

A: The purposes being to make something salacious out of our casting Hope Davis. That Sandy would write her into our next movie as some perverse Hollywood sexual triangle thing.

Q: No, I—

A: Donald.

Q: But you and Ms. Davis—

A: I wish.

Q: Do you?

A: No, no, c'mon, Donald, be a go-with guy. I'm joking.

Q: Oh, ok. So the Hope Davis character—

A: Is based on dreamstuff, is pulled out of the same ether from which Scarlett O'Hara, Mick Kelly and Quentin Compson were pulled squalling from—

Q: I don't—

A: Move on.

Q: Right.

A: So, how you been, Donald?

Q: Fine. Fine. Oh, you're looking for more questions . . .

A: When you're ready.

Q: Ha. Ok. Um, there's a moment in one of your earlier films. The main character, a filmmaker, has just been excoriated in the press for some of his more, uh, personal sexual content. It seems he has used his own life, his own sexual history for his films.

A: Yes.

Q: So, what would you say about this character? Is he you, an aspect of you?

A: The question doesn't interest me much. But, for you, for the sake of your audience, I'll take a stab at answering. You're referring to the film *After You I Almost Disappeared*. My second feature and the first film I made after moving to Hollywood. I was homesick. I was thinking about my past. My first film, *Sunset Striptease*, had its success, you know. It took me to California where I was given a lot of money and told to do whatever I wanted. It's dangerous for an artist to be told, "Do whatever you want." [Laughs.] So, I had all this cash and was told to make a wish list of actors, which I did, putting Hope Davis at the top, of course. And I set to writing a script that would be worthy of all this freedom.

Q: Sandy didn't write this one?

A: Wait. This is a story. I am telling you a story.

Q: Sorry.

A: So, I set about writing this script and I thought, man, they're eating up everything I dish out. I am king of the fucking moviemaking universe. This is what it felt like. Yet, underneath that there was this River Styx of regret and loneliness. I mean, I had left behind everything that was what I thought of as my identity. Memphis was gone gone. So this script was all about the past, all about my past, you dig? And I wrote scene after scene based on people I knew, people I loved, women whom I loved and lost, women whom I loved and left. You know? It's such a seductive topic for a young artist, that rich soil of the past. So I turn the sucker in, I take it to the studio and say, "Here. Here's my next film and here's who I want to play each part." It's laughable now, my hubris. And Marty Sicowicz, at the studio, took this mess home with him. It took less than a day and I was called back in. He smiled a sad smile and handed me back my new masterpiece. "No," he said, and sat back. That was it. I was dumbfounded. Just no. And that really sent me reeling. So to speak. I went home, well back to this amazing house I was renting in Brentwood, and wept like a child. I was really stung.

Q: It hurt, even after all the success.

A: Yes, I was hurt. But another 24 hours went by and I went back in to see Marty. "What do I do?" I asked him. He gave me Sandy's number. And that was that.

Q: That's how you met Sandy?

A: That's it. And, it turned out, unbeknownst to me, she had been called in to doctor *Sunset Striptease*. So, when I say she wrote every one of my movies, I mean every damn one.

Q: Huh.

A: Yeah. And the finished product, the irony of the finished product is that the title is almost the only thing left from my self-indulgent script. Beverly was still there.

Q: The Hope Davis character.

A: Right, the character I wanted Hope Davis to play. Well, it's funny now, but, really, what I wanted was to visualize Hope Davis in the role of my ex-lover, a woman who was as hot as a pepper sprout

Q: And Beverly is her name.

A:

Q: Or not. I see.

A: Right.

Q: Who ended up playing Beverly? I can't recall—

A: Jodie Foster.

Q: That's not a bad fantasy lover either.

A: [Laughs.] You said it.

Q: Huh. So . . . what was I getting at? Oh, yeah. This character, this filmmaker, then. He really is you.

A: No. It's fiction.

Q: Yes, but—

A: It becomes fiction. Everything becomes fiction. Leave it out on the counter long enough and it becomes fiction.

Q: Ok.

A: That's the title of my next movie. *Everything Becomes Fiction.*

Q: Really, that sounds—

A: No, not really. I am pulling your leg.

Q: Ah.

A: Sorry.

Q: Right. Do you have an idea for a movie after this, after *Memphis Movie?*

A: I do.

Q: Can you talk about it?

A: I can.

Q: Will you?

A: Sorry. I will and now. But, with this caveat. I've been cut loose, so to speak. Hollywood has taken me off the teat, you know. So, I can't really say there will be a next movie. The monies for this one, well, have come from private investors.

Q: Folks who will get an associate producer's credit.

A: Ha! Yes. So, anyway, we are working already on our next project. Sandy has been working with a writer, a Memphis writer actually, on a screenplay based on his book.

Q: A Memphis writer? Can you say who it is?

A: I'd rather not at this point. It all could collapse like a dissolving palace of snow. But, the story concerns two middle-aged men and their private conversations. One of them, though happily married, is being tempted by a woman he has just met, tempted by the age-old demon-god, lust. He is contemplating having an affair, but a lot of the action of the story—and we're still trying to make this happen visually— is made up of dialogue.

Q: This sounds familiar.

A: Well, the book, which had no success whatsoever, is written entirely in dialogue.

Q: Ah.

A: Yes, and though that sounds like it's tailor-made for the movies, it has proven to be a sonofabitch to adapt.

Q: Do you have a cast in mind?

A: Yes, Hope Davis will be the wife . . .

Q: Of course.

A: Yes.

Q: Lovely. Well, we're about through here. Good luck on *Memphis Movie* and we're happy to have you here filming.

A: Thanks, Donald. I'm happy to be back.

2.

Eric Warberg always kept a copy of *Malone Dies* on his nightstand so that when he died people would say of him, "He died with Beckett on his nightstand." This speaks of the director's pretension but it also says something about perception, especially as it relates to the makers of movies, an art created of equal parts light and greasepaint and air-castle.

Eric was dazed to find himself back in Memphis, his hometown, the place of his birth, childhood, loss of virginity, young adulthood and tangled love-lines and embarrassments. The first morning he woke up in a strange bed, in a house in Midtown Memphis, rented for him by his ex-roommate Jimbo Cole, he had a Twilight Zone moment.

What am I doing here? he thought.

The light coming in the window was Memphis light, a distillation he could recognize in a flash. The soft buzz in the air was Memphis buzz. The tang in his sinuses was Memphis pollen, a potent blend.

Then he remembered. He had come home to make a movie. Hollywood was far away. It was on another planet, a planet he had once called home and would again. He tried not to picture himself with tail between legs. Instead, he wanted to manufacture a new self: the Returning Hero, come from foreign shores to bless his little backwater hometown with the tinsel and klieg lights of movie magic. That's the ticket, he thought. A triumphant return.

The space next to him in the bed was empty. It was emptier than a bed recently vacated.

Eric thought perhaps that Sandy had stayed up writing on her laptop and he would find her dozing in the den, head on chest. That was a sweet thought and Eric tried to hang onto it.

He stood up slowly. Time, recently, had been digging inside him with its cheap spoon. There were new aches in lower back and legs. He thought suddenly of his father, a man who was hale and hearty and seemingly indestructible until he dropped dead in his driveway while doing yard work at the age of 57. Eric had just crested 50 so the road ahead seemed suddenly dark to him, a country road. The one his father now walked toward Abraham's bosom.

After peeing and splashing his face with tepid water—Memphis water—he went in search of his lady love.

There was no Sandy in the den, no laptop, no drowsy, tender, stirring scene. The den was particularly empty of Sandy, perhaps even more so than the bed had been. Was this because Sandy was not spending as many nights in the bed as formerly? A silly notion, Eric thought.

In the kitchen he found the coffee, the coffeepot. He began the morning routine, the one he and Sandy had cobbled together over more than 20 years together. The coffee, which they had brought with them from the West Coast, was Organic Shade Grown Mexican, the only *real* coffee, as Sandy liked to say.

Right as he was set to hoist the first cup he heard the key in the front door.

Sandy met him in the foyer. She looked like she had been out all night.

This was because, of course, she had been out all night.

Hair hand-combed. Face made of old paint. Eyes like a college student cramming for a final. And her shirt was misbuttoned.

"Jesus," Eric said.

"Good morning to you, too," Sandy said back.

Eric hesitated. He stood on the threshold of a scrap. Did he want to continue? He did not. It was the same fight they had had before but not for a few years. They had both strayed—Christ, it was Hollywood—and both had wept and confessed numerous times. Lately, there had been more amity, more nights together, if not sexually (they still managed to pull it off a few times a month) then *physically*.

"I didn't think you even knew Memphis," he said after a pause.

"I'm in the bathroom, I can't hear you," she called out.

"I said, 'There's coffee,'" he called back.

3.

Eric's ex-roommate, Jimbo Cole, had been hired by the production company to scout locations. Jimbo was a real estate agent in Memphis. It was his phone call that now jangled Eric back to sense and sensibility.

"Jimbo," Eric said. His voice needed a shave.

"Hey, Buddy," Jimbo said, a tad too loudly for this early. "What say?"

Jimbo was given to these kinds of rhetorical questions. The problem was that he expected answers to them. If he greeted someone with "How are you?" he waited for the reply and assumed it would have something to do with general health and happiness.

"I say, 'It's goddamned early.' I say, 'What am I doing in Memphis?'" Eric said.

"Making a movie!" Jimbo fairly crowed.

"Right."

"So, I've been up for, let's see, about four hours now and I think I've got some homes for you to look at. Some homes that would serve as, let's see, Faith Davis's, where the big party scene will be shot."

"Hope."

"You hope?"

"Hope Davis. Yes, never mind. Great. Great, Jimbo. Lemme get dressed here and—"

"Hope Davis. Goddammit. Sorry, Eric."

Eric knew he had to make it ok.

"Jimbo, that's wonderful. You're way ahead of the curve. Great job."

"Goddammit," Jimbo said again.

"Ok, lemme just get dressed."

"Ok, Buddy." Some of the blaze in Jimbo's voice came back.

"Ok."

"Uh, listen."

"Yep."

"Can Aileen tag along?"

Aileen. Jimbo's wife. Jimbo had married Aileen Sour. Eric remembered this now. He hadn't been able to come back for the wedding because he had been filming in Fiji. He thought it was Fiji. And Jimbo had been heartbroken, having promised his wife's family that they would get to meet the director of *After You I Almost Disappeared*.

"Of course," Eric said.

"Great!"

"Pick me up in—let's say a half hour."

"Ok. I'll be there. We'll be there."

Eric hung up.

He could hear Sandy in the shower.

Sandy. What to do?

He waited for the water to stop running but it went on and on. He rapped lightly and then entered the bathroom.

"Jimbo is picking me up in half an hour," he said through the shower curtain.

"Ok. Have a good day. Call me later and we'll meet up at— where was it?"

"I don't know."

Eric felt a little dizzy. Maybe it was just the humidity in the bathroom.

"Ok," Sandy said.

"He wants Aileen to go with us," Eric said with an ironic lilt.

Silence.

"I say, he wants Aileen to go with us."

"I have no idea who Aileen is." Sandy spoke above the water.

"Jimbo's wife."

Silence.

"I say, Jimbo's wife."

"Ok."

Eric stood at the sink. In the mirror above the basin was Eric's father's face. Whiskered and lined. Sandy turned the shower off.

Eric waited. She pulled back the curtain. Sandy's body, never a model's, had grown heavy around the thighs and waist, as if extra modeling clay had been applied, yet it stirred him still. Her tangle of pubic hair, now dripping with water, looked darker and more mysterious. He knew there was grey there.

"Hand me a towel," she said.

"I—" Eric said.

He handed her one of the thick towels brought in especially by the production company at Sandy's insistence. Sandy, Eric thought, was a bit of a hedonist.

"Guess I'll get dressed," Eric said.

Sandy smiled at him. It was the sorriest excuse for a smile Eric had ever seen.

4.

Jimbo Cole was driving a rented car. He had chosen a bright red PT Cruiser. Apparently, the movie company had offered a rental and Jimbo had jumped at the chance.

"Morning, Buddy," he sang out when Eric opened the door.

"Hey, Jimbo."

"You ready to go? I've found some great homes. I think you're gonna be pleased."

"Right. Come on in a sec."

Jimbo swung his head around as if he were standing in the middle of a football field at the biggest bowl game of the year. He let out a low whistle in appreciation.

"I knew this place would suit you," he said.

Eric didn't correct him. This lavish suburban mid-century modern ranch house felt so artificial to Eric that he couldn't relax in it. The furniture looked like Jungle Room rejects.

"Want some coffee before we head out?"

"Stoked on joe," Jimbo said. "I told you, I been up for hours."

"Right."

"Take a shot of something, though."

"Uh, yeah, there's a bar, I think."

"You bet there is," Jimbo said. He located it quickly and just as quickly he was drinking something on the rocks.

Sandy entered, her hair hanging in sopping curls, a bathroom towel cinched around her that showed her somewhat large thighs to good advantage.

"Hey, Jimbo," she said with no inflection.

"Hey Sandy, you look great this morning."

Sandy walked past the men into the kitchen.

"There food in here?" she said over her shoulder.

"I don't know," Eric answered.

"You bet there is," Jimbo said. "At least, I told them to stock it good."

This was not really Jimbo's job but he was trying to become the man-on-the-ground, the Memphis Player you could count on.

Sandy bent to examine the refrigerator's contents. Both men studied her ass, Eric with end-of-the-world melancholy and Jimbo in frank appreciation.

"Great," Sandy said and walked out of the kitchen, back through the living room and down the hall.

"She's practically macrobiotic," Eric said.

"See you tonight," Jimbo called after her.

The men left through the front door.

"What's tonight?" Eric asked as they got into the car.

"Film Commission kickoff party."

"Fuck," Eric said.

5.

"Where's Aileen?" Eric asked as Jimbo piloted the car down Poplar Avenue.

"We're picking her up at Kimberly's."

"Jesus Christ, Jimbo," Eric said.

Kimberly Winks was an ex-girlfriend of Eric's. She was also an actress and had been given a small part in the film, against Eric's express wishes. She knew someone who knew someone and had wrangled a bit part. Sandy was still writing and rewriting her few lines, trying in her way to undermine the starlet. Eric had been hoping to avoid Kimberly Winks at all costs. Their relationship, which she ended abruptly and without explanation, was still a sore spot in Eric's past, a blur in the colored ink of his heart's map. Because she had walked away from what Eric had thought was a good relationship—lots of laughs, lots of sex—and never said why and refused all communication for years, Eric hated her. He hated her just as hard as his ennui would allow.

"What? I thought it would be great since we're all working together now," Jimbo said. "Hey, you wanna stop off at Houston's for a beer first?"

"It's 11 a.m.," Eric said, peevishly.

"Ok," Jimbo said. He knit his brow for a moment. Then his smile crept back into place like a dog reprimanded who knows he is still the favored pet.

Surprisingly, Kimberly Winks still lived in the same house where she had lived two decades or more earlier when she and Eric had been an item. It was a house willed to her by her parents who were both killed in a car accident on Mendenhall Road within a mile from home. It was not the house she grew up in, she was quick to tell anyone interested; that house, which was burnt to the ground when the family was on vacation, was in a tonier neighborhood in Germantown. Jimbo pulled into the driveway as if he had been coming here for years.

He honked the horn once and turned to look at Eric.

"You wanna go in?" he asked.

"No," Eric said. What he really wanted was to go back to Hollywood, eat shit and get a job on a no-budget Disney film or TV show remake or Showtime production. He wanted to kick himself in the ass every morning for the rest of his days and die of skin cancer and be memorialized posthumously with an autographed photo hung at Planet Hollywood. For this moment what he wanted was for Kimberly Winks to not walk out that door and back into his life. He wanted her to forever not walk out that door.

Kimberly Winks walked out the door.

She stood in the bright sunshine and put her forearm to her forehead to shade her eyes. "Eric?" she twittered.

She looked great. Eric hated her now more than ever.

"Hey, Kim," Jimbo called out.

"Hey, Jimbo."

Behind Kimberly Winks's shoulder Aileen's little otter face appeared. She had a black eye.

"Eric, get out of that car," Kimberly said now.

In the sun the dress she was wearing appeared to be gossamer, or perhaps spider webs. Kimberly must have been past 40 by now but she looked 25. She still had her figure, a body that made Eric roil inside as if he had eaten some bad broccoli. She was blonde and white. Her hair was cornsilk and her pale face was expertly dotted with freckles. Her mouth was wide and full-lipped. She was as beautiful as a yellow egg.

He reluctantly unfolded himself from the passenger seat of the PT Cruiser.

"Hello, Kimberly," he said.

She worked her way around the car and put her arms around Eric's neck.

"Oh, I'm so proud of you," she said into his hair.

"And you, look at you landing a part in my film," he said. Suddenly he hated himself also.

"Oh, it's just a little bitty part," Kimberly said. "I tried out for Mandy."

Eric couldn't remember who Mandy was. A character in his movie presumably.

"What are y'all doing this morning?" Kimberly asked.

"Jimbo's scouting locations for us. He's found a few houses for us to look at."

"Don't y'all do that like way ahead of time?"

"Yes," Eric said. His weariness made every word a weight. "There has already been groundwork done for us and filming will start almost right away. However, in small productions like this, it is common to fly by the seat of the pants, finding the right locations quickly and shooting and moving on. It's economic more than anything."

He was boring her on purpose. Because she bored him.

He also wanted to see her naked again right away.

"Well, do y'all mind if I tag along?"

She had already used up her day's worth of y'alls.

"Sure, it's apparently a delegation," Eric said.

"Hello, Eric," Aileen said in her soft, brown voice.

"Hi, Aileen." He bussed her cheek.

"So Hollywood," was her comment.

"Kissing the cheek is Hollywood?" Eric asked.

"Let's roll," Jimbo said. Then after a moment, "Now that's real Hollywood talk. Let's roll."

The women took the back seat. At least that. Eric didn't think he could stand being in the back seat alone with Kimberly Winks.

The drive was pleasant enough. It was a crisp day—Eric thought they called such days crisp—and they drove with the windows down. The houses Jimbo had chosen seemed to all be in a small area of East Memphis. And they all looked alike. Mostly Eric signaled Jimbo to just slow down and then he waved him on. The coffee he had consumed earlier was a small flame behind his sternum.

They stopped at one home. Kimberly and Eric stood alone in the bedroom. Eric was trying to visualize the scene he wanted to shoot there. Kimberly was doing her best to stay quiet while the genius worked. In truth Eric couldn't remember the scene exactly, something about an early morning disagreement . . . no, that was another character.

Eric sighed.

Kimberly Winks took it as an opening.

"So who's playing Mandy?" she said right at his shoulder.

He looked at her with the look that had withered many a grip.

She didn't wither. Her broad, bright face made Eric want to cry.

"Suze Everingham."

"I don't know her."

"She's very good. *Guns Along Main Street. The Escapers.*"

"I didn't see those."

"She's quite good."

"Is she pretty?"

"Oh, yes," Eric said. He tried to bring his focus back to the task at hand.

"Prettier than me?"

Now he turned toward her slowly.

"Kimberly, you gotta understand how these things work. Suze Everingham has a track record, a fan base even. She's a known quantity. Known quantities get films made. The money is there for known quantities alone."

"I don't understand any of it except that my lover is the director." She allowed herself a sly smile, as if to say, you and I understand each other.

"Ex, yes," Eric said. He was tiring of Kimberly already.

"Oh, Eric, there's a part of us that is still alive, don't you feel it?"

"Do you really want to do this here, now?"

"Certainly," Kimberly said and sidled up to him. She actually sidled.

They were in a bedroom in a strange house. In the other room Jimbo and Aileen were laughing in loud snorts.

Kimberly sat on the edge of the strangers' bed. She crossed her still beautiful legs.

"First, and this is just first, not having anything to do with how movies are made, first, you dumped me without rhyme or reason. Many, many years ago, you dumped me."

"Eric, sit here," Kimberly patted the bed as if calling a dog.

Eric reluctantly sat.

"I had my reasons. Don't think it was easy for me."

"Ok. Let's have them. You could have given them to me years ago and I wouldn't have had to live with this hole in my life, a hole of uncertainty that spreads like a stain—"

"You say the prettiest things."

"So, that hole, forget that hole. Now you wanna talk to me. Now that I have returned. Now that I am making a movie, a movie, it does not escape me, that you would like to have a part in."

Eric was almost too weary to form the words.

He picked an Ativan out of the small quantity he kept in his pocket and fisted it into his mouth, surreptitiously, bringing a small amount of lint up, too.

"So, you think I only want a part."

"Yes. That is what I think."

"Oh, hmp."

"Yes, there it is."

"You poor sweet thing. You know I don't think a week's gone by that I haven't thought about you."

"I find that incredible, Kim. I find that without merit."

"Oh, Babe."

"Don't call me Babe."

"I always, I always—"

"I know. It's dead. The name is as dead as Carole Lombard."

"Why Carole Lombard?"

"I don't know, she's always seemed deader than most other stars, perhaps because she died so long ago, at such a young age. Partly because I wish I had known her."

"Oh, Ba—sorry, Eric—listen. I think we need to hash this out. If we're gonna work together."

"I don't—"

"There's a fucking water bed in this other room. Did you see this?" Jimbo was in the doorway.

"Huh—" Eric said, rising.

"Oh, sorry—"

"We're just about—"

"Did you two want this room, that is, do you want us to ride around some?"

"Jimbo. I think we've seen enough here."

"Oh—ok—you like this one?"

"It's ok. Let's see something else. This room is right but I don't like that patio. It looks like something from an Elvis movie."

6.

The quartet stopped at Houston's for lunch. Jimbo's choice. Aileen knew the cook there. It was a dreadful place full of loud diners all dressed in chic casual and all forking oversize portions into their prattling gobs while their wilding children spat food into the aisles and the waitpeople sang and bopped and skipped and the muzak was all Golden Oldies done by soulless muzak bands. Eric thought it was how Hollywood phony culture had become mainstream Americana. He felt dead, dead.

They shared a pitcher, of which Jimbo drank a full half before ordering another.

"So, Scout, what do you think of Atticus, here?" Jimbo asked Kimberly.

"Wouldn't that work better if you said Scout and Jim? I mean, Eric is not her father, nor even a father figure." Aileen smiled at her husband.

"Whatever," he answered her with a sour twist to his mouth.

"It's great to have him back. And to see y'all, too," Kimberly said, smiling her Beauty Queen smile.

"It's been a long time," Aileen said.

"Kim, how come you're not married? I mean, how come you live where you always lived."

"First, Jimbo. No one calls me Kim except Eric. And secondly,

I was married. And we lived in that same house. Funny, huh? I've lived there my entire adult life."

"You were married?" Jimbo said, throwing back some beer.

"I was. Dreadful."

"Dreadful, as in the whole damn institution or just your singular experience?" Jimbo could keep up this kind of chatter for days.

"Both, I guess. He was a real asshole. All my friends told me so. I wanted to get married. Silly, really."

"This was when?"

"Oh." Kimberly waved a hand in the air.

"Right after Eric, right?"

"Y-yes, it was. Shortly afterward."

Eric opened his mouth. No sound came out. Kimberly looked at him with apprehension.

"I know, I know. I told you I didn't want to get serious. I didn't. I can't explain. Richard just came along at the right time when I was feeling at sea and I had no plans and, well, he seemed like the right square to jump to."

"Mixed metaphors aside, Kim, it doesn't matter," Eric said.

Kimberly eyed him as if he were the judge who had just voted her off the island.

"Don't correct my grammar, Mr. Hollywood." Just as suddenly she switched emotional tracks. "Honey, I wasn't right for you then. Didn't you sense it?"

"No, frankly, I didn't," Eric said.

The food arrived then and there was silence while the waitress, a buxom pre-med student, smiled and made phatic conversation, mostly, it seemed, to herself.

"Dig in, comrades," Jimbo said, his fork tearing into the greasy, overcooked pork of a pile of baby back ribs, slathered in spicy red barbecue sauce.

Eric wasn't finished talking. Now that the box had been opened he wanted all the devils out at once.

"I assuredly did not sense it. You left me for no reason. We were sailing along, I was getting very seriously wrapped up in you, as you well knew, and you turned and ran. Still today I wonder why. We seemed, for a brief fiery time, to be just right for each other."

"Sweet," Kimberly said, laying her own fork back down. "You were just more mature than me. I was a kid, I didn't know what I wanted. If I had thought I broke your heart—"

"Kim, you know damn well you broke my heart. I called you something like 20 times and said, 'Kim, you're breaking my heart.' That seems pretty clear. You wouldn't even talk to me."

Kimberly appeared to sulk.

"Woody Allen says 50 percent of life is just showing up," she said, after a pause.

"I don't know what that means."

Kimberly smiled a weak smile.

"You didn't show up," Eric said. "That was just it. Suddenly, you stopped showing up."

The other 50 percent, someone had told Eric once—who?—was having the right office supplies.

Aileen was looking at her plate in embarrassment. Jimbo was tucking it away.

"Ok," Kimberly said. "Ok. Here it is. I was seeing a married man."

The silence at the table was gelid. Even Jimbo stopped moving.

"At the same time I was seeing you I was seeing this married man. He had told me, look, Kimberly, I am happily married, so if you want to do this it will be just sex. And I did want him, even in those circumstances. It was awful, a terrible situation. He would have sex with me, kiss my cheek and return home. And I would lie there and cry and cry. Eric, if you'd only known."

"Yes, if I had I could have dropped you like a replete leech."

"I don't know what that means but it sounds nasty. I guess you want to be nasty to me." Kimberly began to cry quietly. Eric was stunned.

"Ok, Kim. Ok. Stop. Let's eat and go. Ok?"

Kimberly was making little mewing sounds. Aileen reached across the table and gently took her wrist, circling it with her fingers as if with handcuffs.

"What happened with you and the married man?" Jimbo broke the silence.

"I married Richard to get away from him."

"Ok," Eric said, apropos of nothing.

Kimberly snuffled into a Kleenex.

"Check," Eric called out when he spotted their waitress.

She bounced over. Her smile was frightening. She placed a warm hand on Eric's shoulder and looked into his eyes.

"Just the check, please," he said.

"You're Eric Warberg," she said.

7.

Eric's cell phone was pregnant with too many messages. He thought it a good idea to return the calls right away. If nothing else it would protect him from the babble in the PT Cruiser.

"Linn Sitler's office."

"Hi, it's Eric Warberg."

"Eric, yes, lemme get her."

Linn Sitler, a woman of infinite energy and generosity, was the head of the Memphis Film Commission.

"Eric, hey."

"Hey, you called about tonight?"

"I did. Just wanted to make sure you had everything you need, directions, etc."

"Yes, yes, I think so."

"Ok."

"Ok."

"Eric, listen. Little problem."

"Shoot."

"Dan Yumont never checked into his hotel."

"Christ."

"Yeah, I—"

"I'll handle it. Thanks."

"Ok, see you tonight."

Eric hung up. He put a forbidding finger up to stop Jimbo's anxious question. He next called back Ricky Lime, the still photographer for the movie. Ricky was hired after Bill Eggleston opted out. Eric didn't know Ricky and though he had no reason to not trust him, he didn't trust him.

"Hey, Ricky, it's Eric Warberg."

"Eric, I think we need to talk."

"What's up, Ricky?"

"I have to show you something."

"Can it wait? I'm looking at houses with Jimbo Cole."

"Um, yes. I guess so. Yes, I guess it can wait. But not long. I—I don't quite know how to proceed from here."

"Trouble with the locations?"

"No, not exactly."

Why was everyone so exasperating? Eric thought.

"What—exactly?"

"I have to show you something."

"You said that."

"Ok. I can wait."

"Keep taking pictures, Ricky."

"I'm not sure I can do that, Eric. I'm—I'm afraid."

Eric hung up. Jesus.

"How about the place on Audubon?" Jimbo shot out before Eric could begin another call.

"Yes, ok," Eric said.

There were calls from a couple of the stars. They wanted reassurance. Reassurance that the film was still on. Reassurance that there was money. Reassurance that they had the talent to assay their roles. Reassurance that the Big Earthquake scheduled for Memphis wouldn't hit in the next month or six weeks. Eric spent half an hour making his actors feel okay about the unsophisticated town where they had just arrived.

There was no call from Hope Davis. Eric wanted to call her anyway but didn't.

There was also a call from Eden Forbes, the Arizona moneyman. He had made his money in cattle, which Eric found hilarious, a cowboy entrepreneur. Eric didn't imagine that men still made money from cattle. He pictured John Wayne in *Red River*, driving his herd relentlessly to market, men and weather and Indians be damned. Eden Forbes wanted to get into the motion picture business in the worst way, even if it meant giving money to a director who had produced an expensive flop and was going home to Memphis, Tennessee, to lick his wounds and make his next film.

Eric didn't really want to talk to Eden. He felt like a high-schooler called into the principal's office, even though Eden was such a suck-up that he groveled at the feet of Eric Warberg.

"Hi, Eden."

"Hey, Buddy. You in Memphis?"

"Yes, Eden."

"You all got what you need? You got everything you need? Cuz if you don't you need to holler. I don't want this to be a second-rate production. You know that, right?"

"I do, Eden. I appreciate you." He didn't want to mention to Eden Forbes that Dan Yumont was missing.

"That's my Buddy. Sorry I can't be there at the launch party tonight. Gotta court date here. Trying to shake wife number five so I can marry number six."

Eric didn't know if this was a joke or not so he tried a tentative laugh, half bark.

"Har har, that's right, Buddy. You stick with that fine woman of yours."

"Thank you, Eden, I will."

Eden Forbes, of course, had never met Sandy.

"Eden Forbes says you're a fine woman," Eric said to Sandy, his next phone call.

"Fuck him," Sandy said.

"Where are you, dear?" Eric said with an ersatz trill.

"I'm writing. I'm at this picturesque, comfortable habitat writing."

"Ok," Eric said. "You wanna meet us later—"

Sandy had hung up.

"This is my favorite," Jimbo said, pulling into a driveway.

Jesus God, Eric thought. Drive me out of this nightmare.

8.

The search for Dan Yumont had begun that morning. Linn Sitler sent out a team of young filmmaker wannabes who hung around her office. They were instructed to scour the city beginning with the hospitals and police stations and then the bars and sleaze joints. Dan Yumont had been arrested twice before for picking up prostitutes. And once for possession of a firearm without a permit. This was common knowledge, mythopoeic tabloid fodder like Britney Spears occasionally forgetting her panties, or Mel Gibson sometimes turning into Adolf Eichmann when he drinks.

One of the young reconnaissance filmmakers was named Bandy Lyle Most. Word around the city, at the local independent film groups and at the Media Co-op at First Congo Church, was that Bandy Most was the most talented filmmaker to come from Memphis since, well, Eric Warberg. This reputation was based on one short film he made while a student at the University of Memphis. It was called *Madam Sabat's Grave*. Its status was just aborning. For now, Bandy was working at Black Lodge Video. He was known for his arcane recommendations and for pushing Alain Delon movies on lovely young co-eds who thought they wanted to see Mario Bava films instead.

Another member of the search team, at the other end of the achievement spectrum, was a mad young Turk named Hassle Cooley. Most people assumed that the name Hassle came from his reputation as a pain in the ass, but it was actually his given name and, perhaps, had prefigured its owner's temperament. Hassle was 27 years old and had hung on the fringes of Memphis's fringe film groups for years. He seemed to be at every film showing, at every media event, at every art show opening. He was purported to be working on a "mammoth, truth-telling motherfucker of a film," loosely based on *Birth of a Nation*. The film was more rumor than full-fledged proposal.

Out into the bright sunshine of Memphis, Tennessee, went our intrepid searchers. They saw much that was of interest, especially in the rent-by-the-hour motels. Hassle Cooley was first on that scene and was trying to claim all the hookers' stories as grist for his mill alone. One hooker, after only a brief chat with Hassle, was heard to say, "If this fucker wants a pop, it's double."

By late afternoon they had all returned to base. No word of Dan Yumont had they heard. The trail began and ended with the airport search of his bags. Dan Yumont, for all intents and purposes, for now, had vanished.

9.

After Eric and crew had seen the house on Audubon, a nice enough spot but horrible for shooting, with low windows and an almost underground feel to it, they were about to split up and go their separate ways. Eric declared he wanted a lie-down before the party that night.

"Eric, you wanna lie down at my house?" Kimberly asked. "It's quiet there. I won't bother you at all."

Eric was tempted. He saw it all complete before him, the opening credits, the establishing shot, the story line as it stretched out like a red thread, and the smashing downfall of the leading man, who ends up disgraced, embarrassed, cursed and alone.

"Thanks, Kim, I need to get back to my headquarters."

Headquarters? God.

"Ok, Baby," Kimberly said, placing her hand on his forearm. "You know where to find me."

This was the same woman who for years wouldn't return his phone calls or letters.

Once back in his own digs, having dismissed Jimbo with the admonition to pick him up late—not early—for the festivities that evening, Eric wondered at the silence, the stillness of his temporary home.

"Hon," he called softly.

The only answer was the susurrus of the overhead fan.

He headed for the bedroom to lie down in the dark. There he found Sandy, asleep, her mouthed cocked open and drooling. On her chest a sheaf of papers.

Eric tiptoed to the bed. He gently extricated the sheets and took them out to the living room.

Once he was seated and his reading glasses nosed, he read:

—Good.

—Saskia. I've just discovered I like to say your name.

—Many people do. It's an odd name, isn't it?

—Well, I don't know any others. Saskia. Where does it come from?

—Company my father works for.

—That's the name of the company?

—Yes. Art historians.

—A company of art historians? Doing what?

—Providing images—art for—heck, you know, I'm not sure I can explain it.

—That's ok.

—They license images, Jack.

—Ok.

—Right. What do your parents do, Jack? Are you from here, Jack?

—Born in Niagara Falls, New York. My father worked for E. I. DuPont and was transferred to Memphis when I was five. A sort of Southerner. My accent falls somewhere along the highway between New York and Tennessee. An Ohio accent, maybe.

—And your mom?

—Does your mom work?

—She's a college professor.

—Huh.

—Why?

—Mine's a homemaker, through and through. Her generation.

—I think my parents are a little younger than yours.

—Probably. What does your mother teach?

—Russian studies.

—Huh.

—What were we saying—before the waiter—I had something—

—Shiva.

—No—oh, half empty. Are you really that downbeat or are you being ironic? This is the age of irony and sometimes I don't always get it. Not that I'm dense. It's—

—No, I wasn't being ironic. I don't think. I mean, really, I just think—well, that things are serious, that being serious is a, in a way, positive approach to the world.

—And if you're a half-full kind of person? You're not taking things seriously enough?

—To be honest, I'm not really a half-empty kind of guy, either. I don't think the glass has ever had a damn drop in it. And, well, I'm not judging, mind you.

—Aren't you? Aren't you saying that if you are light-hearted you're not paying attention?

Eric put the pages down. It was good. Sandy was good. He didn't really have to remind himself of this. She had been at the top of her craft for decades now and he was lucky to have her. But, there was the other thing: the love thing, the sex thing. Wasn't it always that way? Respect isn't enough. Amity isn't even enough. There has to be love and there has to be sex.

Eric placed his glasses on top of the papers. He put his head down, not really expecting to fall asleep sitting up, chin on chest, but he did. He fell fast asleep and immediately slithered into a dream in which he was called up on stage to sing with Booker T. and the MGs and he had neglected to tell everyone that he could not sing. The spotlight hit him—he was expected to sing, because it was all riding on him, because he was in charge, the whole show, the whole enterprise, was resting solely on his ability to sing . . .

He woke up around 6 p.m. His neck hurt like hell. The light was muted, seeping in like syrup under the heavy drapes.

Sandy was in the kitchen making coffee.

"Hey, Bunky," she said, softly. "Coffee and cake? They've got some pretty nice chocolate cake in here."

"Yes, thanks," Eric said, shaking the cobwebs away. "How long did I sleep?"

"Dunno, don't know what time you came in."

"Oh, yeah. Oh. Wait. The pages—they're wonderful. Just the right touch for Hope's character. You've really nailed it."

"Thanks, Bunky, My Little Cabbage. Come get some cake."

Eric struggled out of the recliner. His bones hurt. After he rose he picked up the pages to take them to the kitchen table. Something fell out from between the pages.

Eric groaned as he bent to pick it up. It was a photograph.

"What's this?"

Sandy looked up from her cake.

"Ricky Lime brought that by. Look at it."

Eric went back and put his reading glasses on. The photograph was of a city street, a shot down one sidewalk, street with moderate traffic on the right side. There was a sign in the foreground. Central Barbecue.

"So?" Eric said, settling down. He picked up his coffee. "Thanks, Sweet," he said.

"There's a ghost in the picture."

"What, this blur?"

"Uh-huh."

"So Lime isn't the best still photographer. I'll get him replaced. I don't know where he came from anyway."

"No, no, look closer. The—ghost—"

"Is—oh, no—is wearing a white cape."

"Yep."

"A white, spangled cape and jumpsuit."

"Yep, that's the puppy."

"It's blurry."

"Well. He's been dead for so long."

10.

The Film Commission sent a limousine to pick up Eric and Sandy. The limousine driver handed Eric a note. It read: DAN YUMONT STILL NOT FOUND.

Eric sighed.

The driver smiled as if he were driving a hearse.

He handed Eric a second note.

Eric studied the messenger. He had that lean and hungry look, the one most often associated, in Eric's experience, with someone who wants to break into films.

"Thanks," Eric said, investing the simple word with as much endgame as he could muster.

The second note was from Eden Forbes. Why didn't he just call Eric's cell?

It read: DIDN'T WANT TO CALL CELL IN CASE SANDY ANSWERED. I WANT YOU TO ADD MEMPHIS WRITER TO SCRIPT. NEED MORE LOCAL FLAVOR OF WHICH SANDY HAS NIL.

Oh, this was gonna go over well. Eric looked at his paramour. He smiled a tight smile.

"Who's that one from?" Sandy asked. She was dressed in a gown so low-cut that a fingernail-paring-size slice of aureole was visible on either side.

"No one," Eric said.

"Hm," Sandy said. "Is no one female?"

"Now, there's a question."

"Hm," Sandy hmmed. She had already lost interest in the query.

"Why this note passing like we're in school?" Eric mused out loud. Had he mused it out loud? He thought so, though Sandy moved not.

"Everything all right?" the limousine driver asked.

Eric studied his eyes in the mirror. Even his eyes were lean and hungry.

"Yes, thanks," Eric said into the mirror.

"My name's Hassle Cooley," the driver said into the mirror.

"Hassle. Cooley."

"Right."

"Ok. Thanks, Hassle."

"No hassle," Hassle Cooley said.

"Ha. That's funny," Eric said.

Sandy rolled her heavily made-up eyes.

"I make movies, too," Hassle Cooley said.

"Ah," Eric said.

"Maybe later I can tell you about a couple of projects I have in mind."

"Sure."

"Really?"

"Yes, why not?" Eric said.

"You won't be sorry," Hassle Cooley said.

Eric was always sorry.

11.

The party to celebrate the launch of *Memphis Movie* was held in a downtown restaurant called the Arcade. The restaurant sat on South Main, across from the Amtrak Station with its gorgeous and frightening architecture. The building adjacent to the station loomed high above the street, gothic and unkempt, its dirty stone like a hanging garden of soot and age.

The Arcade itself, though unpromising from the outside, inside was a bit of a Memphis time machine: quaint and funky, alive with Memphis mojo and serving up the best hummus in the city. Its walls were obscured by a plethora of photographs of Memphis greats: Elvis, Rufus Thomas, B.B. King, Big Star, and a new addition, a lovely dun-tinged photo of the recently deceased Arthur Lee. The restaurant was closed for the movie party and the two shotgun rooms of the place were packed so tight it was impossible to move. In each booth sat at least six people, animated to the point of public disgrace, creating, overall, a din akin to the roar in the Roman Colosseum during a bloodletting.

Eric and Sandy were greeted by loud shouts and incoherent toasts as they entered. At the doorway stood someone from Linn Sitler's office, a lovely young woman named Mimsy Borogoves. She offered Eric a soft, thin hand, which he took the way a retriever takes a shot dove into its mouth, gently, with only a deeply buried desire to crush it. Was it Eric's imagination, or did the young beauty hold his hand a little too long, a dangerous half-minute longer than she had held Sandy's?

They had reserved a place at the head of a long table for Sandy and Eric. When they were seated plates of appetizers were placed before them. Sandy immediately began to eat. Her appetite recently was something to behold.

Eric eschewed the food and looked up and down the main table. Here were the chief ingredients for *Memphis Movie*. The actors; the cinematographer, Rica Sash, whom Eric had never worked with but was excited to get the chance, Rica having just the previous year shot the new Roman Polanski film, for which he had received an Oscar nomination; Ricky Lime, looking worried and smug simultaneously; much of the crew; and in the chair marked for Eden Forbes sat a round little man with eyes like a tax accountant's. Eric made a mental note to avoid him.

Eric ad-libbed a little speech. It was a short conglom of fervent words. Five minutes after he sat down he couldn't remember what he'd said. Had he said anything worthwhile? Anything new? Did it matter?

Sandy was asked if she wanted to add anything, after being introduced as "Eric's wife and writing partner." She waved a half-eaten chicken wing in the air, signaling that she would rather not speak. A small phobia of Sandy's, the getting up in front of crowds. Eric hated it too, but it never frightened him. He had about him a bit of the ham.

Later, in the crush of the crowd, Ricky Lime pressed up against Eric and breathed heavily into his ear.

"Did you see the picture I sent over?"

Eric nodded.

"What do you think?" Ricky fairly shouted.

"Can we talk later? It's hot as hell in here."

"I have more. Nearly 50 percent of the shots have some kind of—of anomalous image in them."

Eric nodded. He wasn't sure if he was agreeing to anything. He just wanted to get out of there.

"Some younger, some older," Ricky was saying now. Had Eric missed part of it? "When can we get together? I also think I'm being followed."

Eric nodded one last time. As soon as he could he would have Lime fired and replaced with—anybody.

Eric greeted most of the cast at least briefly. Kimberly Winks seemed to spend most of the evening in tight conversation with Ike Bana. Eric could only imagine what delicious ambition was being generated between them. At least he was spared Kim for the night. Many of the actors were expressing overly ardent worry about Dan Yumont. Eric was all calm reassurance. He felt, actually, something less than calm about it. A small qualm, would be how he would put it.

At the end of the evening, he pulled Hope Davis outside. They stood on the sidewalk under the neon and Eric felt a bit less harried outside in the relative quiet.

"So, how do you like Memphis?" Eric was suddenly a high school nerd looking for a date.

"What I've seen is charming." Hope Davis spoke in her Hope Davis voice. Eric's heart fell through his body like a cake dropped from a second-story window.

"It can be. Charming, that is."

"Yes, you grew up here, right?"

"I did. If I grew up."

Hope Davis laughed a warm and polite laugh and placed her hand on Eric's bicep.

"Now I think I'm ready to crash for the night," Hope Davis said.

"Is your room nice? Did they do right by you?"

"Oh, yes. The Peabody. The view of the river is quite—quite hypnotizing."

"Sleep well," Eric said.

Sleep well. Shit.

Where was Sandy? Did it matter whether he waited for her or not? How far had they gone down *that* road?

Eric could see the maniac limo driver across the street grinning like an ambitious Moonie.

Just as he was about to start for the car a hand arrested him by grabbing the back of his shirt. It was a disconcerting, though oddly sensuous feeling.

Eric turned and was staring into the exquisite face of Mimsy Borogoves. She had pale skin with a natural rose blush to her cheeks and eyes the color of luminous fish scales. Her hair was a soft brown nest.

"You don't remember me," she said.

"I—I don't."

"When you came back in . . . uh, 2000, to give a workshop at the U of M."

"I—"

"There's no reason you should remember me. You must have talked to hundreds of people that night. You said something that night, a joke that flopped, that I have remembered ever since. Some hotshot young actor challenged you concerning Memphis's theater history, something about you not supporting local actors enough. And—do you remember this?—the young Turk made a reference to the Memphis State production of *Hair*, how groundbreaking it was and—"

"I don't—"

"The punch line, anyway, was, 'You, sir, are no Keith Kennedy.'"

"Ah."

"I think I was the only one who laughed."

"A joke too insider to make a ripple."

"It still makes me laugh."

"Ah—afterward—at that professor's house—"

"Yes."

"You were—well, you were a child."

"I was 19."

"Yes, but—"

"I know. Late bloomer."

"Well."

"Yes, I just—I wanted to say, that talk that night, it sorta changed my life. I dropped literature as my major and went full-steam into film. I graduated last spring."

"Well—aren't you the big girl now?"

There was a pause—and then they both laughed at the ridiculous phrasing.

"You've really turned into a beautiful woman."

"The swan from the duckling."

"Not exactly that—"

"It's ok. I'm enjoying blowing off all the guys who didn't look at me just five years ago."

"Ha! I imagine that is a distinct pleasure."

"It is."

"And now you—you work for Linn?"

"Linn? Oh—"

"How's that going?"

"Oh, it's wonderful. I get to do so many—creative things. And I get to meet you again."

There was a modicum of warmth to that last phrase. Sexual?

"I am happy for that as well," Eric said. Just in case he faked a flirtatious geniality.

"I got Kimberly Winks put on the picture," Mimsy added.

12.

Eric rode back to the house alone in the limo. Alone except for Hassle Cooley, whose anxious eyes appeared to Eric like T.J. Eckleburg's peering down in judgment over the valley of ashes.

The filmmaker-driver outlined one of his many movie proposals. He said he had "scads of ideas, ideas raining down like falling angels." Eric squirmed at the metaphor.

"Here's one, and I'm just grabbing one off the top of the pile, so to speak, right?" He was holding Eric's eye in the mirror. Eric answered quickly, if only to prevent them from plowing into an oncoming car.

"A sequel to The Fly, ok? Except rather than the transformation making the poor mad scientist into something superhuman, and evil, like the Jeff Goldblum version, the fly DNA only makes him pissy and annoying. Get it? He, like, he shows up at dinner time without asking. Or makes phone calls at inopportune times. Or tries to talk to you when you're like two or three pages from the end of a book. See? Little annoyances. Like he hangs around wherever food is. And he talks in this sort of incessant drone. He kinda hums. He's just annoying but he doesn't realize he is."

Like a wannabe director buttonholing someone in a limousine.

Actually, Eric had to laugh at the idea. It was clever. Of course it would make a one-note movie but there were dozens of one-note movies playing right now. Hollywood wasn't making anything more complex than this and they were laughing all the way to the bank.

"That's very clever," Eric said.

"You laughed," Hassle Cooley said.

"I'm sorry, I—"

"No, I meant it to be funny. See, it's a comedy?"

Eric was suddenly very, very weary of the talk. And the constant need for reassurance this poor sap exhibited. They all exhibited this—the wannabes—the draw of Hollywood was too damn seductive.

"I'm very tired," he said.

"Right. Be there in two beats. One and a half beats maybe at this hour."

"Thank you," Eric said.

"No, thank you," Hassle Cooley said, inflection-less.

Eric couldn't read the madman's answers, couldn't find the correct nuance. Perhaps he was just tired. Or perhaps Hassle Cooley just wasn't that good at social intercourse.

Eric closed his eyes.

He woke up in Hassle Cooley's arms. The fool was carrying him to bed.

13.

Dan Yumont woke up in a strange bed. Should you call it a strange bed when he was used to waking up in beds that were not his?

Dan squinted. It was a trademark of his. Dan Yumont's squint was right up there with Audrey Hepburn's neck. Or Clark Gable's pursed lips. Or Jimmy Stewart's stammer.

He squinted and what he saw was a blonde head on the pillow next to him. Looked like real blonde, too. The light coming in the window was lemonade light. The room was decorated with posters of rock stars and school pictures with glitter hearts around them and red and blue bunting. It looked like the room of a teenager because it was the room of a teenager.

Dan sighed. Her name?

Donna? Zora? Dora? Dudu? Surely not Dudu.

He met her at a bar called the Buccaneer. Now he remembered. She wore a see-through shirt made all but invisible by her sweat. She was really sweating. She was dancing to the music of a band called Great Bear. Now she was naked beside him in a room that looked like the top of a birthday cake. She looked like birthday cake. Dan pulled the covers up to admire her one more time.

He reached for his cigarettes on the nightstand.

"Hello, Lover," the sleepy voice beside him exhaled.

"Good morning," Dan said, putting a cigarette in his mouth.

The blonde's upper lip was stuck to her upper teeth. She looked like a feral dog.

Dan offered her a cigarette.

"I don't smoke, Sweetie. We talked about that last night. It would play hell with my cheerleading."

"Of course," Dan said.

"And, really, if you smoke in my room my mom might smell it."

Dan Yumont felt ill. He looked at the teen again. She really was pretty, in that Southern Sorority Sister way.

"Listen—" Dan said.

After quite a pause she said, "Dudu."

"Your name really is Dudu?"

"Nickname."

"Ah."

"Oh, real name Sanhedrin. Sanhedrin Orr."

"Right. Listen, um, Dudu. This is on the QT, right?"

"Sure, Baby."

"Ok, then."

Dan pulled the covers back for one parting look. Dudu smiled with the confidence of youth. Of course the man would want to look at her body. She had tits like Marilyn Monroe. Dan thought he had better take her one more time since he would never see her again.

"Ooh," she said as his intentions became clear. "Remember, really quiet."

Then after a few moments, just as Dan was digging in, "When are we due on the set?"

14.

Interior bedroom. Grey light.

When Eric Warberg awoke on what was to be the first day of filming he was initially pleased to see that the pillow next to him showed a definite indentation. A head had lain there in the night. Not that he would remember. Upon returning home last night, after extricating himself from the apelike arms of Hassle Cooley, Eric had not so much gone to sleep as swooned. It was the best night of sleep he'd had in ages. He had even forgotten to take his antidepressant before retiring. Which is perhaps why he felt prickly, as if the world were set to bedevil him. It was creating a galvanic reaction upon his epidermis.

He could hear Sandy humming in the kitchen.

Sitting before standing, Eric felt his newfound friend, backache, twist its rusty coil. He stood slowly, awkwardly. He made his way into the bathroom and downed his Remeron. Was it okay to take it in the morning if he missed his p.m. dosage? He couldn't remember. There was too much cerebration involved in taking a maintenance drug, or three as Eric did. He spent too much of his day trying to make sure his chemical mix was correct.

That was the double-edged sword of medicaments. Would you rather feel bad about having to rely on a drug or would you rather feel . . . crazy?

"Morning, My Little Cabbage," Sandy said. She was scrambling eggs, or what looked like eggs. Maybe egg substitute or tofu scramble.

"Hey, Sweet," Eric said, filling his coffee cup.

"Ready to go?" Sandy positively shone. What was going on behind that crash of sunshine her face offered?

"I hate first days."

"I know you do. I did some good pages last night."

"Jesus, when did you have time to do that?"

"Lover, you were comatose when I came home. I worked for a couple of hours in the den."

"And still woke before me and fixed breakfast."

"Yeah. Funny, huh? My hunger woke me up. I am ravenous."

"Is that tofu?"

"Nope. Real eggs. From the supermarket delivery we have been honored with here."

"Huh."

"Did a great little bit of dialogue between Hope's character and Dan's."

"Great. Uh, listen. Got some rather awkward word from Eden. Which we can choose to ignore if we are confident that he will only squawk and not raise holy hell."

"Or we can just weather the holy hell and make the best movie we know how to make. We've done that before."

"Yes, when we were more secure."

"I see." A chill entered Sandy's demeanor. "Maybe you better gimme the word."

"Yeah. He wants to hire a Memphis writer to supplement what you're doing, someone with some, you know, local flavor."

There was a crisp silence at the breakfast table. The toaster ticked. The refrigerator gargled.

"That's a good idea," Sandy said. "Got anybody in mind?"

Eric was stunned into aphasia.

"I say, got anybody in mind?"

"Uh, yeah, yes. I thought maybe my old pal Camel Eros."

"Camel Jeremy Eros." Sandy said it so flatly it sounded like an idea as absurd as the Spruce Goose or Joseph Smith's other harebrained schemes, the ones before he hit on a religion in which men could not be monogamous.

"Sure," Eric said like a sheep.

"Camel Jeremy Eros."

"Yeah, I said, yes. I haven't talked to him in ages but he sure knows Memphis."

"I thought he was living on the West Coast."

"Word is he moved back here. He and Arthur Lee were making some plans together before Arthur passed."

"Camel's a burnout, 1960s roadkill. Like his buddy Skip."

"It's worth a shot."

"Do you have any idea how to get in touch with him? No, scratch that. Of course you do or you wouldn't be proposing this. Are you proposing this?"

"Yes. My idea is, let's give the whole crew a day off to get acclimated to Memphis. Let Jimbo continue to scout locations. Let Rica get the city right in his eye. Let Reuben do whatever it is A.D.'s do and you and I will go meet with Camel. What say?"

Reuben Wickring was the A.D. He had been hired by Eden Forbes and Eric had never met him. He had been in Memphis for two weeks already, apparently had even put some film in the can, though that was obviously an inchoate accomplishment since Eric and Sandy had not yet finished the script, nor had they finalized *anything* to do with the story.

"You've already talked to him."

"No, no, I haven't. I only found out where he is. I wanted to see how you would take it first. And I must say you are taking it remarkably well."

"Well, Cabbage, it's just moviemaking, right? What's the word on Camel?"

"He's better."

Sandy snorted a laugh. "He's better!" she crowed. "By all means, let's go see him and cement this deal. It sounds so promising."

Eric couldn't help but laugh. At least they were laughing together. At least they were together.

15.

When Dan Yumont saw fit to call Eric's cell that morning he was prepared for a tongue lashing. It was what he was used to. It ran off him like lick whiskey off a Peabody duck's back.

Instead all he got was a Pass Go card.

"Hey, Dan," Eric said. "Listen. Check into your room, ok? And take the day off. We're doing some other things first. Tomorrow, bright and early at the Pyramid, ok?"

Dan Yumont was grateful. Most directors, even the ones who feared him, at least expressed disappointment or perturbation. This guy, this Eric Warberg, he just might be a cool cat.

Now the day spread out before Dan like a newspaper on a teenager's bed.

Which was just what Dan was looking at after ringing off.

That and the teenager herself. He had slipped out, running into neither mother nor promised family dog, gotten a newspaper, some coffee and donuts, and returned to find his bedmate showered and looking like an orchard apple.

Now she was reading about the opening party last night and eating a donut as if it were manna. She was yellow as saffron, shiny as burnished metal, with a body that did things even in its stillness. Even clad in a silky Simpsons bathrobe.

Dan sat on the bed next to her.

"Hey, how come we didn't go to this shindig last night? The Arcade is tops, man. They make the best hummus. How come we didn't go rub elbows with these famous people, eh? Look, here's Hope Davis—she's pretty, isn't she? And Suze Everingham, wow, she's like *so sexy*. She's naked in every movie, is she gonna be naked in this one, do you know? Do you get to be naked with her, that would make me a little jealous but I understand it's just a job for you, still, Suze Everingham has a body like Jessica Simpson, you know? Oh, Ike Bana! I love Ike Bana! He's like so muscleman handsome, you know? Like he could break you or take you, know what I mean? Ike Bana! I didn't know he was gonna be in town. So how come we didn't go last night?"

The "we" was like a small scalpel inserted into Dan's eye socket in preparation for the lobotomy.

"We only met last night," he said. He put a comforting hand on her hip. Then slid it away.

"Yeah, that's true. So, how come you didn't go to that Arcade thing? I mean, I am glad you didn't because if you had you wouldn't have been at the Buccaneer and wouldn't be here now enjoying these tasty sweets with me, right?"

"That's right," Dan said and patted her shapely rump through her bathrobe.

"Jew meet Mama?" Dudu now asked.

"No, of course not. I thought this was taboo. I mean, it's certainly taboo in the courts." Dan smiled a whiskery smile.

"Yeah, I guess you're right. I guess she might freak. But seeing as how you're a movie star and all, it would probably make it ok. I mean the starfucker thing. I think she would trip to that, you know? I dunno. Did you see Bush?"

Dan assumed Bush was the dog. Named after the president? God.

"No, no Bush," he said.

"He's not named after, you know, W. Bush. He's named after the group. Are you into Bush?"

He had to get out of there fast.

"Listen, um, Dudu, I gotta go check into my hotel room. I was supposed to last night of course. So, thank you—"

"Great!" she sprang up like a spark from an anvil, slopping a kiss across his cheek. "Take me two secs to get dressed." She had yak breath.

When she closed the bathroom door Dan Yumont quietly left.

16.

Poet Camel Jeremy Eros lived in Midtown Memphis in a ramshackle, remodeled, shotgun house on Rembert Street, amid an overly profuse garden, wherein could be found daisies, rhododendrons, buttercups, zinnias, false asters, real asters, mushrooms, tomatoes and other veggies, and two healthy marijuana plants. There was a colorful, hand-lettered sign amid the profusion: WE'VE GOT TO GET BACK TO THE GARDEN.

Ever since he had moved back to Memphis in 2004 his house had become a haven for runaways, musicians, artists of every stripe, political outlaws and what passed for bohemian culture in Bush's America. He was the kindly grandfather figure to many young neo-hippies, when he was not the lover to many young neo-hippie chicks who wanted an authentic "beatnik" experience.

Camel's lifelong love, the willowy artist Allen, she of the boy-chest and drop-dead hips, she of the sculptures that defied both gravity and grace, had died in 2002 after a protracted battle with cancer. It damn near broke Camel's heart and, back in Memphis, he was both woeful and tranquil. He had danced with Death. He now saw the downhill of life and it pleased him, though without Allen he was also sad as a neutered dog.

It was a rainy morning that found Eric and Sandy on Camel's front doorstep. They had called ahead but were unsure whether their message had gotten through. The answering machine said: "Commander Cody's Air Force and Rehabilitation Union. Please drop your name and maybe someone will pick it up. Then again, there's the other thing."

Eric said, "Camel, Sandy and I are coming by this morning. Hope that's ok."

The machine cut him off between *o* and *k*.

Now, they stood under one umbrella, ringing the doorbell. Faintly, they could hear a vaguely familiar tune.

"What's that?" Sandy said. "It sounds—"

"Camel calls it 'Tubular Doorbells.'"

"Ah."

Nothing happened.

They rang the tune again.

Still nothing.

They turned toward the street and looked around. Between them and the street was the overgrown front yard: Camel's garden.

There was a rustle amid the cabbages. What looked like a gargantuan toadstool turned out to be Camel's back in an ecru Macintosh bent to the task of plucking small worms from his Mary Jane plants.

"Camel," Eric said into the drizzle.

The becoated figure turned.

"I'll be damned. Craig Brewer!" Camel exclaimed.

"It's Eric, Camel. Eric Warberg."

"Of course you are," Camel said.

Camel Eros looked much older than Eric was prepared for. The death of Allen had taken a great toll on him; his weathered hippie face looked like a map running in the rain. He still favored shoulder-length hair and a vest of many pockets and pants patched with symbols of peace and communion. His mustache hung loose and morose, dripping.

"Come in, come in," Camel said now. "If I'd known you were coming—"

"We left a message on your machine," Eric said.

"What machine?" Camel asked, seeming genuinely perplexed.

"Your answering—"

"Got rid of that years ago," Camel said, ushering them inside.

An enthusiastic border collie met the group at the door. He seemed to engage his whole body in his tail wagging. It was a dance unlike any Eric had ever seen.

"That's Fido," Camel said. "Smartest dog on the planet. So smart when I leave the house I leave him written instructions."

"It's a border collie, right?" Eric said.

"Yes. They're shepherds. I haven't lost a sheep since I got him."

Camel seemed to mean it, to value the dog's innate abilities and his intact flock.

Stepping into Camel's house was like stepping through a door into a Lost World. It looked as if it had been decorated in 1969 by Abbie Hoffman and Wavy Gravy and had never been dusted since. The posters, rugs, ojos, lamps, macramé, albums, all seemed foxed with age, scattered, scrambled and stacked, yet timeless. Sleeping on a sprung sofa was a near-naked teenage girl. She was short, blonde, Slavic in her features. She was perhaps Hungarian; her people were perhaps Hungarian. Her breasts were round cups of pleasure and her little curved belly softly inviting. Someone had drawn a peace symbol around her navel, a pouting outie. She was sound asleep, sucking her thumb.

"That's Lorax," Camel said. "At least I think that's what she said her name was."

"She a friend?" Sandy asked with a worldly smirk.

"Don't know, don't know," Camel said. "Showed up last night. Said she just got to town from Louisiana. Boyfriend in Memphis

somewhere, hence my couch. I think she's on the way to California, or maybe that was someone else."

"Uh-huh," Eric said.

"So, whatcha doing here, my man?" Camel asked. He gestured
as if they should all sit but there were no empty chairs.

"I thought someone had contacted you. We are looking for a
writer to punch up our script. To, you know, add some Memphis
Mojo."

"A writer, eh?" Camel seemed to go into a fugue of thoughtfulness. He was genuinely pondering the question.

"I don't know," he said after a time. "I used to write."

"Yes," Eric said. "We're here to ask if you would be that writer."

"Oh, oh, I see."

Sandy found a beanbag that might be a chair and dropped
onto it.

"You remember Sandy, right?" Eric said. "She's my—my script-
writer. She's—well, we're here to make a movie."

"Yes, yes, I'm getting it now," Camel said.

"What do you think?"

"I, that is, I don't know. Can I throw the I Ching and get back
to you?"

"Camel, sure, whatever. We know you can do this."

"A movie. I haven't seen a movie since—since *Porky's*. That's a
hilarious film. Have you seen *Porky's*, Sandy?"

Sandy didn't even look up. She was doing something with her
BlackBerry.

"*Porky's*. Yeah. But, Camel, you don't have to technically know
movies. We're looking for local color. Someone to add poetry to
Sandy's strong storyline."

"Hm-mm. Poetry, mm. What *is* the story?"

Eric looked for someplace to sit. Finally he sat yoga-style on the carpet. Under his ass was the Monkees' *Headquarters* LP. It crackled.

He laid out the bare bones of the story for Camel, who paced during the telling.

"Huh," he said when Eric was through.

"What, I ask again, do you think?"

"First, I'll need some reds."

"Uh-huh."

"I don't know, Craig. I guess I can give you some help."

"Great, great," Eric said. He looked to Sandy for encouragement. She was text-messaging someone. Eric only briefly considered that it might be her lover from their first night in Memphis.

"Hey, you guys want something to drink?" Camel said now, a smile creasing his soft leather face.

"Whatcha got?" Eric said.

"Oh. Nothing. There's nothing to drink here, Craig. I thought maybe you'd buy me a libation."

Sandy finally spoke: "Yes, let's do that," she said. "Let's please start drinking."

17.

"That's a little too much gun for household use, but lemme—"

"I like it. I like the heft of it. I like the rubber grip," Dan Yumont said.

"Yes, it's a beauty, the Raging Bull they call it. Too much gun, really. But, look, look at this honey. This little puppy will do the do. Feel it in your hand."

"Hm, yeah, I like it. I do like the way my hand hides it."

"That's our bestselling piece. That's all you need. The other, the Bull, will stop anything short of a rhinoceros."

"I have some friends who are short of a rhinoceros so this'll be good."

"Heh, yeah, look, Jack, let's put the other, let's put that cannon back."

"I like them both. But I want the cannon."

"Oh. Well, sure. I mean, I'm here to sell guns."

"How much? How much for the Raging Bull and a box of shells?"

"Well, lemme tell you, that's gonna set you back. Now—"

"I'll give you 1,500 for everything, as long as there are no strings."

"Well—heh—the strings, we can maybe let that slide a bit, but—"

"Seventeen-fifty."

"Yeah, yep. That's a deal."

"Good. Load 'er and I'm on my way."

"Load it?"

"Problem? Load it and I am on my way."

"Ah, cash, well. Lemme—you know—you look familiar. Something about the way you hold that piece. I can't place it."

"You see many movies?"

"Movies, nah. I don't go out much. The wife, she's got phlebitis, she don't like to go out much."

"Like this, if I hold the gun like this?"

"Wait. Wait. Oh. Oh, shit. Yeah, *Murder Among Friends*. Or, what was it? *Murder with a Vengeance*? You're—you're Harrison Ford."

"Close enough."

"Really? Shit. Wait till I tell the wife."

"Nice to meet you—eh—"

"Tom."

"Tom, nice to meet you."

"You here to make a movie?"

"Nah. Nah, no movie. I'm here to make a hit for a friend. Don't tell anyone, ok?"

"Heh-heh, right. Listen, thanks, Mr. Ford."

"Yes, Tom. Thank you."

18.

The bartender, accustomed even to early morning drinkers, still seemed perplexed at his patrons. They seemed exotic, from some other place. Perhaps it was Camel's flop-brimmed hat.

"The story," Eric was saying, "is about cynicism. It's about how irony only takes one so far and then you discover that you are tightrope walking without a net."

Camel was nodding, sagely, into his beer.

"It's all but written," Sandy added. "Though, typically, what we do is keep the script fluid, malleable, especially when we go on location and we're unfamiliar with the local zeitgeist. That's where you come in."

"Local zeitgeist," Camel said.

"Sure," Eric reassured him.

"Will I, like, be on set?"

"No, not necessarily. We're hoping you can communicate with us by email as we go. We'll give you pages and—"

"Email," Camel said.

"You don't have email," Eric said. It wasn't a question.

"That entails a computer, am I right?" Camel suddenly sounded like a schoolboy.

"Sorry . . . um, we can work differently. What do you think, Sand?"

"Well, we can work . . . differently."

"Yes," Eric said.

"Ok, sure. Gimme some pages and I'll see what's what."

"That's great, Buddy." Eric was straining his effusiveness. He was about out of it.

"And you can get me drugs?"

"Sure."

"Hollywood drugs."

"Sure, Camel. Hollywood drugs."

"Hey, did you see that special on Dylan last night?"

"No—I didn't—"

"He's gone electric," Camel said.

19.

Sandy and Eric gave Camel a working copy of the script. First, all three of them had to go to Kinko's to print a copy from Sandy's laptop since giving Camel a zip drive of it would be inane.

"Memphis Movie," Camel read, weighing the pages in his hand as if they were so many tomatoes.

"Working title," Eric said.

"I like it," Camel said. "It's kind of like 'This is not a pipe,' except you're saying it is, it is a pipe. Or in this case, a movie."

"R-right," Eric said. "Take it home, live with it for a few days. But we need to get rolling, so, you know, ASAP (he pronounced it "ay-sap"), anything you think you can help us with."

"Yep," said Camel.

After they dropped him off on Rembert Street Eric had to take a call from Jimbo.

"Hey, what's up?" Eric asked.

"Have you been drinking?" Jimbo asked.

"A beer."

"That's my dog."

"Yes. What, I repeat, is up?"

"Since we're not shooting today I thought you'd want to see the grocery store I found, you know, the one Ike's character owns."

"I'm sure it's right," Eric said. "Use your best judgment."

"Um, ok. When should we get together?"

"Later. I'll call you later this afternoon."

"People to do, things to see, right?"

"Yes, later—"

"Ok, Buddy, I'll—"

Eric hung up.

"I have someplace to be," Sandy said.

"Someplace," Eric repeated, stupidly.

"Yes."

"Ok, I'll drop you."

"Just drop me at Huey's," Sandy said.

"Huey's. Yeah, you know, it's almost lunch time. I could use a burger."

Sandy looked at him with every single year of their being together knit into her brow.

"Right," Eric said.

After she kissed his cheek on Madison Avenue and he had driven away, Eric felt like he couldn't make this movie. Not here in Memphis, not ever. It was all coming apart, he thought, though really it hadn't had a chance to come together.

He stopped at a Piggly Wiggly parking lot to check his calls.

There weren't as many as he had expected. The cast were probably happy about the day off, the crew probably pissed that they had to work. No further call from Dan.

No call from Hope Davis. Hope doesn't spring eternal. It doesn't spring at all.

There was, however, a call from Mimsy Borogoves. Eric got a particular buzz dialing her number, a schoolboy buzz.

"Hi, Mimsy, this is Eric Warberg."

"So formal. I can see it's you, you see. It says so on my phone. And I chose to answer it unlike you who only call back later."

Was she ragging him or flirting? Eric never knew. Eric never knew.

"I was in a meeting," Eric said. Jesus, what a Hollywood answer.

"Uh-huh."

"With a writer."

"Uh-huh. I thought your wife wrote all your scripts."

"She's not my wife. No, what I mean is, no, she does write all my scripts but there is always input from other writers. That's just the process. Do you know Camel Eros?"

"Camel Jeremy Eros?"

"Yes."

"Really?"

"No good? We're barking up the wrong dog?"

"No. I don't know. Camel. I haven't seen him in forever."

"Oh, so you know him."

"Well, who knows Camel? He was a friend of my father's. They went to jail together. This was, oh, I don't know, the garbage strike—was that 1968?"

"Yes, I think that's right."

"Camel, huh."

"So, what for you call me, Mimsy Borogoves?"

"Wanna get some lunch?"

"I do. I really do."

"Huey's?" she asked.

"Um, no. Let's—I don't know—let's go someplace far away from Huey's."

"Ok, Mr. Mystery. Do you know how to get to Gus's? Best fried chicken in the world."

When they were seated in the large room at a small square table Eric couldn't help but think that Mimsy Borogoves was even prettier than he remembered. She was white like spirit matter, pale as ghost orbs, the backscatter in a photograph. She was positively lucent.

"What's good here?" Eric asked.

"Get the chicken."

They laughed a mutual laugh, one of those that makes a bond, a warmth transmitted. He wanted to put his hand on her hand, which rested next to her water glass. The light through the water glass lit her hand, making it resemble fine marble, or glazed pottery.

He put his hand on her hand.

"Tell me things," he said.

Mimsy Borogoves looked long into his face. She was deciding something but Eric could only guess what.

"It's true, isn't it, the Hollywood stereotype? The director who beds women left and right because every female has illusions about being in the movies. That's you, isn't it? That's who you've become."

"Is that why you wanted to get together? To castigate me for my profligate ways without even knowing what those ways are?"

"I'm sorry." Mimsy Borogoves lowered her gaze.

Eric removed his hand.

"What then?" he asked.

"I want to be in movies," she said. Then, after a beat, a nervous laugh.

"You're beautiful enough," Eric said, gallantly.

"He said gallantly," Mimsy said.

"Well, really—"

"I don't want to act, Silly. I want to direct."

"Ah."

"So, can I sleep with you for *that*?"

Eric and Mimsy shared another laugh. Eric wasn't sure whether she was serious or not. Sleeping with Mimsy Borogoves would be about the best idea he'd had since coming to Memphis.

20.

Midday. Exterior. Medium shot.

Dan Yumont is buying lunch at a Stop'n Go. They sold the best gyros, he had heard. He carried the dripping sandwich to the parking lot where he ate it leaning against his rented car.

A guy on a Harley pulled up next to him, the din all but swamping every sense for a few seconds. Until he turned the hog off Dan was deaf, dumb and blind. The world was eclipsed.

In the silence afterward the two men made uneasy eye contact. Dan never backed down from a staring contest.

"Hey," the biker said with a head bob.

"How's it going?" Dan answered with a shit-eating grin.

"You're Dan Yumont," the biker said.

"Who?"

"I must be wrong. Sorry. You look like someone."

"I hope I am. I hope I am someone."

"Right. Sorry."

"Have a good day," Dan Yumont said.

As Dan was finished his gyro the biker was re-saddling his bike and, with a cautious nod, off he roared. Dan stood in the dust and midday silence and squinted. As he squinted he was reminded of who he was and being reminded, he wanted to use it to—do something. There was power there and power begged to be used.

Suddenly Dan was horny again and he wished he could remember how to get back to Dudu's house. It was in Midtown somewhere. But, he then reflected, she was probably pissed now that he had left so abruptly.

So he set out again. A knight errant.

Where else to go? A college campus. Dan Yumont was practiced in the ways of seduction. Ever since the Oscar, of course, it didn't matter whether he was practiced in those ways or not. Women came to him. Yet, still there was the thrill of the hunt.

Dan parked on Southern Avenue across from the campus of the University of Memphis, formerly Memphis State. A train separated him from his hunting ground and he stood smoking a cigarette and watching the cars rush by.

"Aren't you Dan Yumont?" he heard at his elbow.

He turned to find a round, cheeky face under a mop of black hair. One pierced lip. Yet, underneath some scabrous clothing there was a body to die for. This was too easy. Too easy.

"Nope," Dan said.

The little black figure eyed him as if he were a trig problem.

"You are," she said. "You're here to make that movie."

Now Dan turned fully toward her.

"Hi, Sweet," he said. "Who are you?"

"Name's Candy," she said.

"Ah, and I called you Sweet. Must mean something."

He squinted at her.

She smiled an engaging smile.

Well, Dan thought, might as well.

"That must work on dipshits," Candy said. "You're a bad man, Daddy."

And with that she walked away. Across the tracks where there had been a train only moments before.

Dan laughed at himself. Some days the magic works and some days, well, it works less well.

Dan Yumont found the student center and parked himself on a bench in front of it. He lit another cigarette and surveyed.

The campus was so alive with humanity at this time of day that Dan could hardly see the trees for the forest. Then he saw her.

She was with a couple of other young women but she erased them. Her beauty, her confident beauty, positively swallowed up anyone else around her. She was tall, about six feet, with long legs, about which she was rightly proud because she wore a short, tight jean skirt. Her hips worked like a runway model's and her breasts were perfectly round eyes in the center of her body. They stared at Dan and he stared back. And her face—she was a Botticelli angel. She was white-blonde and looked a little bit like Heather Graham, whom Dan had dated briefly back in the previous century.

Dan stood. The angel had not noticed him yet. She was chattering angel talk to her friends.

Dan stepped into her path like a gunslinger.

"Hi," he said, ignoring Friend Left and Friend Right. "Can you tell me where Chemistry is?"

The blonde squinched up her face.

"Y-yes," she said. Her voice was throatier than one would have imagined. "Chemistry," she repeated.

"Yes," Dan said and smiled.

"It's behind us, over that way."

"Hm, I'm new—I don't—"

"Fuck me," Friend Right said.

Everyone turned to her.

"This is fucking Dan Yumont. You are, aren't you?"

Dan looked at the blonde. And then—he squinted.

"Jesus," she said.

"I'm Trudy," Friend Right said and stuck out her hand. "Pardon my Franco."

"Hello, Trudy," Dan said, taking her hand and never letting his gaze fall away from the angel's face.

"I'm Ray," the angel spoke. "Ray Verbely."

"Ray Verbely," Dan Yumont said.

Friends Right and Left cowered. The energy level approached the red zone.

"Will you take me to lunch?" Dan asked.

Ray Verbely spoke as if ensorcelled. "Of course I will," she said.

"Wonderful," Dan Yumont said and he slipped an arm around her waist.

21.

The call from Eden Forbes came as Eric and Mimsy were leaving Gus's Fried Chicken.

"Excuse me," Eric said to Mimsy. "Gotta take this one."

Mimsy smiled and walked a few paces down South Main. It was still a fairly bleak area.

"Hi, Eden," Eric said.

"Eric! I hear you're taking a day off!"

"Yes, I did. I needed to talk to the Memphis writer you wanted to bring aboard."

"I love nautical metaphors," Eden said. There was a pause and Eric thought he was supposed to speak. Then Eden said, "So, how is that working out? This writer you talked to—can he deliver the goods?"

"Yes, I think so."

"Good, good. Throw money at him if you need to. Hammer it home to him that we want funk, right? Memphis funk?"

"Yes, Eden."

"Good, good. Listen, I was fiddling around last night with the opening credits."

Eric was stunned into silence.

"How's this sound and I'm just roughing it out here so, you know, we can spitball. Like this: An Eden Forbes Production, in association with William Pilgrim Pictures and Chair Ass Productions, a Big Rear Crew Movie brought to you by Oust Berserk Book Pictures, a subsidiary of God Is Alive Magic Is Afoot Productions, a Thespis Slam Dunk Movie. How's that sound to you?"

"I'm speechless. Except to say that we haven't started shooting yet."

"Yes, yes, I know, I'm just excited from my end and wanted to line up the ducks, so to speak. I think I got everyone in there, and elegantly, too."

Eric didn't know who these mysterious production companies were except for Big Rear Crew, which was his and Sandy's company.

"As long as we don't say based upon," Eric said, sardonically.

"Wha—"

It was Eric's contention that any movie that began "Based *upon*" rather than "Based *on*" was off to an unlucky and pretentious start, as in "Based upon Vladimir Nabokov's *Ada* . . . " Moviemakers that say *upon* probably don't read real books.

"All good, Eden. Got to get going here."

"Right, right. You are gonna start rolling some film, right?"

"Yep. Second unit has already begun. Gotta get a few" (here he almost said "ducks in a row" but caught the repetition quickly) "things done first."

"Yes, yes. You know moviemaking. I trust you're doing the right thing."

"Thanks, Eden."

After he hung up Eric scanned the sidewalk. About 50 yards away Mimsy was talking to a black guy with pants around his thighs and a jailhouse rag on his head.

Eric hustled toward her.

"Mimsy—sorry," he began.

The black guy gave him a quick once-over.

"Eric, this is Sean Meezen," Mimsy said. "He worked on *Hustle and Flow*."

"Oh, nice to meet you," Eric stuck a hand out, tentatively, unsure whether he would meet a soul brother, a businessman or a fist. Movie people everywhere, he thought. He might as well be back on Santa Monica Boulevard.

"Mimsy was a big help to me. She put me on the path. You thought I was a street tough raggin' on your lady," Sean said. He shook hands in a straightforward way.

"No, no—" Eric tried to regroup. "I'm from Memphis," he added.

"Oh, ha, then you're practically black!" Sean said.

They all laughed. It was like a little cloud of noise underneath the thin Memphis sunshine in the middle of a crumbling downtown street.

As they headed back to the car Mimsy slipped her hand into Eric's.

Eric's body reacted. His libido was drinking milk.

22.

Camel laid out his medicaments.

On the glass-top coffee table he had a little Thai stick, some Mississippi Thunder Weed (a gift from Ernie Abel, Camel's postman), some Alabama Slamma, bubble bags of hash (German and Middle Eastern, some Maui Wowie, and a small amount of Amsterdam *Uitbarsting*). He was preparing his tools to begin the arduous process of plumbing the ether for words, for magic words. It was an old ritual but one he hadn't practiced in over a decade. His tools—his mental tools—were rusted.

Lorax, still with sleep locusts in her head, sat on the couch watching the ceremony. She wore panties and the blanket she had slept in, wrapped around her Native American–style.

She thought about smiling. Smiling seemed like a good idea. She would hold it in abeyance. Soon, she would smile.

Camel looked over his paraphernalia and thought that it was good. It was meet and right.

He sat back and opened Sandy's script to page one.

He brought his full concentration to the page. And he read.

Ten pages later he looked up.

Lorax tried that long-dreamt-of smile.

"It's not very good," Camel said to Lorax.

"I'm sorry, Baby," the teenager said.

"Furthermore, I'm not very good. I have no words left. I used to have words but now I am bereft. I am wordless."

"I'm hungry," Lorax said.

Camel smiled at his houseguest. "Go find some food," he said.

He meant for her to begin the quest at, say, Piggly Wiggly.

Instead she headed for the kitchen where there hadn't been food since Abbie Hoffman cooked Minute Rice in there. Except for a counter stacked with vegetables.

Fido, for one, was tired of brown rice and vegetables. He longed for a little piece of ham, a little twist of bacon.

Camel watched Lorax walk by him. He thought about her breasts, which were lovely, in a young body sort of way. Lovely like beach sand early in the morning before the children come with their pails and castle-dreams.

"There's no food out here," Lorax said. "And Fido is hungry."

"I know," Camel said. He thought about reading another page. Instead he lit a pipe and sat back to gather moths.

Reenter Lorax.

"What should we do?" she asked. She truly thought it a metaphysical puzzle.

Camel just smiled his Buddha smile.

"I guess we could ball instead," Lorax said, scratching her decorated belly.

Camel thought, yes, perhaps that would be best. Script doctoring be damned. There were more pressing needs and one of them was the wiggle in his willy.

"Come here, Sweetheart," Camel said.

23.

Eric emerged from Mimsy Borogoves's bed newly washed in emotional well-being. He knew, briefly, the secrets of the universe, a flash-knowledge only, a presque-vu.

And when he stepped outside, after tender goodbyes and soft kisses, the sunshine was like balm to him. It was two o'clock in the afternoon. Suddenly, and for the first time, he thought, I have come home. And I have come home for one reason only, to make the best damn movie I have ever made.

His cell rang.

"It really is *him*," Ricky Lime said. "It's clearer in the ones I took last night."

"Ok, Ricky. Good. Let's get together—uh—later tonight—and we'll see what's what," Eric said.

"I've got a swimming pool for you," Jimbo sang into the phone. "It is THE swimming pool, I'm telling you. It looks like it was designed for Sandy's script. I'm not kidding."

"Ok, Jimbo—uh, pick me up at the house in about an hour."

"Right, Chief," Jimbo said.

Chief.

"Did you get my fax?" Eden said.

"Uh, no, I haven't been—"

"Jesus, boy. I got it all laid out. I'm working my ass off here. I expect you to be, too."

"Right, Eden. I'm heading home now. I'll get it in five minutes."

"Tell that driver to make it in three," Eden said, with a laugh as phony as Shirley Temple's Oscar.

"Right," Eric said. He didn't want to tell Eden why he thought it was better to rent a car for the day.

"Eric." Hope Davis's purr came through the phone with some heat.

"Hope!" Eric crowed. "I was just thinking about you. Everything ok?"

"Yes, yes, I was wondering if you and Sandy could run some lines with me tonight. I'm a bit unclear on a couple of scenes, where I'm going. If I don't know where the character is going I can't, you know, do her *in the present*."

"Of course, Dear," Eric said. He didn't tell her that the script wasn't finished. "Let's get together tonight, say, around dinner?"

"Ok. You wanna come here?"

"Yes, let's do that. Have some food sent up maybe."

"Yes. Ok, thanks, Eric."

"Ok, Love."

Oh my God, Eric thought. I just called her Love. I called Hope Davis Love.

Still, he hoped that Sandy would be tied up tonight and that he and Hope Davis would have the evening to themselves.

Because—

He didn't know why. He had been in love with Hope Davis for ten years, ever since he saw *The Daytrippers*. He wanted her—talent—for his films. But, he had to be honest with himself—he wanted more than that. Just what was hard to say. And now there was Mimsy Borogoves, whose pale, rose-colored skin still hummed in his hands. He could still feel her on his palms. And the things she whispered to him, the magic things, things most sentient beings are unaware of. He was born again in her bed. And THAT was something that he could tell no one.

24.

"Hope Davis wants to run lines tonight. She says she's not clear on the direction her character is going."

"Well, that makes sense since we don't know."

"Yes. I didn't tell her that."

"Smart Cabbage."

"Can you make it?"

"What—tonight?"

"Yes, can you come with us?" Eric's voice stuck briefly.

"Does Cabbage want to run with Hope by himself? Does he want to run away with Hope perhaps? Run with Hope. Not a bad title," Sandy said, and tapped it into her laptop in a file marked simply, "Notes."

"I don't care either way," Eric said. And suddenly he didn't. It was all too much. The rosy glow he had picked up from Mimsy Borogoves was beginning to corrode at the edges.

"Oh, c'mon, talk to me."

"I really don't care," Eric said, with more conviction.

"Ok." Sandy bent back toward her keyboard.

Eric stood uncertainly in the middle of the room for a minute.

"Hey, did a fax come?" he asked.

"Yes. From Eden."

Eric found it on the end table. It was the opening credits just as he had read them over the phone, it seemed. Then Eric saw the small difference. Big Rear Crew had been replaced by something called Worm Credit Pictures. What the hell was Worm Credit? What did this mean? And, further, did Eric have the wherewithal or the balls to challenge it? Did he even care? All he wanted to do was make a movie.

"Apparently," Eric said, "Our production company has been dropped from the picture."

Sandy held up a finger.

"I'm working here," she said.

Fuck her, Eric said to himself. Suddenly, he was enraged. An ancient anger welled in him. On his way to the bedroom he glanced back at Sandy. Her screen was open to gmail. She was answering her fucking email, he realized.

Script? What script?

In the bedroom he sat on the bed and took out his cell.

He dialed Mimsy's number.

"Hi," she said.

"Hi."

"You sound blue. That's not much of a compliment."

"Mimsy Borogoves, I don't know where you came from. But you're about the best damn thing that's happened to me in my return home. The only good thing, I should say."

"That's better."

"Well—"

"What is it, Eric? Tell me."

"This movie. I can't do it."

"Are you being serious? Aren't there like gargantuan machinations—like large semi-trucks full of equipment and Oompa Loompas—already in place so that you can't *not* do it?"

"Yes. Hundreds of thousands of dollars. That's what trumps. Money trumps. You know what Dorothy Parker said about

Hollywood? She said, 'Hollywood money isn't money. It's congealed snow, melts in your hand and there you are.'"

"Only hundreds of thousands?" Mimsy sounded disappointed.

"Yes. Disappointing, eh? My last film's budget was 20 million."

"Oh, Eric. Is that it? Just the detritus of that failure?"

"No, no, it's—"

Eric realized he didn't know what it was. It *was* that failure. But it was Memphis, too. It was returning to Memphis with a moribund relationship—one that was hopelessly entangled with his business—and no real story to film. The only thing they really had was the idea to make their movie in Memphis. It sounded like genius at the time.

"It's Memphis," Mimsy said.

Her prescience scared him a bit.

She said, "Memphis is like that. The city you can't shake. The one you return to and nothing has changed. Though you've gone through massive changes, the city treats you the same and you try to act like you're the same. It's a subtle form of torment."

"Mimsy, how do you know this? One so young as you?"

"I've seen it, Love. I've paid attention."

She called him Love.

"Can you come to me now?"

"Eric, where's Sandy?"

"She's in the next room emailing her lover."

"I see."

There was a frozen silence, one packed in dry ice.

"Never mind," Eric said. "I have things to do, strings to tie together. Lots of messy strings. This is my job—I'm a knitter, not a director."

"You're making a movie."

"Yes. Mimsy, I am. I'm making this movie."

They hung up with a few inchoate endearments.

His cell rang immediately.

"Love, can you come get me?"

Eric was temporarily staggered. It took him a moment to realize it was not Mimsy's voice. He couldn't figure out whose voice it was.

"Um, I— I'm busy here," he stalled.

"Eric, you mooncalf, it's Kim."

"Hello, Kim."

"Eric, Love, can we get together? I sorta am aching for you."

"Kim, what are you talking about? I'm here with Sandy."

"Eric, I know about Sandy. C'mon, it's Kimberly. Talk real to me. Be real."

"Real?" Eric's anger began to simmer again. "Ok, real. Let's see. I'm trying to pull this fucking movie together. I've got actors running around all over town, not one of them reading the script. I've got a script that is unfinished, perhaps unfinishable, that a burnt-out hippie is supposed to save. I've got the money men squeezing me. And then I've got you. My ex-lover who left me without explanation, without even a glance back. And now she's a day player. A bit player in the movie and in my life. Ok? that real enough?"

"Fuck you," Kimberly Winks said. "Fuck you, and your big head and your big dead movie."

That, thought Eric, was real. That was how it was supposed to go. That was following the script. At least I have Hope, he thought. And he laughed a fairly cheerless laugh.

25.

Dan Yumont had not really wanted lunch. He only wanted to take Ray Verbely to some place semi-private and remove her clothing. Ray Verbely looked like she desired to have her clothes taken off, as if her clothes were the chrysalis she needed to shed. Her body moved about underneath that fabric like a snake's, a sexy snake.

Ray ordered a salad. Dan ordered a salad, too, with steak on it.

They were sitting in a bar-restaurant near the university campus. They were surrounded by the Greeks and the jocks and the people who pass for glitterati in college. Ray was trying to show Dan Yumont that she had some eminence also, that she had her own set of fans.

Dan couldn't have cared less. It was all he could do to make small talk.

"I loved you in *Evil Going On*," she was saying now. Dan's eyes were weak slits. He was weary.

"Thanks," he said, and moved a piece of steak deeper into the bowl, obscuring it with greenery.

"You were so . . . " Ray was searching for a word. Dan was betting she wouldn't hit it.

"So *mean*," she finished.

Dan smiled.

"And in *The Tin Woodman Objects*. You were so different in that. So . . . " Again the search began.

"Mean?" Dan asked.

"No, just the opposite. Um, you know, *sweet*. How do you do that? Be two different people?"

Honey, you have no idea, he thought.

"Listen," Dan said, after waiting for Ray to eat half her salad, "you're very pretty."

Ray Verbely was taken aback.

"Thanks, Dan," she said, falling a little in love with him.

"You wanna fuck a movie star?"

Once they were inside Ray's apartment, itself close to the campus, Dan Yumont began unbuckling his belt.

"You're really needy, aren't you?" Ray Verbely trilled. She was nervous.

"Yes," Dan said. "Take all your clothes off."

"Ok, Dan," Ray said. "Lemme just check—"

"Now. Right there."

Ray Verbely stopped in her tracks. She was about three yards inside her apartment.

"Ok, Dan," she said, and began an awkward striptease that Dan watched with only half interest.

Ray Verbely, naked, was everything Dan had hoped. She was as pretty as a movie star.

26.

Rembert Street. Interior, lights low.

Camel had read four pages of *Memphis Movie*. He sat back and puffed at his pipe.

There was something there, something that clicked with him, something that turned an old tumbler. Inside Camel's head letters began to line up as if for drill. Almost all 26 of them appeared, polished and ready for action. The ones missing he could do without. He'd done it before.

Now words came. Old words. Words that led to other words. Words he thought he had left behind in San Francisco.

Which reminded Camel of a song, but which song?

Was it something he had heard in his youth, something his mother sang while she cooked for him and his father, frying, that's what she did, she fried everything? What was it she sang? And his father, sitting there as if he had spent all his conversation in his youth and had none left for his child or wife. A sad man, a man beaten down by working all his life for Grace Chemical, adding figures for them as if without adding them up they couldn't make their millions. Was he even listening to the song his wife sang?

She sang all the time. Camel thought she was writing her own songs.

Lorax, as if channeling Camel's dead and now-dream-bidden mother, walked about the house singing also, little Sibyl songs.

Fido followed her if she were piping him to and fro. Fido had taken to Lorax like a peri to Queen Mab.

Once Camel had written a song—collaborated, really—with Grace Slick, a song that never made it onto an album but did appear on a European bootleg of the Airplane live. Those were good days.

Why was that the only song he had written? Surely, he had other songs in him.

Perhaps even now.

You're never too old to write a song.

Perhaps he should try to write a new song. He could call Ardent and see who's still hanging around there; maybe all the old guys weren't gone. Maybe Buddy could help him.

Buddy was dead. That was a hard truth.

They were all dead, all Camel's old crowd. And Allen. She was even deader.

She died on Camel.

She left him bereft.

Camel sat and cried quiet tears.

He couldn't write a song. He couldn't write a movie script. And he couldn't bring Allen back. Every bit of his magic had gone the way of all flesh. Is anything sadder than exhausted magic?

Lorax watched sleepily from the couch as Camel cried.

"Hey, hey, Camel," she said from her dreams. "What is it, Baby?"

Camel looked at her with thousands of years of heart-breaking shortfall. He looked at her the way Father Time looks at Death, when Death shows up fresh-shaven and natty at the party, carrying a bouquet of black roses and grinning like Youth Rampant.

"What is it, Camel? Can Lorax do anything for you?"

Camel thought about the thing that they had just done. He had almost not been able to complete the transaction. His body, like his soul, had lived too many lifetimes.

"It's ok, Sweet," Camel said, at last. "I need to lie down, I think. My head is full of locusts."

Lorax smiled a teen imp's sempiternal smile. It was the prettiest thing Camel had ever seen.

"But, first, you know," Camel said, hesitantly, "I think I'm gonna help these poor movie folks and their raggedy script. I think I have just the right words to help them."

And Camel smiled, too.

27.

When Eric saw Jimbo Cole bouncing on his doorstep like a dog anxious for its walk, Eric's heart sank a bit lower. This was what his career had led him to, a reunion with a friend he was not friends with, in a city where he had never been comfortable.

"Hey, Buddy," Jimbo said. "Where next?"

"Listen, Jimbo, we gotta meet with Ricky Lime. Do you know where the Ornamental Metal Museum is?"

"Yeah, yeah, of course. You know every time I go there I make that wrong turn that takes you across the bridge into Arkansas, no way off, gotta go all the way across the bridge and turn around. Every damn time."

"Ok, so, that's where we're meeting Ricky."

"Ok, sure, let's go." There was a hesitation. "Who's Ricky Lime?"

"The still photographer."

"Right. Eggleston's son."

"No." Eric could almost not summon the energy for discussion. "No, not Eggleston's son," he finished.

"Ok, great, let's go."

The drive there was part silence, part uncomfortable rehashing of the past. Eric and Jimbo had had some unfortunate head-buttings, involving Jimbo's relentless pursuit of any female that Eric had the fortune of accompanying. Jimbo's dick-measuring contests were almost comical. All in the guise of friendship. They had led, of course, to a split.

"You know, after she ratted on me—I mean the one girlfriend of yours I didn't sleep with—after she said I hit on her and you exploded on me. And rightly so, rightly so, I'm not saying. Anyway, after that, I really felt the loss of our friendship. I blamed myself totally. I mean it. I just saw it all for the first time, what I was doing wrong, you know?"

Eric didn't even remember the incident. How could it matter now?

And yet it did, if only to Jimbo.

"What's that?" Eric asked as they drifted through downtown Memphis.

"New entertainment plaza, or, what's the word? New entertainment extravaganza. No, that's not it, anyway, Peabody Place, movie theaters, mall, bowling alley. You know?"

Eric didn't. But it didn't matter.

Downtown had changed considerably; it almost sparkled. Eric imagined it was the NBA team and its new downtown arena, the FedEx Forum. A mammoth mushroom that had sprung up from the decomposing soil south of Beale Street, swallowing all the surrounding housing projects and cheap grocery stores. It looked like a spaceship. A space mushroom. Something alien.

And there were tourists everywhere. Eric imagined that his entire cast wandered among the crowds, sparkling too, signing autographs, smiling Hollywood smiles, getting back that energy stars crave and hate, the fan adoration.

Eric hated his business. He hated the movies.

Ricky Lime was standing on an Indian burial mound looking at the river. He didn't even turn as Eric and Jimbo approached. He had circles under his eyes like thumbprints of pitch, as black as Vulcan in the smoke of war. His voice was floating, detached.

"You know, this river, think about it: it's older than anyone alive. It's as old as the universe. And it still has such—*vigor*. Think about it," Ricky Lime said.

"So, Ricky, show me what you've got," Eric said. He was busy. This was business.

"What I've got," Lime said, pulling his gaze away from Big Muddy, "what I've got is proof of life after death. A dark truth. I set out to frame the look of your film and I got proof of life after death. Now, what are we going to do about it?"

Eric sighed. He tried to hold Ricky Lime's eye but had to look away. It was like falling into a well.

"Look, Lime," Eric said. "I have to have what you've shot. Ghost and all. Ok? I have to have it now and I have to have your commitment to this project. Not to some Uri Geller fantasy. Ok? You with me or not?"

Ricky Lime looked like he was going to cry. His face crumpled like a rejected page of prose.

"Sure, Eric. Sure. I just wanna do my job."

"Ok, then. Tomorrow. Tomorrow, you and I and Rica will take some time to sit down and talk about the location shooting. Ok? It's at the Pyramid tomorrow. Early. 7 a.m. Ok?"

"Yes, of course, Eric," Ricky said, clearing his throat.

"Good. Ok, now why are we here at the museum?"

"I wanted to show you—that is, this, well, here's the picture."

It was a picture taken inside the actual smithy shop at the museum. In Eric's film something mysterious happens in this shop, something involving sparks off the anvil. Something that leads Dan's character to suspect that Suze Everingham's character is hiding something behind her private school teacher's prim demeanor. The something hadn't been decided yet. That is, the script stalled at the doorjamb of the mystery.

"This is a nice shot, Lime. Nice. The murky atmosphere like

some infernal workshop where Old Scratch forms his army of darkness," Eric said, holding the picture above his head to catch the right light.

"Yes!" Lime's face was contorted into Dwight Frye–level dementia. "Yes, my God help me. You see it!"

Eric pulled back. He thought the photographer might be rabid. "What the hell—"

"In the picture. There in the shadows—my God, look!"

Eric squinted at the picture. There was something there, a murky form.

"What—what is it?"

"See him!" Lime nearly exploded.

It was just a shadow, probably. Eric lowered the picture and handed it to Jimbo, who mimicked Eric's way of seeing the photo clearly.

"It's just a shadow, probably. The smithy's shadow," Eric said.

"It's a shadow that looks just like Satan," Jimbo Cole said.

28.

Exterior. Long shot.

The sun was sinking into the river. The river was the color of a rotting tangerine.

Eric's cell phone was suddenly full of messages again.

The first one was from Eden Forbes.

"Eric, how the hell are you? How's our movie? You get that writer I suggested?"

This was phatic conversation. Eric didn't feel bound to answer literally.

"Everything's ok," he said.

"Good, good," Eden said.

"I'm gonna be working with Hope Davis tonight and then to bed early. We're starting at the Pyramid tomorrow at 7."

There was silence.

"Eden, that's it," Eric said.

"Sorry, sorry, Eric. I was listening on the other line to my wife. Ok, Buddy, lemme know how the new pages look. And, Eric."

Eric knew his line.

"Yes, Eden?"

"You call me if you need *anything*. Got it?"

"Yes, Eden, thanks."

Sandy had called, too. No message. She knew he would call back.

"Hey, Baby, how you doing?"

"Great, Cabbage. Where are you? Did you see Lime's ghosts?"

"Yes, yes. We're down by the river. Lime's taken off. I think I'm gonna kick his new age ass. He's got Jimbo worked up now."

"When is Jimbo not worked up? Listen, about tonight. You go. Don't worry about me. I was being bitchy earlier. You go and run lines with Hope. Call me if you need any clarification. Though you know the script as well as I do."

"Have you written more? Gotten any closer to a denouement? Is this movie gonna have an ending?"

"It will, Cabbage. It will end when and how it's supposed to."

"Ok, Sweet. I got a call here from Camel, I see. I'm betting we're gonna have to go elsewhere for our local funk. At short notice I don't really know which direction to go. I'll worry about it tomorrow."

"Ok, Scarlett."

"Ok—" Eric heard hesitation.

"Oh, and Cabbage."

"Yes, Sweet."

"I love you," Sandy said.

"I love you, too, Baby."

Eric called Camel and that stray picked up. Her name? Lorraine?

"Hey," her sleepy voice said. "This is Camel's house but this isn't Camel."

"Hi, this is Eric Warberg. Is Camel available?"

"Hi, Eric, it's Lorax."

Lorax. Right.

"Hi, can you put Camel on?"

There was a snuffling laughter coming through now. The sound a puppy might make wagging its tail in a silk dressing gown.

"Lorax?" Eric said eventually.

"I'm not putting Camel on," she said, giggling.

"I don't—" Then Eric saw the joke. "Oh, ha, yes, I'm sure you wouldn't. Ahem, can you give Camel the phone?"

There was a sort of silence. He could hear music. He thought it was the Doors.

"Hey, Eric," Camel said.

"Hey, Camel. Am I disturbing you?"

"No, no, man, I'm in the bathroom."

"I'm sorry," Eric said. He hated disgusting images. They played havoc with his personal well-being. They played hell with his visual dictionary, the library he kept in his head of useful, meaningful images, from which his movies came. Also, he didn't trust his body and hated imagining anyone else's personal eructation and necessaries.

"No, I'm not, you know, number twoing or anything. At least I don't think I am. I am—"

Again that soft-edged silence.

"I sit in here to write. That is, I used to. So, I thought if I was gonna write again, I should try it in here. It's quite a happy space, you know? The colors are nice, the chrome of the pipes, the smell of recently used soap."

"Listen, Camel, if this is too much for you—"

"*Movie Man*," Camel said with a sense of urgency. It brought Eric up short. He prepared himself for something from left of left field.

"I've written you some damn good dialogue."

"Camel, that's wonderful."

"Can you gimme a few hours? I'm thinking I can write all night here and have something near to what you're looking for."

This was so unexpected Eric didn't know what to say. Camel lucid was the Camel of old, creative, energetic, amusing. Eric's gratitude made him feel blubbery, blurry at the edges.

"Camel, you're a prize. We'll talk tomorrow."

"Ok, Craig."

Eric called Mimsy Borogoves. She whispered whispery endearments. He invited her to the 7 a.m. shoot at the Pyramid and she said that she would be there.

He talked to Rica Sash, who assured him that he had a visual style that Eric was going to love. "Yes," he said, "I can work with your photographer's images."

Eric took a call from Ike Bana and one from Suze Everingham. Both only wanted assurances that the movie would begin shooting tomorrow. Not having ever worked with either actor before, Eric was a little on edge. He felt challenged somehow by Ike's aggressive manner. Did he have to assert so early that he was in charge?

Suze Everingham, however, sounded warm and friendly. She was about to break big this year, with two already acclaimed independent films being released just about simultaneously. There was already Oscar buzz about her. Eric only knew that she was as sexy as a flame. She was bicycling, Eric knew, shooting a movie with Miranda July simultaneously with his.

Suze Everingham had a funny/sexy persona on screen, a blonde Sarah Silverman, with that same kind of killer body. Eric was anxious to work with her and the part Sandy had written her was key, a real plum role. "This part," Sandy had said, "this is our Independent Spirit Award for Supporting Actress."

Eric had no call from Dan Yumont so he checked in with his wayward star.

The phone rang a dozen times. The rings sounded tired.

"Go," Dan said when he picked up.

"Hey, Dan. Just wanted to make sure you had everything you needed. You need a wake-up call, a limo in the morning?"

"Eric!" Dan howled. He sounded coked to the gills. Maybe even beyond the gills. "Man, I'll be there. I'm gonna walk, Buddy. Shit, the Peabody is in the Pyramid's backyard."

Eric didn't like the sound of this. It was walkable, of course, but he didn't think it was safe to have his star on the street. Maybe at 7 a.m. it would be ok.

"Ok," Eric said. "You did check into your room, then?"

"Not yet, my man. I am about to. I might need to crash early."

"Ok. Um, where are you? Do you need someone to come get you?"

Dan Yumont didn't rightly know where he was. Somewhere near the college.

"See you in the a.m.," he sang out.

"Ok, Dan," Eric said.

He had a bad feeling about Dan Yumont. The insurance policy on him was a pain, an expense that Eden Forbes balked at initially. Then relented. Eden Forbes knew Dan Yumont was the ticket, the money. The policy stipulated daily drug tests. Eric hoped they didn't follow through on that.

29.

Eric was nervous about meeting with Hope Davis. He felt as if he were dressing for a date, as if he were a high school swain with a crush on a cheerleader. Luckily, Sandy had vacated the premises prior to Eric's preparations. God knows where she went.

She missed him putting baby powder in his underwear. She missed the extra deodorant, a swipe down his sternum to his pubes. She missed the cherry Binaca.

"Goddamn fool," Eric said to the mirror. He wore a T-shirt that read, THE REVOLUTION WILL NOT BE ADVERTISED ON T-SHIRTS. And an expensive sport coat. Urban chic.

When he knocked on the door to Hope's suite, his heart answered the brief tattoo of his fist. She opened right away and Eric was caught in mid–deep breath.

"H-hi," he managed.

"Come in," she said, stepping gracefully back. Her face, so luminous on the screen, was more luminous in real life.

Who builds his Hope in the air of your faire looks, lives like a drunken sailor on a mast.

"I can't believe we've never worked together. Never even crossed paths," Eric said, entering.

"I know, isn't that strange? And we're both so—Hollywood?" She tinkled a laugh. It was golden.

"Yes," Eric said.

"I loved *Spondulicks*, by the way," Hope Davis said.

"Oh, Christ. Only you." Eric groaned.

"No, no, the smart people loved it. The smart people are disappearing."

"Yes," Eric said, uncertainly. He thought it best to sit down and dropped into one of the stiff but elegant chairs in the room.

"Let's sit over here, can we?" Hope said, gesturing toward a table, on which sat her script.

"Right," Eric said. He groaned, standing. His back spoke harshly to his head.

"Do you want something," Hope Davis asked, "from the bar?"

"Yes," Eric said. "Uh, gin and tonic?"

"Right. I'll join you."

Once he was seated at the table, so near her, Eric's face burned. He sipped the drink, which hit his cortex like a jolt of moonshine. He smiled with half his mouth. God, she's beautiful, he thought.

"So, my scenes," Hope Davis said.

Eric swallowed hard. Oh no. She hates the script. She hates the part. Why did she take it? Sandy will die if she hates the words. Why didn't I make sure Sandy came?

"Yes," Eric said.

"I *love* them," Hope Davis said.

Music rises. Cymbals clash. There is balm in Gilead. There is Hope!

"Wonderful," Eric said. He took a longer sip of his drink. It burned like school.

"I'm having a stumble, though, in my scene with Paul." She smiled, sweetly.

Who the hell is Paul? Eric thought. Was he an actor that Eden had hired without telling him? Was Eric supposed to know Paul?

Had they ever worked together, dined together? Oh, God, Paul is someone large, someone Eric, if he knew half of what his work was about, would know immediately and thoroughly.

"You know, Dan's character," Hope Davis continued. "The scene where Dan and I go to the adoption agency and he has to answer for his past, for his drug use. That is a sticking point with me. It's a powerful scene, pivotal I'd say. I'm having a hard time—I guess, with Dan's *involvement.*"

"I'm not sure I follow," Eric said. He was lost. Had he missed a meeting? Was this movie going on without him while he was left at the starting gate?

"I just don't see Dan playing this, I guess is what I'm saying."

"Ah," Eric said, stalling. "You—you've never worked with him."

"Oh, I love Dan. Yes, we've done two films together. You *know, Meanwhile in Love?* He is wonderful. What I am asking is, will he say these lines? I'm betting not. You know he's a notorious ad-libber, rewriting his lines at will?"

"Yes, I know. This is something Sandy and I have discussed. It'll be fine. But you—you're lost as to what is going to happen here if Dan goes off on his own?"

"Yes, I guess that's a good way of putting it."

The meeting went a little smoother after this.

Eric almost relaxed. They ran lines for a while, Eric, who was no actor, feeding her Dan's lines, sometimes giving her a couple of options, a couple of *maybe* lines, some ways Dan Yumont might take his character.

They drank a bit more. Once Hope Davis laid her hand on Eric's arm. It was what the character might have done. Yet it hit Eric like the spark Prometheus stole. He wanted her to do it again, he wanted her to do it forever, but the gesture was never repeated.

He tried to keep his mind on his movie. His movie. Hope Davis was so committed, so professional. He thought that she could see that he was faking it, going through the motions. Perhaps not; perhaps it was only his personal mistrust.

At the end of the evening, he kissed Hope Davis on the cheek.

"Tomorrow will be grand," she said. Was this to comfort him? Did he seem at sea to her, in need of rescuing?

"Yes," he answered.

All the way back to his house his lips were numb as if he had ingested alum.

He recalled a line he had read once but could not remember where: "Hope has left you like a painted dream."

REEL TWO: UNFAITHFULNESS

I have a lot of tics and phobias. I hate to travel. I hate to go to festivals. I hate it when somebody gets close behind me. I'm scared of the darkness. I hate open doors.

—Ingmar Bergman

30.

There was one long table, where kings of ancient civilizations might have held their summits, a coarse, wooden monstrosity surrounded by folding chairs like suckling pups. Eric sat at one end of it, Sandy just to his right. It was early in the morning and there were a lot of groans and a lot of jokes about coffee.

Here it is, Eric thought as he surveyed the table. Here is my movie.

Even saying it he didn't believe it. Didn't believe it was his. Didn't believe it would ever get made. It had been a rough road getting here.

The missing chair just next to Sandy's was Dan Yumont's. The places weren't marked but it was left empty anyway, in deference to him, the wayward star.

Eric rose reluctantly.

He had no prepared words. These read-throughs—how many had he managed in his long career? They were tiresome, being the first step, the baby step before the movie learned how to walk, much less dance.

"It is with a heavy heart that I tell you that we are about to begin the long and arduous process of dragging this movie into the light."

There were smiles. He was being breezy, he thought. Perhaps breezy was beyond him. Perhaps it was behind him.

"Ok, so Dan's not here yet. I'll read for him. Any questions before we begin? I've talked to all of you individually so you know the score here. The script is almost finished. If it seems that we're on a road to nowhere, fret not. Sandy has written some pages that are shimmeringly beautiful. And, many of you may already know this: we've hired Camel Eros, the famous beat poet, to punch up the story, to add Memphis Mojo. His blues—that is, his blue sheets, should be with us in the coming days."

Sandy added: "The story hasn't completely come together yet but I've got a visual concept, at least that, a good visual concept."

He looked up and down the table. These were pros. They knew the score. They recognized the bullshit for bullshit. They knew that they were working at the thin end of Eric's career, his last gasp perhaps. Yet, they showed up here in Memphis enthusiastic and prepared. Eric caught Hope's eye and her smile was cool suasion, a reason to continue. They were all pros, Eric kept saying to himself. Except, of course, Kimberly, who wouldn't meet Eric's eye. She sat in gleaming silence next to Ike Bana, who, in a sleeveless shirt, looked like the preening, egotistical tennis star, Rafael Nadal. (And like Nadal, Bana was forever picking the back of his pants out of his ass. Was this a nervous tic, or just bad grooming?) Who was Bana preening for? Eric wondered. Could it be Kimberly? Let him do it. Let him open up her head full of snakes.

The reading went as well as these things go. There were many questions about lines. They tried to wrestle with them, make them all cohere. Sandy was a tigress when working. She defended her words, yet was always open to questions, to the struggle to make it work. And Eric was reminded of her hard-nut intelligence, how she could twist language as if it were her own thick hair and she making a French braid.

Eric's own reading of Dan's lines was stiff. He was no actor. Hence, the scenes he attempted to limn were going poorly. Then, suddenly, right before they broke for lunch Dan Yumont strode in. His face was a dark path. His attempted smile a poor approximation. He looked as if the complicated geometry of dressing was beyond him.

"Hello, Dan," Eric said, without inflection.

"Hello, people," Dan said. "Sorry. Traffic."

A ridiculous statement, of course. Perhaps Dan had forgotten he was in Memphis. Perhaps he didn't know he was in Memphis.

Dan bussed Hope Davis and she laid a sweet hand on his whiskered cheek. He greeted a few others in friendly terms. Many of those gathered were in awe of Dan a bit, despite his dishevelment, or maybe the dishevelment was part and parcel of his image, his animal power. This was, after all, the creator of Pat Lucy in *Harmon's Dilemma*, of Bob Canaletto in *Bob Canaletto*, of Johnny Niagara in *Bible of Dreams*. And his Iago was still the textbook Iago, the one that would be studied forever. Ditto his Rodya Ralskonikov. Ditto his Pozzo.

Eric was temporarily befuddled. He had lost his place, seriously lost his place. He started to introduce his wayward star as if he had to both apologize for him and explain who he was. Absurd, Eric thought, and caught himself.

Then, before Dan sat down, he spoke as if from a dream: "The bus that used to stop at this stop does not stop at this stop anymore. You can stand there all day and no one, I mean no one, will even tip his hat. The rain is the most insistent thing about this place. We give it another name."

Everyone held their collective breath. Kimberly Wink's eyes welled.

It was a line from the movie, unmistakably one of Sandy's lines that helped shape Dan's character. He recited it now as both a mollifying agent and as a warning: do not underestimate me. I do what I do well.

The day went better from there. Even the lunch was good, some Memphis barbecue thrown in with the requisite chicken and vegetarian dishes, and the conversation during it lively and warm. This quickly they were becoming a troupe. Eric was grateful. At the end of the day he was more than grateful; he was almost pleased.

Late in the day, when weariness began to set in, Eric called for a break. Dan's reading was the talk of the troupe; it was rough, unmannered and so meticulously thought out that the character Sandy had seemingly only sketched had sprung magnificently to life. And this was only the first day.

Then there was a commotion at the entrance. One of the security people was trying to catch someone's eye, anyone who could tell him what to do with a madwoman who was trying to break in.

Just as Eric rose to go see what he could do, a female voice cut through the air like a cat in heat.

"I'm in this goddamned picture!" it howled.

And Dudu Orr broke from the guard's grasp and headed toward the illuminated table where the kings and queens of make-believe were holding their meeting. The glittering gathering seemed to stop Dudu Orr dead.

Everyone at the table looked lost. Slowly, some of the faces turned inevitably toward Dan Yumont.

It dawned on Dan, gradually, that something was expected of him.

He looked toward Dudu Orr, standing there in her high school finery, a cheerleader frozen in the headlights, and turned back toward the actors.

"I've never seen her before," he said.

31.

That morning Camel told himself he was ready to work. He had fallen asleep the night before with rain gently falling on his cabbages and lines from Sandy's script dancing in his head like psychedelic mushrooms in an off-Broadway *Fantasia*. When he awoke he was mildly surprised to find that it had not rained the night before.

After a wheat-germ shake and his handful of medicaments, some prescribed, some experimental, Camel sat on the sprung couch with a legal pad and a rollerball pen. His back ached from the activity he and Lorax had practically invented the day before. He watched her sleep now, curled on the rug like a dog, thumb in mouth, hair stuck to her pretty forehead with sweat. Ah, youth, Camel thought, and his mind went back to the day, to the time when he and his friends wanted to change the world. The world changed with or without them. Had they done any good? Camel thought so, if only in the small spark of individualism that still lived in the lunatic youth like Lorax.

Camel smiled one sad smile at Lorax's nakedness. Her perfect little nuciform body only vaguely stirred him. Something deep inside him turned over once. His engine did not engage. Yet, he knew she was beautiful. He still knew that.

To work:

Camel put the pen point to the paper. A small dot appeared. A beginning.

Camel looked deeply into the dot. He imagined it was a hole, and he was traveling downward. Or was it upward? A wormhole in space. He was traveling; that was the key. Then, abruptly the dot was an egg, a black egg, the future Leda's child. The egg that held the key to the story Camel had to write. But how to break in? How to break the shell, peacefully, nonviolently? He stared long and hard at the egg.

Process. That's what this was.

He had to remind himself that writing was a process. This seemingly pointless woolgathering was writing, too. Not writing was writing, too.

He thought Gary Snyder had told him that.

Now, the pen was poised above the pad again. Just to the right of the egg.

Camel thought that a pretty name for a poem. Just to the Right of the Egg. He could see it laid out on the page, could see it in a small chapbook of poems, a letterpress edition. It would be the collection's cornerstone. The edition would quickly sell out and reestablish Camel as a force in poetic circles. Were there still poetic circles? Camel thought of them as the circles that were still spreading outward from the stones that he and Brautigan and Snyder and Corso had thrown into the jade pool.

A word. That was what was called for. Camel had it now.

When Lorax awoke she thought Camel had died and rigor mortis had set in. She was preparing in her head the story of his death, how he died doing what he loved, pen in hand, poised to spill his guts, unaware that the Angel of Death was his final editor.

Then he blinked.

"Oh, Jesus," she said. "I thought you were dead."

Camel blinked a few more times.

"What time is it?" he asked.

"How would I know?" Lorax said, kindly.

"Could you look at the clock for me? It's on the table behind me."

Lorax sighed. She stood up. Her pubic hair glistened like ambergris in front of Camel. Camel managed another sad smile.

"It's almost noon," Lorax said. And then, in Pavlovian response, "I'm hungry."

"Feed your head," Camel said.

Almost noon. A full morning's work, Camel thought.

He laid the pen down and followed Lorax into the kitchen.

"Want me to pick some tomatoes?" he asked her.

"For breakfast?" she asked, squinching up her little animal face.

"Yes!" Camel said. "Omelets!" And he hustled out the front door.

When he returned with three tomatoes the size of softballs Lorax had dressed, if by dressing you mean she had shrugged on a T-shirt.

"How's the movie?" she asked, her bright, chattery brain awake now.

"Ah, the movie," Camel said, slicing his bright vegetables. "I'll tell you about the movie."

Lorax sat on a tall stool. She was a good audience.

"Movie exists because it exists. There is no reason for Movie any more than there is reason for housefly or pond. Movie is. So, where does Camel come in? How does Camel approach Movie? That's the question. And here's what I have figured out. Camel comes to Movie with hat in hand, the outsider, the beggar. See? So, how to be beggar and still contribute? Ah, now we're getting somewhere."

Lorax was already getting drowsy again. She loved Camel. She didn't care if he made sense because the world didn't make sense.

"So, have you, like, written any lines for them?"

Camel looked at his guest as if she had just invented physics.

"My dear, Camel always does what Camel says he'll do."

"You're a sweet Camel," Lorax said, her smile as soft as the place where her neck met her shoulder. "How's that omelet coming?"

"I am about," Camel said, raising one finger like Archimedes, "to break some eggs."

32.

Eric and Mimsy Borogoves met for dinner that night at a Midtown eatery called Tsunami. They sat at an outdoor table and relished the Memphis evening, so cool you could hold it in your hand or rub your cheek against it. The surrounding Cooper-Young neighborhood was like a liminal space made of color, kites and butterflies and music, music so solid it stood straight up on its stalk.

Mimsy had not come to the set that day as planned. Eric had forgotten, in his boyish excitement at seeing her again, to ask why she hadn't.

"Hello, Mr. Director," Mimsy said, holding his hand.

"Hello, My Lover," Eric said. The day's problems, the entire, overwhelming problem of the movie, seemed miles away.

"Tell me about your day."

And it all came back. Such a brief respite.

"Ach," Eric said. He was hoping that said it all.

"Not going well?"

"Oh, it's going well enough. I mean, the first read-through went well enough. Dan—well, hell, he's Dan Yumont. And despite one of his illegal consorts breaking into the set he was—almost professional. Jesus, what he can do with a single line. I mean, he can make it his own so quickly. Do you know what I mean?"

"I do," Mimsy Borogoves said. "I loved him in *Godot*."

"You saw that?"

"Yes, I did. I was in New York meeting some old girlfriends and one of them got us all tickets. He was—well, masterful."

"Yes. Yes. I mean, I didn't see it, but, yes, I can imagine it."

"So, what is it? What's bothering you?"

"I can't—" and here Eric came up against it. What was bothering him? Suddenly, honesty came from him like nausea. He was sick with honesty.

"I can't direct anymore," he said. His head felt heavy. His hands thick.

"Oh, Eric," Mimsy said. "Of course you can."

"No, really. I have no idea what I'm doing."

"All artists feel that way."

"At the outset, yes. At the beginning of their careers, everyone feels like a phony. But, Mimsy, I—I'm dried up. This is why Hollywood spit me out."

"No, I don't accept that. You're in an unforgiving business, in some ways, an unappreciative business. But, dammit, you've got moviemaking skills that make most directors look like pikers. Come on. You can direct this in your sleep."

"That's what I'm doing. I'm somnambulating through the damn thing. And, Mimsy, listen to me now. This movie—there's nothing there. Sandy hasn't written a story. She's written a set of snappy scenes, some worthwhile dialogue—but Sandy's gone, too. She and I do not touch, even tangentially. There is no connection between what she's written and me. We might as well be doing different projects."

"You don't believe in her story."

"There is no story! That's the dirty secret. There is no story. And I think the actors sense it. I think that's what sweet Hope Davis was getting at by inviting me to read with her. She knows there's nothing there."

They sat in smoldering silence while some elaborate plates of food were set before them. Eric looked at his fish as if it were a work of modernist art that he couldn't comprehend. Mimsy pushed her plate aside and put her elbows on the table. She leaned toward Eric.

"What can we do?" she asked.

They wound up at Mimsy's apartment, on her bed, which was as large as an inland sea. There was a TV at the foot of the bed, lending the room a sort of hotel suite quality.

They had kicked off their shoes and slithered downward onto the coverlet. They had eaten too much.

"What's on TV?" Eric asked, propped up on pillows.

"Let's see. A lot of bad movies. Cheese factor five."

"For instance?"

"Well, I mean, I'm going on stars, though I hesitate to say, seeing as how you might know these folks and/or have worked with them."

"Talk to me," Eric said.

"Well, you know, certain actors, actresses, you don't really have to check into the movie; they raise the cheese factor by name alone. Jeff Fahey."

"He's a good friend."

"Oh, shit—see—"

"I'm kidding. Yes, Fahey's cheese factor is high."

"Any of the Love Boat crew, or Charlie's Angels. Connie Sellecca, Dean Cain, Billy Zane, uh, Richard Grieco, Shannen Doherty naturally, Lorenzo Lamas, Christopher Lambert—almost anything on the Lifetime Channel."

"Uh—Tom Wopat—"

"Obviously."

"Ken Wahl. Yasmine Bleeth."

"Yes! . . . Sybil Danning, Sean Young, mostly, Michael Landon."

"Little Joe!"

"Ok, maybe we shouldn't play this game."

"Well, I get it, anyway. What's really on?"

"Hm, here's something that may make your head explode. *L'eclisse* is on Sundance, opposite a Shannon Tweed thriller."

"Ha. Let's watch both."

"Really?"

"Sure. Flip back and forth."

"Our heads might explode. There. There you go."

"I've had a crush on Monica Vitti ever since—"

"The spy spoof—"

"Yes! She was Modesty Blaise! And I met her once. This was back in . . . whenever. I wanted to cast her as Magda in *Cracker Hobgoblin*."

"Why didn't you?"

"Studio wanted—"

"Huh."

"Monica Vitti's smile."

"Yes, a wonderful smile."

"Monica Vitti's smile is totemic, like the light behind Tuesday Weld's hair in *Play It as It Lays*, or Cary Grant's cool . . . And her laugh, it's infectious. She's lit from within. And those Antonioni silences. They seem to go on for weeks, the attenuated silence between people."

"Here."

"That was an abrupt segue."

"Let's hear you wax poetic about Shannon Tweed's dimpled chin."

"Ha. I'm pretty sure she's a man."

"Except for those."

"Yes."

"You see a lot of those."

"Well, that's her calling card. This isn't Pinter."

"These Tweed thrillers. They're teases, mostly."

"You've studied them?"

"Well, hell, there seems to be one on at all hours of the night. And I know all hours of the night. The education of the insomniac."

"I see."

"Anyway, these sex thrillers, they take you up to the moment, time and time again, and let you down. Frustrating."

"Antonioni is sexier."

"Probably."

"Though, well, that is pretty sexy."

"Well . . . "

Eric placed his hand on the inside of Mimsy's thigh. On the screen Shannon Tweed's panties, so white between her legs, were being kneaded by her hunk's hand.

"Get it, girl," Mimsy said.

Eric's pinkie moved to the middle space where it was soft and warm. Mimsy Borogoves spread her legs wide.

"Turn it back to *L'eclisse* and take me," she said.

33.

Meanwhile, Dan Yumont was holding the hand of his teenage conquest as they stood in the parking lot of an abandoned K-Mart, leaning against Dan's rental car. Across a ragged field they could see the twin screens of a drive-in. Simultaneously they could watch either Bruce Willis or Dan himself in *Jackpot Jeopardy!*

"So, anyway, I thought, you know, that you might be mad at me for today, for almost breaking into the set, for disturbing the filming and all, but, really, it didn't seem like you all were doing anything, just sitting around, and I know that maybe the part you said they'd give me might not even be written yet, she seems like a bitch, the writer, I hope she's not a friend of yours but she didn't seem all that friendly to me, but, then I thought, maybe I should make myself available so it could all proceed, you know? So that they could get a look at me and know what I can do, you know, Danny? I didn't do wrong, did I?"

Dan Yumont squinted.

Cicadas in the trees at the edge of the macadam played a Ravi Shankar tune.

In *Jackpot Jeopardy!* Dan was holding a gun the size of a waffle iron. He was squinting there, too. Bad guys were squinting back at him but, really, their squints were overshadowed by Dan's more formidable squint. The camera closed in on Dan's eyes.

"Don't call me Danny," he said, at last.

It had been a long day on set. They had quit after 6 and, for Dan, that meant a whole day without his personal freedom. He was 45 years old, still in great shape, but he didn't suffer fools any longer and he didn't let much stand in the way of drinking and fucking. This was his code as near as it could be articulated.

But, he was also a professional actor and that had its responsibilities. Though he had box office clout like few male stars of his generation he was still a craftsman, a perfectionist. Though it came easy to him he still took it very seriously. This was part of his mystique, of course, the ability to create such memorable performances in the midst of such a messy life.

Dudu was stung. She bit her lip and lay back on the hood of the car. She tried to watch *Jackpot Jeopardy!* but her eyes were teary and the screen was blurred. She only wished Dan would turn toward her and look right now. She was wearing a tube top and her flat stomach and perfect breasts were practically speaking for themselves. She only wanted Dan to want her again as he had in her bedroom. She imagined herself back in her room, amid her stuffed animals, sitting across Dan, holding a plush manatee in his mouth to muffle his coarse exhalations. She was trying to will him to turn toward her. She was his little fuck bunny. He said so. Look at your little fuck bunny, she thought, squeezing her eyes closed to hold back the tears.

Dan turned toward her.

She smiled.

"I'll talk to Eric tomorrow about a small part for you," he said.

"Oh, Danny!" she said, throwing her arms around him.

34.

"So, what do you know about this photographer, this Ricky Lime?"

Eric and Mimsy lay in afterglow, the satiny sheets pulled halfway over their naked bodies, the television set to low burble. Eric had one momentary twinge of guilt—an ancient reflex—and thought, briefly, about Sandy and where she might be. Then he looked again at Mimsy Borogoves and thought her beautiful in a way he seldom encountered, beautiful right through, deep like soul-deep. Is this love? he wondered.

Mimsy was balancing a glass of whiskey on her flat stomach.

"I don't know him very well," she said. "Why?"

"He keeps coming to me with these, um, anomalies in his photos, these blurry images that I think he thinks are ghosts."

"Ghosts? Isn't there practically a whole school of ghost photography, most of which has to do more with bad-quality film than anything occult?"

"Well put. Yes. But, well, I've seen these photos . . . and they do seem eerie."

"In what way?"

"Don't laugh. There is a whole series of Elvis photos."

Mimsy smiled. Her mouth was busy swallowing a titter. It may have been a titter, or perhaps a guffaw.

"I know, I know. It's just that the sap is so insistent. I think I ought to fire him."

"Well, Eric, I wouldn't throw out the baby with the bathwater. How are his stills for the film?"

And there it was again, stalking him like a ghoul, the evidence of his own detachment, his own lack of passion for the project. Surely it showed in everything he did and didn't do. For instance, lying in this plush bed with the beguiling Mimsy Borogoves rather than doing—well, a dozen or more necessary things to make sure this film came together.

The question before him was: how are Ricky Lime's stills for the film? Grand? Inspiring? Germane?

Eric had an opinion, surely. He'd seen the photos. He knew the city. What was the sticking point? Oh, yes, he had no real vision for this movie, no real consistent vision.

"Yes, I suppose so," he said.

"Then—forget the other. Let it slide. Use his images of the city for the movie and grin and bear it when he goes all new age on you."

Mimsy Borogoves was a rock, a foundation upon which you could build a church.

"Yes, yes, that's best," Eric said.

"When do you anticipate location filming beginning?"

"Oh, I don't know," Eric waved a hand in the air like a dithering kite. "When—when? I suppose, well, the sets are ready. I guess we should, should—" His voice died away. His brow wrinkled.

"What?" Mimsy said. A small furrow of concern passed over her face.

"I don't remember what the locations are. I don't remember what to do next. I have no clear idea . . . " His voice died again, one of the birds sent from Ararat that didn't return.

"Eric," Mimsy said, taking his hand. "Talk to me. Are you having some kind of performance anxiety about this movie? What's going on?"

"Mimsy. Mimsy Borogoves," he said, dreamily. "I—I have no idea what this movie is about. I have no connection to it. I don't remember the story, if there is one. I don't know who is in it or what it's gonna look like, or what my role is, if I have one. What would happen if I just showed up and turned it over to the techies, to Sandy, to—to you—for instance? What would happen? I tell you what. It would still be made. Movies, once begun, are a snowball gathering momentum. All kinds of things will be picked up, gathered on the decline, and the increasing speed of the snowball will either be a good thing or a bad thing, but it won't matter. At the bottom will be this big, motherfucking snowball, perhaps ugly with mud and debris and the accrual of everyone who threw things at it as it rolled downward, ever downward. Perhaps, and this is the magic part, just perhaps it will look like a glorious, clean, glistening snowball, all white and sparkly and seemingly smoothed by experts. But at the bottom, beyond all the folks who pitched in, all who stood by the slope and cheered or didn't, at the bottom there will be a snowball. And, so, I don't matter, see? It's just as well that I am confused, lost, uninspired, fearful. None of it matters."

"So, what's your worry?" Mimsy asked, stroking his hand as if it were a kid glove.

"Ah, so what's my worry? My worry is this: Art. Ok? See how foolish? Art. It's what I set out to do, it was my whole life. I wanted to make art. Now, I find myself back home, making a movie I am almost forced to make if I am to reclaim my career, and I have my mind still on Art. As if I could still wrestle it from the darkness and bring it, flickering into lit-up life."

"Art kills," Mimsy said.

Eric turned to her now. Art kills? he thought. Jesus, that's a frightening thought. Is it true? Eric found himself in the position of being willing to believe anything Mimsy Borogoves told him.

"Does it, Mimsy?" he asked. His voice was weak, drained of its humanity.

"It does, Eric, dear, if you let it. Art, like life, happens when you're doing something else. When the magician makes you look elsewhere."

"It seems simple when you say it."

"No, it's not simple, Eric. It's hopelessly complex."

"What do I do?" Eric asked her. Briefly, for a flaming instant, he believed she could tell him.

35.

Lorax had gone off. She said she had met some people and she was going off with them. Camel considered this. Where had Lorax met some people? She never seemed to leave the house. It didn't matter.

Camel had packed his pipe with some rich homegrown.

He sat, meditatively puffing on it, while a wobbly 33 was spinning out a song called "Magdalene, My Regal Zonophone." Camel believed he understood the song. Herbal insight. The record wobbled so much the singer sounded as if he was gargling. Camel thought this was the way the song was supposed to sound because, for him, it had sounded that way for a long time.

On Camel's lap lay the screenplay to *Memphis Movie*. He had read it 14 times.

And to its jerrybuilt structure he had added two aperçus and one bit of poesy that he filched from an old Lawrence Ferlinghetti paperback.

Was this how I used to write? he asked himself. Yes, I always kept open books next to my legal pad, words of thaumaturges and friends and poet-priests. It's called inspiration. It's called seeking inspiration. Yes, yes, this was just.

Now, he had become intrigued with the liner notes to a Dylan album. He was immersed in the nonsense lines. Something there turned a key, a rusty key.

Camel inserted a line of dialogue into a conversation on page 13 of the script.

Page 13.

Camel stopped and thought about that.

The number 13 held no special significance to him. He was not triskaidekaphobic. And yet—yet—why poke the sleeping demons, even if they were not your sleeping demons.

He erased the line he wrote.

Somehow, at some point, the record had stopped emitting music. He looked long and hard at the turntable. The record was still spinning, the needle lost in some dead groove. The sound was not unlike what a raven makes asking to be let in, scraping its beak upon your bust of Pallas. *Scritch, scritch, scritch.*

He knew a woman named Pallas once. She was lovely in her bones, a deep-souled Southern woman with legs like a spectral dobbin. Pallas Something. Another bird, Camel thought. Pallas Gnatcatcher? No, it was alliterative. Pallas Pipit? Pallas Plover?

Too puzzling.

Screenplay. He must concentrate on the screenplay. He tossed the Dylan album cover aside. Once there had been a record inside that sleeve, a record wherein lyrics were enunciated and proclaimed with the cauterizing voice of an ancient scop.

An album. A record.

Camel considered the words, their many meanings. What was missing?

The music.

He rose, reluctantly, and pulled a record from the derelict crates that housed them. He reached in at random, trusting providence to deliver to him the music that he needed at that particular time.

He didn't even look at the disc. It spun. That was important. He placed the needle carefully at the beginning of the record.

This was crucial. Begin at the beginning. Not that Camel believed by doing so one could find the straight path through.

No. Nothing was that simple.

The music began. Gypsy muscle music. Music from the fen.

A droning voice. A song called "I Just Sit There."

Yes.

Whose voice? Not Dylan, Dylan-lite. David Blue? John Kay? Janis? Perry Como? Camel knew this voice. Was it Sonny Bono? Sonny, dead now, Camel mused, telling him, from the beyond, to just sit there.

Camel returned to his chair and just sat there. He trusted the message as it had come to him through honest channels.

And as he sat he cleared his mind. There was no more clutter there now. No more random seekings after names that alliterated or did not. No more woolgathering. No more lines of poetry.

No more lines of poetry.

No more writing.

No more writing.

Camel put his face in his hands and wept. He wept.

Later, he used the telephone to call a friend.

"I have to get out," he said. "I have been locked in this detention center by men in suits, alcaides with money, Baal worshipers with their deceitful gods and corrupt dreams, dreams that twisted and warped and bled. I have to get out."

His friend said that she would come right away.

Camel sat back in his chair. It would be better now. There were people alerted and they were coming. They would take Camel out of the house and show him the variegated world and how he could fit back in. He would be shown that even the most outside outsider has a place in the human parade. Camel began to smile.

And then to laugh.

When his friend got there Camel was sitting in his chair laughing like a moonstruck amadan.

36.

Eric left Mimsy's bed grudgingly.

And, upon finding himself outside her apartment building, he couldn't remember how he had gotten there. Cab? Or his driver? No, not that.

Oh, Mimsy had driven him. Should he go back and remind her? No, actually he felt like walking a bit. It just might clear his head. And it just might reconnect him to this city. He figured he could hail a cab when he got tired.

Downtown Memphis at night was quite a sight. Not what he remembered. It seemed to hum with life and glow with neon light. He walked east on Madison, heading away from the river and the city lights.

After a bit of walking he found himself inhaling the smell of baking bread. It hit him like a madeleine. The Wonder Bread factory. Does one call it a factory? He remembered it from his elementary school field trip there, where they gave you free samples at the end of the tour. He remembered how disappointing the little hunk of white bread was after imbibing that smell. It was like a stolen sip of vanilla. But, surely they weren't baking bread now, at nearly one a.m. Was this sense memory? Or the ghost of his youth returning with olfactory hallucination? He laughed to himself and thought of that crazy Ricky Lime.

Eric realized pretty quickly that he was bone-tired and that to walk, even another mile, would lay him out. He also realized— or recalled—that one doesn't hail a cab in Memphis. There are no cabs to hail. His choices were calling Mimsy and taking the chance on waking her up and having to explain to her why he was a couple of miles from her apartment building. Or he could call a cab company, which meant finding a phonebook. A fairly daunting task. Or Jimbo—no, he wouldn't call Jimbo. Or he could call Hassle Cooley. He wasn't sure how that worked except that poor, moonstruck Cooley was on call 24 hours a day.

He chose the latter.

"Cooley," Cooley answered.

After Eric explained where he was, Hassle Cooley didn't even ask why.

"I'll be right there. Lemme slip my pants on. Oh, I have something to tell you anyway," he said.

As Eric continued to stroll eastward on Madison Avenue the streetlights glowed like Christmas morning and the street, nearly deserted, seemed to shimmer like a desert mirage. Eric saw Cooley's car approaching from a great distance. Cooley was speeding his way, pedal to the metal, the cavalry arriving where, really, no cavalry was necessary. He passed Eric, braking hard, spun 180 degrees and pulled alongside the pedestrian, screeching to a full stop. He was grinning madly.

"Boss!" Cooley shouted as Eric entered the back seat.

"Don't call me that, Cooley," Eric said, suddenly so tired he laid his head against the cool glass window.

"How's it going? You didn't need me today? I was ready. You see how much I was ready?"

Eric neither answered nor opened his eyes.

"How's the movie? That's the important thing, am I right? How the movie is going."

Eric opened one eye. It was amazing that Cooley could keep the car on the road since his attention was mainly on the back seat.

"How much have you filmed? Get anything good? How's Dan Yumont to work with?"

Hassle Cooley was jangled on something stronger than caffeine.

"I'm tired," Eric said.

"Right," Hassle Cooley said. And he gave Eric about 30 seconds of silence in which to relax.

"I had a weird dream," Hassle Cooley said.

Eric had heard enough. This jobbernowl was about to iterate a dream as a basis for Eric's next film. How many fools had he suffered thus?

Eric said, with some heat, "Cooley, dammit. To say you had a weird dream is kinda redundant, don't you think? I mean, dreaming itself is weird, a gateway into otherness. And, if you think for one minute that a dream makes good drama, that it can be transcribed into a boffo screenplay, you're sillier than even the most addlepated cabbie."

This came out a little uglier than Eric had intended.

Cooley let his eyes rest on Eric's for a tense second. Then he drove on, his concentration seemingly only on the road home.

After his gorge had subsided a tad Eric thought he should offer a mollifying comment, something interesting from his day, something about film. A scrap to the begging dog.

He could think of nothing.

"We haven't started filming yet, of course," Eric said.

Cooley glanced briefly toward the rear seat.

Fuck him, Eric thought. So I've hurt his feelings. Poor driver.

The hum of Midtown Memphis was buzzing past outside. Eric saw many places from his past, many haunts that were still haunted. Zinnie's, Huey's, Paulette's. Overton Square, which, when

Eric was a young man, was the hottest spot in town, clubs, restaurants, music halls. He saw Billy Joel there before Joel broke big. He saw the Mark-Almond band after their one-hit fame had dissipated. Now Overton Square was three-quarters deserted. Why? Eric pondered.

But there was something new, something that made Eric smile. A movie multiplex. Studio on the Square, which sat just off Madison Avenue, like a cake at the end of a banquet table. He had heard talk about this new space, with its wine bar and welcoming lobby. And every small theater with the new stadium seating. No bad seats! It put Eric in a friendlier frame of mind.

"Look, Cooley," he offered. "I'm sorry. It's been a rough day. A couple of rough days."

"Sawright," Cooley said, tersely. But the evidence of thaw was observable.

Eric smiled to himself. He was doing well. He was making with the small talk when, really, all he wanted was bed and oblivion. He did not live in an ivory tower, or mansion. He was still a regular guy.

"So, I've got another idea for a movie," Hassle Cooley said now.

"Of course," Eric said. "Tell me all about it." He lay back and closed his eyes. Behind his lids another movie was taking place. In it Mimsy Borogoves was slipping her silky slip off, letting it slowly fall from her perfect, glossy tabernacle.

"Ok," Cooley said. "It's a sequel, sort of."

Eric swallowed a groan. Mimsy, Mimsy . . .

"I'm thinking now that there is a huge ethnic market, right? I mean, with some of the top box office stars being black, there's a whole new audience, I mean, one that was there all the time but untapped. Will Smith, Sam Jackson, Ice Cube, Halle Berry. You know what I'm talking about. So, I'm working on this ultimate ethnic cash-in movie."

The pregnant pause was meant for something. Eric wasn't following the script. *Sam* Jackson?

"And the title—" Cooley said.

Eric opened his eyes. He smiled his readiness.

"It's called *The Color Purple Rain.*"

37.

At 2 a.m. Dan Yumont found himself kissing his teenage lover good night. He kissed her long and hard, their tongues alive, their eyes wide open. Dan gripped her in all her curvy places and pulled her close.

"Good night," Dan said, a sweetness to his face heretofore unseen.

"Good night, Dan," Dudu said, and rolled over.

Dan looked at where he was. Inside the birthday cake, shadowed like some film noir, frilly coverlet pulled up to his goozle. Ridiculous, he thought.

Yet, there was this woman-child, body like Monroe's. She stirred him. There it was. Simple and not so pure.

She now pushed her lovely rump against his hip, body language for "spoon me." Dan wrapped himself around her, his well-used Johnny almost springing to life one more time.

But, no, no. Sleep beckoned. Tomorrow they were going to actually attempt to shoot a scene. Dan didn't know whether he trusted his director to actually pull it off. Dan Yumont took a laissez-faire attitude toward most of his moviemaking time. He did his job; he limned the complex characters written for him. He was a master at it.

Still, he wanted, occasionally, reassurances that the project was moving forward, that there was a vision involved.

Tomorrow he would see. If the movie was to become a movie much would be told by the first scene shot.

This was what Dan was thinking as sleep began to engulf him and the 16-year-old girl inside his spoon began to hum a Justin Timberlake tune. Dan had no idea what the song was but it carried him, like a rocking child, into dreamland.

38.

Eric came home to an empty house. He was too tired to worry about where his paramour was sleeping these days.

He sat on the edge of the bed and undressed. When he was down to his skivvies he repaired to the bathroom for end-of-the-day duties. Then he turned out the light, caught his hip painfully on the door jamb and shuffled into the kitchen for some milk. On bad days he took a glass of milk with a shot of bourbon in it. It was medicinal.

He went through the house turning out lights. The idea that he was not anticipating Sandy's return was too depressing for him.

Back in the bedroom he found the ghost of his father sitting on the edge of the bed in the identical posture he himself had occupied only minutes before. At first Eric thought he was seeing himself, an eidolon that was the result of his fatigue, or his bisected feelings toward this current movie. Then his father raised his head and it was the careworn face Eric knew from the last days of his father's life, the times when he was in and out of the hospital. Eric feared that face. He imagined the face exhibited fear, fear of the coming cessation of life and what that might bring. His father, a stoic like his entire generation, showed little emotion throughout his life, but, there, at the end, he seemed to be caving in like a poorly constructed tower, one built originally to safeguard the keep, and one that now appeared to be made of decomposing pastry.

"Dad," Eric said, weakly.

"Hello, my son," Eric's dad's ghost said.

"I, I guess I didn't expect you. At this time," Eric said. He took a chair opposite the bed. In the dim grey of the bedroom this tête-à-tête seemed to be happening underwater.

"I've always been here," his father said.

This seemed astonishing to Eric.

"I've missed you," he said.

"I know, son. But, listen. I wanna ask you something."

"Ok," Eric said.

"This movie. It seems a mistake to me."

Eric was pulled up short.

"That's not a question," he said, a bit peevishly, as if this were a debate and he was looking to score points.

"The question is why," his father said.

"Why? Why am I making this particular movie at this particular time?"

Eric took the silence to mean that he had hit the proverbial nail on its proverbial head.

"Dad, I had to." That seemed simple enough to Eric, plain to see.

"You don't, of course."

"I was practically tarred and feathered," Eric said. "I was run out of Hollywood on a rail."

"Hollywood," the ghost spat. "That faux city, that non-place. Eric, stand up straight. You don't need Hollywood any more than you need fame. You want to wear the suit of lights, that's up to you. But don't hand me that horseshit about 'You had to.' Whatever you do you've decided to do."

Eric was thinking, is this my father? Is that the way he talked in life, so blunt, so full of rock-solid advice? He honestly couldn't remember.

"Dad, I—"

"Eric, when you were younger, you were the golden boy, the kid that was always accomplishing things, precocious things. By college it was already predetermined what you would become, what your destiny was. We all saw this as a good thing, a remarkable thing. Who gets such a solid future at such a young age? Who is promised this? But, now, I'm thinking, you feel like it all was your due, which has now become your cage. You are damned to fame."

Eric was sure his father did not know that this was the title of a biography of Beckett, *his* Beckett. It was only one of life's useless coincidences.

Now, Eric smiled ruefully. His father had come back to help him steer this rocky part of his life, this whitewater stretch.

"When nothing seems beyond your grasp, you lose your rootedness, you lose the earth beneath your feet. What do you really need, Eric?"

Eric's father's ghost was losing his voice. His words sounded gargled.

Eric rose and stepped toward the bed. His father wavered like bad TV reception and just when Eric reached him he disappeared with a distinct pop.

"Pop," Eric said to no one. The room was as silent as a crypt.

There was nothing to do but go to bed, perchance to dream, perchance to wake in a city called Home.

39.

Interior bar. Low lights. Jukebox music.

At the Lamplighter Lounge Camel and his friend, Carla Binnage, were sitting in a booth, quiet the way best friends can be together. Carla had been through the wars with Camel, a frontliner who in the 1960s was known in the movement as Carla Starla, committed street fighter and heavy advocate for peace, women's rights and free love. Her lovers included John Sebastian, Don McNeil and, briefly, but most famously, Stokely Carmichael.

She had moved to Memphis in the 1990s to be near her mother, who was dying of Alzheimer's. And she and Camel had rediscovered each other. Camel's attention to Carla's mother, his nearcommunication with her sad and diminished state, had created a bond between the old comrades that was more solid than red bricks. Carla would do anything for Camel and Camel knew it.

Now, she was swirling her finger in some spilled beer. The jukebox was playing Johnny Rivers. Carla's grey hair, which swept down her back like a cataract, had not been cut since Abbie died, her personal tribute.

"You wanna tell me what triggered this tonight? You ready to talk about it?" Carla said, laying her hand on Camel's.

"Bad juju," Camel said. He looked into Carla's grey eyes. They were almost the same color as her dramatic hair.

"Mm, hm," Carla said.

"Movie madness. Film dumb."

"Ah. You saw a movie that set you off? What was it?"

It sounded logical.

"*Red River*," he said.

"Uh-huh. What about *Red River*?"

"Stealing sugar can kill a man," Camel said. Yes, that was it.

"Hm," Carla said. She appeared to think this over. "It's true," she said.

"Exactly."

"So, now what?"

"I don't know. Now what? Sheesh, that's it, isn't it?"

"Yes, it is."

"Whew. Now what?"

"Another drink?"

"Sure. Are they trying to close?"

"Let 'em try."

"Right."

"What is that you're drinking, by the way?"

"They call it a Salinger here."

"Hm. What—"

"Ketchup in the rye."

"Oh. Oh—ha! Camel, that—ha!—that's priceless."

"Is it?" Humor is one of the first disconnects, a signal of real trouble.

"Camel, really. It's not *Red River* that's bothering you."

"No."

"What then—think—what is it?"

"I'm writing for the movies. I'm writing again. That is—wait—I think I'm writing again."

"Jesus, Camel. You can't write for the movies. You hate the movies."

"I do. I loved *Red River*."

"I know. I mean, you hate the kind of crap movies Eric War-berg makes. Whatever possessed you to—"

"They asked me."

This stopped Carla's rant. She rubbed Camel's hand again.

"Of course," she said. "Of course."

"They asked me," Camel repeated.

40.

Eric is holding the blues, the sheets of dialogue Camel had sent over first thing. That curious little hippie chick, barefoot and grimy, who was living with Camel brought them. She smiled as if she were delivering honey, or a peace accord. What was her name? Laura?

She skipped away like a sprite, down the middle of Front Street. The sun was a ball of white light into which she skipped, like a Bacchante. Then she wasn't there anymore. Eric rubbed his eyes. Morning mist, he told himself, eyes full of sleep. A skipping hippie chick doesn't dematerialize. Of course, one's dead father doesn't rematerialize either, but, for now, Eric was putting that on the psychic back burner.

Eric was trying to decipher Camel's hand, which was spidery and tight as if he had been holding the pen in a death-grip fist. Small black marks like mashed ants. And in pen yet. Perhaps he should send a computer over to Camel's and teach him how to email his work in.

Even as Eric was able to decipher some of the script his head goggled. It was either the most surrealistic flights of genius anyone had ever tried to shoehorn into a movie or it was unintelligible crap. Eric wanted to believe the former even as his sinking sense of just how badly this movie was going was telling him otherwise.

And, practically speaking, he couldn't imagine Dan Yumont saying, "I don't think peace is just for chimpanzees." It was an absurd line. Was it supposed to be?

Eric also realized that Sandy was scrutinizing him, anxious to see just how far he would let someone bastardize her script. She couldn't wait to get her hands on the blues.

So he pretended to read and reread in deadly earnest. His coffee cooled on the table next to him. He was only partly aware of the cast milling about, some clearing throats and running lines. He was only partly aware of Kimberly Winks practically standing on Ike Bana's feet. She was dressed like a hooker—her skirt was impossibly brief and showed off her outstanding legs, legs that seemed to have stood the test of time. Eric's crotch stirred with deep memory, the kind of wasted energy that causes ulcers and wars. He couldn't tell whether Ike was buying her act or not. What man wouldn't at least play along?

Now he read: "Hoagy Carmichael's cigarette wants to take you home, staying till the eggs run out, underneath buttermilk skies, in the land of the unfortunate colored man."

It's a beautiful line, Eric thought. But, dammit, it wasn't even clear from Camel's notes who was saying it . . . and why. Eric sighed and looked up. Sandy's stare was a gorgon's.

"Ok, ok," he said, tossing the pages onto the table. "You try and make sense of this. And when you're done you decide whether the Camel experiment has already failed. Ok? I've got to get this first scene set up. I'd like to get one scene shot today. I think it would make us all feel better, feel more like we have a movie simmering here, inchoate, yes, but a story begins with one line, right?"

Eric hadn't intended to make a speech but when he was through he realized everyone had stopped and was looking at him. Hope Davis smiled her encouragement and he was gone. This was what he did, he thought. He made movies. This is how we create something from nothing.

And as he stood up he noticed two things: Kimberly had her tongue down Ike's throat. And standing next to Dan Yumont was the cheerleader who had busted into yesterday's session.

Fuck it, Eric said to himself.

To those gathered there he said, portentously, a corny line he didn't remember ever speaking before: "Let's make a movie."

41.

The day's shoot had gone well, all things considered. Dan was particularly sharp and the scene, shot ten different ways to accommodate his eruption of ideas, was made whole, was realized like Eric never thought it would be. Perhaps, he thought, for the umpteenth time, we have a movie after all.

During the course of the day Eric was also aware, on the periphery of his concentration—and he concentrated well when filming—that Sandy was angry. Her eyes shone with a fire that he had rarely seen. Upon reflection he began to think that her perturbation had something to do with Kimberly and Ike Bana.

Being driven back to the house that evening Eric kept his cell phone to his ear. Partly because he had to make his daily calls, with rue to Eden Forbes, and with growing concern to Mimsy. He had been unable to reach her all day. Her cell phone was sending a strange message, something about *members* punching in their numbers at the beep. Eric assumed they were connecting that night—he prayed it was so, since Mimsy had become his anchor as he free-floated through this nightmare. No, it wasn't a nightmare. They had shot some film today. It was what he did, directed. It was good.

Partly he kept the phone to his ear to prevent Hassle Cooley from spewing forth new ideas for movies. This evening, though, Hassle seemed off in his own little universe and he didn't even glance backward at Eric. Eric's cell phone mummery was perhaps pointless.

Eric was not using Hassle Cooley to avoid his old running buddy Jimbo. Jimbo had been assigned to scout and he hadn't been around much. This neither concerned Eric nor pleased him. Jimbo was part of his sticky past. Eric did not want to shed that past, even as he had moved so far from it.

Working with Rica Sash was a pleasure. His ideas on every shot were inspired. He was a quiet man, short like Roman Polanski, with black eyes and dark bangs. He spoke only to Eric and then it was in a confidential whisper. His voice low, he would suggest something in Eric's ear. It was always exactly what was called for. Eric wondered, not for the first time, if a film could be made without a director. After all, the screenwriter and the cinematographer and the great unwashed cattle (actors) all seemed to work independently of him. Not to mention all the techies who did their particular jobs with quiet integrity, rarely seeking or needing instruction from Eric. It relaxed him somewhat to think he was not necessary. To think that this million-dollar boondoggle wasn't all his responsibility.

When Eric arrived back at the house, the setting sun coated the front door and walkway with red light. Eric thought perhaps he was entering a gate to Hell. He was surprised to find Sandy inside when he entered.

"Hey, you," she said.

"Hey, why didn't you just ride back with me?" Eric asked.

"I had to talk to Ike Bana about some of his lines. He was, uh, stuck."

"Uh-huh."

"Uh-huh, Mr. Articulate. What are you doing tonight?"

It seemed an innocent question. It never was for them. It was always barbed, weighted.

"I don't know," Eric answered, truthfully.

"Ok," Sandy said.

"Ok. What—what are you going to do?"

"Right now, I am going to shower. After that, once cleansed from dome to arch, I am at loose ends. Up for just about anything really."

This chipperness rubbed Eric the wrong way. He wanted— well, he didn't know what he wanted from Sandy anymore— something *different*.

"So to the shower," Sandy said. But she stood there.

Eric was looking into the middle distance. He felt as if he were standing on a ledge above a street peopled from Actor's Equity.

"Join me," Sandy said. She said it simply, without real feeling. But she smiled. And Eric loved her smile.

In the shower they lathered each other like kids. And when Eric slid into her from behind, standing up, he felt like a kid again. This was the sort of unexpected sexual horseplay they used to engage in frequently. They were younger then. It was an old story.

Yet, as Eric hung there in the warm mist, joined to Sandy at the waist, his arms around her as if she were a life raft, his mouth on her wet neck, Sandy muttered loving endearments, the kind of thing missing from their lives.

Sandy said, "There, there now, My Little Cabbage, there, there now, it's all ok, yes, yes, let it all go, there you go, let it flow into me, it's all gonna work out fine, you know it is, yes, yes, yes."

Eric began to cry quietly. Sandy put her cheek to the tile and felt as if she could sleep there, as if the world had suddenly stopped and peace had entered them, the peace of the affectionate estranged.

42.

Camel was smoking his hookah pipe with the TV burbling lowly, a *Gilligan's Island* episode that Camel could recite along with the actors, such was his knowledge of all things Gilligan. But he wasn't reciting witticisms from the castaways. He was writing lines of dialogue for Eric's movie. His pen was flowing over the pad of blue paper in his lap. He was also humming "Take It Back," Cream's version.

His mind was crackling with purple and green fire. This was the old magic. Camel recognized it as such.

Lorax came in from the backyard. She had been practicing her yoga, naked, on a towel. Which was quite a feat since the outdoor temperature was a crisp 45. Her skin was red as if rough-toweled. Her hair hung in squiggly lines over and around her round face.

"Camel," she crooned from the kitchen, "why is there a bowl of peel-less bananas in here?"

"I didn't need the meat, Sweet," he returned.

"Camel, Camel, Camel," she sang as she danced through the house. "How I love my Camel, tra la la," she sang.

Camel smiled. "You are my Ianthe, you know," he called out. "Though I know an actual Ianthe, Richard's daughter, a lovely woman. Ianthe, traditionally, is a woman conjured by poetry. What say?"

The world seemed a hospitable place at that moment and Camel was not one to let such a realization pass him by. He paused and smiled. He smiled at his hookah pipe. He smiled at the blue paper on his lap, covered with magickal words, enchanted words. He smiled at Alan Hale, Jr., doing his best (or worst) Oliver Hardy. And he smiled at Lorax as she pirouetted in front of him, her lovely young puckery body a peach blur.

"Hey, hey, Camel," she trilled. "You writin'?"

"I am, My Dear."

"That's a wonderful thing, Camel. That's a solid gold wonderful thing."

"Thank you. It is. When it works it's the world's best theurgy."

"You say good things, Camel."

"You're sweet."

"Hey, hey, Camel," she said and stopped. Her body made Camel's heart swell. She was just about the prettiest thing he'd ever seen. And he thought of his lost Allen. Lorax's bright, shiny youth recalled Allen's bright, shiny youth, beauty speaking to beauty. "What's that poem you recited to me? You know, the one with machines in it."

"Yes. 'All watched over by machines of loving grace.'"

"Yes, that's it!" Lorax's eyes grew wide and shimmering. "Did you write that, Camel? Did you write that beautiful line?"

She was breathless.

"No. My friend Richard wrote that."

"It sure is nice. Where's Richard now, Camel?"

"He's with Allen, Baby. He's with the angels, the angels of the last rebellion."

"Aw, Camel. Aw, Camel."

"So many," Camel said. "So many gone."

Lorax moved toward Camel. She placed her rounded belly against his cheek. Camel looked up into her young eyes, eyes that had seen nothing, nothing. Eyes that would, inevitably, see too much. He put his hoary hands around her and pressed his cheek harder against her midsection. He gently began to caress her bottom as if it were a holy orb.

"Oh, Camel, Baby, oh my Camel," she crooned over his head.

43.

Twilight. Carmine smudges on Big Muddy.

Dan Yumont had done good work that day and he knew it. He could pull his particular gift out of a hat. It's what made Dan Yumont Dan Yumont. And after a good day's work he wanted simple things, human things: drink, food and sex.

He took his teenage lover with him to a park by the river. They walked there from the Pyramid, hand in hand, like childhood sweethearts. The park was a long sward of green, manicured and benched and designed for the tony upscale community that had sprung up like prefab glamour on the northern end of Mud Island. Dan knew none of this. He only knew that it was the kind of place that sent thumps through the hearts of young women. It was also the kind of place where you could stand on a bluff and squint into the distance across the chugging, chocolate waters.

Dudu hung on Dan like a fallen comrade. She was agog after watching him work.

Dan was thinking about Dudu's work on the set. She was set to read lines with Hope Davis and it was horrible, embarrassing in a way that left a stench in the room. Eric kindly put her on gofer status for most of the afternoon. Dudu, for her part, didn't seem to be fazed by her public awfulness. Dudu was blissfully unaware of her Duduness.

Dan was not unaffected by her young body in heat, yet he seemed far away. He was almost introspective.

"What is it, Dan? Tell Dudu."

"Nothing, child. Nothing. Thinking about my part, working some things out in my head."

"You're beautiful when you act. You're dreamy."

Dan supposed that dreamy was part of the youthful argot currently.

"Thank you, Dear. Let us repair to yonder village and see about some libations and alimentation." Dan gestured toward the upscale village.

"Sure, Baby, sure. I'm ravished."

Dan smiled at the misspeak.

"Soon you shall be, Sweetmeat," Dan said.

They were seated at a small restaurant, a cozy place with little business. The menu was eclectic, which normally meant nothing was bad and nothing was that good either. Dan wanted a steak, a big red steak. Dudu, predictably, ordered a salad, though her chunky, overly voluptuous body was not built with salads.

"This is a great place," she said, holding Dan's hand, nervously pulling his ring off and on.

"Only the best for you," Dan said.

"My parents took me and my little brother here once. My brother freaked out. He had to be talked back to his seat and assured that there wasn't really something called Death by Chocolate."

"Ha, that's funny," Dan said.

But something was bothering him. Something was prickling his nape. He did a slow turn and there, about 15 feet away, in a booth, sat two college-type beauties. Dan squinted. One of the beauties looked up.

It was Ray Verbely.

She recognized him immediately and four or five emotions flashed across her face. Dan smiled. She didn't return the smile but she didn't look away.

"Hang on a minute, Baby," Dan said to Dudu. "I see someone I need to confer with briefly."

"Sure, Love," Dudu said, reluctantly letting go of his hand.

Dan moved into the booth beside Ray. He sat so close to her she could feel his breath on her cheek.

"Stranger," she said.

"Ray, Ray," Dan crooned.

"Stranger, this is my friend, Sansher Myers."

"Sansher?" Dan said.

"Yes, don't ask."

Sansher Myers was small and dark like an idol. Her close-cropped hair surrounded a girlish face and an extremely wide and wet mouth, with substantial lips. Dan couldn't take his eyes off that mouth. Dan held her small, moist hand for a good minute.

"Sansher is a barber," Ray said.

Sansher pulled her hand out of Dan's so she could take a mock swat at her friend.

"I cut hair," she said. "I own Hair of the Dog out in Bartlett. "

Dan could care less. Though he still wanted to think about her mouth.

"So, Mr. Big Shot, how's the movie going?"

"Oh, shit," Sansher Myers said. "Goddamn. You're Dan Yumont. Fuck me."

"Yes," Dan said.

Surprising, really, that Ray had not mentioned her tryst with a movie star to her friend. Perhaps their relationship was not like that. Or perhaps Ray was just that private.

Ray looked at him as if he were a hoodoo.

"Well," she said, the kind of prelim to conversational conclusion that was universally recognized.

Dan took his eyes off the barber's mouth and turned to Ray. He leaned even closer. She moved slightly away, and slightly back, such was her ambivalence.

"I'll ditch my date. You ditch yours," he whispered.

Ray pulled away. Her look of shock was short-lived. Dan's face was composed iniquity.

"I'm gonna go to the bathroom in a minute. Meet me out back. I hope you have a car." He didn't wait for a response but returned to his table.

"Who's that?" Dudu asked, her teenage emotions bubbling so close to the surface Dan thought she might cry or worse. "I didn't see her on the set."

"She's the producer's secretary," Dan said. It was such a smooth lie Dudu bought it at once.

"Where's our food?" she said now, brightening.

"Hm, yes. I'll check. But first I must air the pizzle."

He leaned over and kissed Dudu's cheek and walked toward the rear of the restaurant without a glance back.

Five minutes later Ray rose and met him out back. He was leaning against her car.

"How did you know that's my car?" she said.

"There are free porno movies at my hotel," Dan said.

"Dan Yumont," Ray said, unlocking the car, "you're a bad man."

Dan squinted at her.

"I skipped out on a steak, Baby," he said. "Let's get room service, too."

"Ok, Dan," Ray said.

"Your barber has a blowjob mouth," Dan said as the car pulled away from the curb.

44.

"Do you want to have dinner together? That would be radical. That would shake up the tabloids," Sandy said, smiling.

"There are no tabloid reporters in Memphis," Eric said. He was dressing. Sandy sat on the side of the bed, still wrapped in a towel.

"Ok. So, dinner, that was the real point of my inquiry?"

"Yes, yes, I do want to have dinner with you," Eric said.

"Where shall we go?"

"I don't care. You pick."

"Let's get away from movie people. Movie people with their movie minds and their movie bodies and their profligate movie ways. I am tired today of movie people."

Eric barked a quick laugh.

"East, let's go further east. Perhaps Germantown—or Collierville. Or, if we keep going we'll end up in Alabama. I know a great Mexican place in Tuscaloosa."

"I don't want Mexican," Sandy said.

"Let's drive to Germantown and see what inspires us."

"Yes, let's," Sandy said. And then, "Oh! Will they let us drive our own car?"

"Yes, well, we won't tell them," Eric said.

Sandy had a rental, an American compact.

Eric's cell phone rang. He prayed it wouldn't be Eden, who

during an earlier phone call was expressing his doubts about Camel Eros. He called him a beatnik and suggested another writer, a guy known primarily for his nonfiction, books about music and Memphis. He was ready to take Camel off the picture but Eric had talked him out of it. Eric had called Camel's blues some of the wildest stuff he had ever seen for movie dialogue. He made "wildest" sound like the highest praise. For the record, it was more customary for added dialogue, for rewrites and revisions, to come in on multihued sheets so that the "final" script looked like a rainbow but Camel refused to work on any color other than blue. "Blue is peace, well-being, heart's ease," he said. Hence, "Camel's Blues" became a catchphrase on set.

The call was from Mimsy.

"Mimsy!" Eric fairly shouted. Sandy jumped and then left the room, dropping the towel behind her.

"I've been trying to call you," Eric said. "Your cell—"

"I know. Sorry. Lemme make it up to you and take you to this great new fish restaurant in Cooper-Young. Can you come?"

"Yes, of course I can. Should we meet there—or will you pick me up?"

"Meet there. Can you do it in 45?"

"Yes, yes," Eric said. He felt like a yeanling.

Sandy reentered the room. Magically she had dressed and seemed to shine with some kind of greedy lust—for something else, something Eric did not have.

"Bye-bye," she said.

"Sandy, I—"

"Skip it," she said. "I have other plans, too."

Eric didn't doubt that she did. His heart sank.

"Sandy, I—well, fuck, I love you."

"I know, Cabbage. I know."

45.

The restaurant's interior was bathed in blue light. Eric sat nervously scraping the tines of his fork over his napkin. The nearly invisible rows he was making recalled some movie—what was it? Parallel lines played a part in some poor amnesiac's mysterious past. Was it James Garner? Or Gregory Peck?

Then Mimsy entered. She walked toward him and her body swayed with glittery magnetism. Eric's admiration was palpable.

"Mimsy, finally," he said, as if they had been parted by the swells of time.

"Hello, Sweet Man," she said, bussing his cheek.

"God, I've missed you," Eric said.

"Have you, Eric? I've had you on my mind a lot. I mean, a lot." Eric felt the angels hover above them.

"Where—where have you been?"

"Working, you goob."

Mimsy Borogoves used words like *goob*. It broke Eric's heart. It really did.

"Yes, yes, of course. I thought—well, I guess I thought you'd be around the set and all."

"I'd love to, believe me. Your project, unfortunately, is not the only thing on my plate."

"Yes, yes, of course," Eric said. Just holding her hand stilled him. "How's it going?"

Eric paused. He could be honest with Mimsy. Yet, his knee-jerk impulse was to damn the thing again, throw his hands up in disgust and pour his heart out about his lack of direction. His lack of direction. Then, he changed emotional gears.

"Actually, we had a productive day. I think—just perhaps—that there is an embryonic movie in the middle of all the uncertainty, a movie that's trying to come out of its egg."

"Well, for God's sake, don't be optimistic." She smiled.

"I know. I know. It's all felt so muddled, so end-of-career fumbling. Then today, when that bastard Dan Yumont was running Sandy's lines—lines which, I swear, up until today seemed dead on the page—well, I don't know, something *alive* happened. Some kernel of human truth emerged. Is that overstating it?"

"I don't know, dear. But it sounds grand. Just grand."

"Yes, it is. I guess it is."

The waiter came and they both ordered some expensive fish. They seemed to settle into a comfort that was balm to them, especially to Eric, whose quest for peace wavered like barometric pressure.

"Tell me about the script. Tell me about your friend, Camel."

Mimsy had that gift. She asked about what you wanted to tell.

"Oh, I don't know. I don't know."

Eric fretted for a second.

"You know what I should do?" he asked. "I should let you judge. Would you? Would you mind looking at it and telling me whether it's just crazy meanderings or if there's sense there? I trust you implicitly."

"You overestimate my abilities, dear. But, sure. I'll look at the pages."

"Wonderful. Can we do it tonight after dinner?"

"Sounds like a plan," she said, and patted his hand. Her slim fingers looked like something ripe and wholesome over Eric's hoary, veined appendage. He would wonder again, and not for the last time, how lucky he was to have her near, to have her during this time.

Back at Mimsy's, Eric took his shoes off and propped them on the coffee table, a mahogany monstrosity that surely came from a yard sale. He was watching a basketball game with the sound off while Mimsy, next to him, glasses on nose, bangs over forehead, was intently studying both the script and Camel's wild addendums to it.

Memphis had become an NBA city since Eric had gone west. He was trying to make out who the star player was on the team. They were holding their own against Detroit and Eric felt a ridiculous surge of pride for his abandoned hometown.

"Stop picking your cuticles, Dearheart. It sounds like flesh tearing."

Eric looked at his cuticles. They burned red.

"Sorry," he said, under his breath.

Perhaps that lanky white guy with the beard. Perhaps he is the star, Eric thought. His moves around the basket were deft and sweet. He held the ball like Lady Liberty holds her torch and quickly slipped it over Chris Webber's outstretched hands. Ah, Eric said to himself. Ah, he's the man.

"Eric," Mimsy said, finally. "Hm."

Eric waited.

"It's wild, ragged stuff, isn't it?"

She was hedging, waiting for his agreement to see where she should go.

"Is it—is it workable? Does it fit somehow?"

Mimsy tapped her pen against the paper.

"You know, I'd say, if you were able to incorporate these wild thoughts—well, hell, it might just raise a moribund story into another place—a place of invention and wit and mystery. It's certainly unlike anything else in the movies today. What do you think?"

This was palliative. Eric smiled as if he had just been promised the Oscar.

"Yes," he said.

"You look like a kid who's just been told about Christmas."

"Yes," Eric said again.

Then a beat later: "Can we talk now about these ghosts I've been seeing?"

46.

Just past sunrise. Downtown.

Eric had to meet with Rica Sash and Ricky Lime. They were moving toward a visual style and Rica had asked for the meeting because he had some fresh ideas. Eric thought again that the secret of this film, the thing that might unlock its mysteries, might lie with his esteemed cinematographer.

Eric was also feeling lighthearted and confident. Mimsy's reassurance had bolstered him. He arrived at the Pyramid very early. The air was chill and the sun a white spot behind muslin, clear as a fresh apple hanging over Poplar Avenue. He was unshaved and his mouth tasted of bitter coffee but he was as happy as he had been since coming to Memphis.

He was met in the parking lot by Camel's fay, the light-footed hippie child who ran his errands. In her small fist was a bouquet of blue pages.

"Hi, hi," she said. "Lorax. Camel's friend."

"I know." Eric smiled at her the way he would at a friend of his daughter's if he had a daughter.

"Camel stayed up late over these. I think it's really powerful stuff."

"Do you?" Eric said. He was honestly interested but his tone must have been awry because the young pixie frowned.

"I do," she pouted.

"Hey, I really want to hear what you think."

She brightened. It was like turning on a dazzling light.

"Well, he's a poet, you know. This stuff is poetry. The first he's written in so long. So, like, hey, I really think it's important stuff."

She smiled as if she had made it all clear.

"Ok," Eric said.

They stood together awkwardly. The pixie was looking out over the river.

"Would you like to visit the set?" he asked.

Lorax seemed to think this over.

"I guess I would," she said.

"Come in. I'll introduce you to my assistant and she'll show you around. I've got to meet with my cinematographer. Ok?"

"Yep," Lorax said.

During the meeting the three men seemed to come to agreement fairly quickly. Ricky Lime was obviously cowed by Sash's reputation and his heavy accent. Lime barely spoke until Rica complimented him on some shots he had done at the Ornamental Metal Museum.

"This has really been a cue for me," he said, waving one of the photos. "The dark forge—it's given me some thematic ideas that I think will color the whole film."

Lime grinned as if his own high opinion of himself had been seconded.

Eric thought it quite humorous and he was happy he had not fired Lime. The two men now were talking shop like old pros. The visual style of the film was made clear at this little confab. Eric was praying, however, that Lime wouldn't spill about the ghostly images he'd captured. It seemed as if he had moved beyond his new age predilections and was happy now talking camera work. Sash grounded him, perhaps.

"And here," Ricky Lime now said, "I've captured something precious, I think." He was showing Rica the image of Elvis on the sidewalk. "What do you think?"

Eric felt the coffee burn behind his sternum.

"It's Presley's ghost," Rica Sash said, matter-of-factly. He handed it back to Lime and smiled.

"Right," Ricky Lime said, and put the photo back in his portfolio case.

When Eric got back to the set the actors were being put in place for another shoot. Sandy was sitting at the big table in deep conversation with Lorax. They both looked up when Eric approached.

"Hello, Baby," Sandy said. "Lorax was telling me how Camel works. His—what did you call it—*organic* way of working."

It was hard to tell if Sandy's ironic and sharp tongue was being honed.

"I love your wife," Lorax said. There was no irony here. One wondered if this child had ever approached irony. She bled sincerity.

"We're not married," Eric said but he grinned wide to let them both know he meant it with love.

"Oh, well, wow, that's cool. I've not been married either."

Sandy laughed.

"Listen, Eric," Sandy said, quickly. "I think this is gonna work. I think Camel's words complement the script in a, well, magical way. I think it's gonna be the Memphis vibe we were looking for."

What was happening? Eric thought. Everything was blithe and chirpy and they were making a movie, right here in River City. I am blessed, Eric thought. I am one lucky washed-up filmmaker.

47.

They were working out a scene with Dan Yumont and Suze Everingham. The young starlet seemed nervous working with Dan the
first time. It was a love scene and the kiss they were practicing
was alternately deep and meaningful and awkward. Eric couldn't
figure out what was going on between them. Suze Everingham
was either deeply involved in the kiss or she was scared shitless.

Here's what Eric didn't know.

The night before, when Dan had brought Ray Verbely back to
his hotel room, there was someone already there waiting for him.
It was Suze Everingham.

Ray Verbely was nonplussed. She had already ditched a friend
that evening. Now, what was this?

"Oh, hi," Suze Everingham said. She was willowy and blonde
and her slim, perfectly proportioned body glowed with heat. She
wore a shirt made of some shimmery Hollywood material, hung
so loosely on her frame that breast and shoulder and belly were
all simultaneously on display.

"Hello," Dan said, tossing his jacket over a chair. "Suze Everingham, Ray Something. Suze works on the film. Ray, here, works
on me."

Suze Everingham laughed. Ray did not. She crossed her arms
over her chest and thought about huffing. She only thought
about it.

"Didn't know you were bringing anyone home tonight," Suze said.

"What's on your mind?" Dan asked. They had never worked together. He knew her slightly from some mutual acquaintances and they had danced once at a party at Jack Nicholson's. Suze had made her name—her minor fame—through a small movie titled *Their Eyes Were Watching Todd*, a gay coming-of-age story, made by a first-time filmmaker who won an Independent Spirit Award for the film. Though Suze won no award she was widely discussed for her portrayal of Todd's girlfriend, who is destroyed by his coming out. She was the hot young starlet for a while, the one everyone was using in supporting parts. She was destined to play only supporting parts for her career, it seemed, if career she was going to have.

"I wanted to practice the scene we're shooting tomorrow," Suze said, lounging back on the couch so that her body's catlike warmth seemed to fill the room with musk. Dan, who catches on to such things with a preternatural instinct, understood the intention of the young minx. Ray was still on the sidelines, understanding little.

"It's a sex scene," Dan now said to Ray. He smiled through a mean squint.

"Oh," Ray Verbely said.

Awkwardly they all gathered on the carpet of the large suite. They sat like Hollywood Indians with a peace pipe, save that peace was coming hard.

"How do you see the scene unfolding?" Suze Everingham asked.

Dan thought.

"It's a smash-up. It's a thunderstorm. It's as sudden as a car wreck."

"Yes, yes," Suze said, excitedly.

"Wait," Ray said.

Everyone stopped. Dan sighed. Here we go, he thought.

"I saw you in *Mitmensch*," Ray said now to Suze Everingham.

"Yes," Suze said.

"You were fantastic. I love that movie. I didn't recognize you at first. You've cut your hair."

"Yes, thank you."

From there the track was greased.

"Shall we practice?" Suze said with a leer, after a while.

"You guys want me to move on," Ray said.

"Not necessarily," Suze Everingham said.

Dan Yumont thought, I love this young actress. I love her so much.

Suze Everingham undressed Ray Verbely gently, like a costumer working on a star. Ray kept looking at the floor until Suze lifted her chin. She kissed her deeply and Ray's eyes widened.

It was only a short time until they were all over each other, a lubricious tangle.

So it was, the next morning, in going over this scene, the one scene on the schedule that day, that Eric seemed to have come late to the party. He couldn't figure out where they were going with the scene, but he liked the energy of it. They were really into it. They were, he thought, real pros.

48.

Afternoon. Rembert Street. The weather has turned slightly warmer. A misty rain falling. The home of poet Camel Jeremy Eros soaks in the steam like sponge cake.

Inside Casa de Camel there is a record player (and here we may still speak of record players) warbling out a wobbly, low-fi CSNY "Déjà Vu." Camel is seated, cross-legged on the floor, his old man's body still spry enough, just barely.

In his lap he holds a legal pad. He is furiously scribbling away, the lines accumulating like moss on the North Side of the Ancient Tree. They almost flow off the edge of the page and pool on the floor but Camel manages to keep them corralled with a sharp-edged simile here and a lovely aperçu there.

The light in the room is fairy light, refracted through moisture like putting phosphorus in a blender. Camel sways as he writes.

Outside, in Camel's mailbox, there is a letter from New Directions Press. An editor there has come up with the idea of *Collected Poems of Camel Jeremy Eros*, a befitting accolade for one of the last of the hippie writers. But Camel is blissfully unaware of this late-life tribute, this opportunity, which, truthfully, he thought would pass him by as it has so many. What was he but one more forgotten writer? And sympathy for forgotten writers was at low ebb, such were the times we live in.

No, Camel does not know that he is about to be memorialized, honored and collected. Instead he is, for the moment, concerned with how to get one actor to say one line, a line so perfect it is inevitable, like Death, like Forgetting. The line must be said. It's the best thing he's written in many years, this line. Yet, he could not lead his actors—which is how he has come to think of them—up to that crucial and absolute line. He shut his eyes and squinted hard. He remembered an old gift, a facility with language that was close to godhead. Inside his brain a small star was exploding, the light flowing into his pineal gland. This was how it happened, Camel thought. This is how it happens.

Somewhere, out on the edge of thought, somewhere even beyond Neil Young's life-affirming descant, Camel was aware of some small distress. Earth was calling on the Cosmic Cell Phone and Camel, slowly, like a titan emerging from the enveloping sea, raised his head. He could hear moaning from the bedroom.

Slowly, he unfolded his body upward. He stood.

Yes, there was moaning from the bedroom. It was not the moaning of physical love. It was Lorax and she was in misery.

Camel moved to the bedroom door. His bedroom was a dark cave. The windows had been covered years ago with Indian blankets. The walls festooned with memorabilia from a life lived for pleasure, for art, for love. Many photos of Allen hung in the bedroom, from her youthful slim-waisted days of power and beauty, right up until her once-lithe body, wrinkled and greyed, was twisting inward like a question mark, folding up into the final obscurity.

On the bed, profuse with blankets and afghans and scarves and gauzy tie-dye, lay the moaning child, Lorax, holding her little belly as if it contained new life.

"Lorax." Camel spoke softly.

He moved to the bed and placed a hand on her hip. Lorax was wearing low-slung jeans and a long-sleeved work shirt. It was the most clothing Camel had ever seen on her and he wondered, briefly, where it came from.

"Oh, oh, Camel," Lorax bombinated.

"What is it, My Sweet?"

"My tummy. My little tummy hurts something awful. Oh, oh, oh."

"Lemme see, dear. Lie flat. Stop tensing."

Lorax straightened out. Camel placed a consoling hand on her stomach. Her body relaxed some. Only some.

"Isn't that a little better?"

"Yes, Camel."

"That will be better."

"Yes, Camel."

"Good, good."

"Oh, and Camel?"

"Yes, Sweet."

"It really hurts."

"Hm," Camel said. "Show me where."

"Here and here," she said, placing her own palm on her mid-torso and lower.

"Dear, dear," Camel said. "What have you eaten today, or yesterday?"

"Mm, mm, mm," Lorax hummed. "Lots of bananas, Camel. I ate your bowl of bananas. You told me it was ok."

"Of course it's ok, Sweet. Bananas. Yes. I think maybe, just maybe, you've blocked yourself up but good. Have you had a BM lately?"

"Poop. Oh no, no poop, Camel. Not today. Not yesterday. Um, the day before . . . is that bad, Camel?"

"Not too bad, Sweet. We can fix it, yes?"

"Oh, Camel, can you? Can you make it not hurt, wonderful Camel?"

"Stay with me. This is what I'm thinking. This may startle. Back in the day here's what we did. A cure that came from Abbie, I think. Or Grace. Or—well, no matter. Richard called it the Boo Enema, because he loved ghosts."

"Your good friend, Richard. Richard the poet."

"Yes."

"What, what do I have to do?"

"You have to do little, My Dear. Relax. Trust me. Take your clothes off. How does that sound?"

"Yes, Camel."

Lorax rose, painfully, purring little *mm*'s, and removed her shirt. Camel helped her pull the very tight jeans off her lovely hips and legs.

"Lie on your stomach, sweet, and I'll get us some reefer."

"Camel, do you always use lay and lie correctly?" she asked, softly.

"I try, Pumpkin."

"That's beautiful, Camel. You're a beautiful cat."

"Ok, Pumpkin."

While he was gone Lorax thought about Camel, his lovely soul, his wisdom, his gentle way of moving through the world. What benevolent gods led her to him, led her here? She thought that she loved him just about more than anyone she had ever met.

Camel came back in, pulling on a toro-sized joint. The sweet smoke filled the dim room. He sat on the bed next to his guest's small, naked body. It seemed especially white against the piled bedclothes. It seemed to glow in the murk.

Camel stroked her back and ass and thighs. While he did so he hummed and toked, hummed and toked. Lorax thought this part would go on forever and didn't mind if it did. Her stomach still hurt like hell but the ministrations felt heaven-sent.

"Ok," Camel eked around a mouthful of smoke. "Relax your ass and spread your legs."

Camel positioned himself behind her and took a great long pull on the doobie. He leaned in close. Between her legs Lorax smelled of forest damp and leaf rot. Camel parted her round cheeks and placed his mouth gently between them. And, even more gently, like a genie's best feat, he released the smoke into Lorax's little anus. And, having released his smoke, he lingered there, pulling the cheeks around his face like a mask. Then he tenderly licked down her deep crack and darted his tongue, once, twice, into her now smoky anus. He rose from her reluctantly.

"Oh my Camel, oh my brilliant Camel," Lorax sang. Something was happening but she didn't know what. Camel was sitting upright now, stroking her body.

"We can repeat as often as necessary," Camel said.

"Hm, hm, hm," Lorax said.

She sat up slowly. She seemed a bit dazed. She materialized like a photo developing.

"Oh, my Camel," she said, dreamily.

"How do you feel?" he asked.

"Oh, oh, Camel, something is happening."

"Relax, sweet."

"Oh!" Lorax said, suddenly. "OH!"

"Yes, sweet," Camel said, brushing a strand of hair from the corner of her mouth.

"Here we go," Lorax sang, and passed an elongated, melodious fart that somewhat resembled the swirling organ in "Like a Rolling Stone." Or maybe it's "Inna-gadda-da-vida."

"Better?"

"Much better, oh my precious Camel," Lorax said, throwing

her arms around him. "I love you, I love you, I love you."

"I love you, too," Camel said.

"I gotta go real bad," Lorax said.

"Yes, that's good, My Sweet."

"Come, Camel, come sit beside me while I poop. Oh, please, come talk to me."

And he did. He talked to her while the sun departed and the Memphis night crept around their house like the shadowy whisperings of the angels. And he never did go back to his legal pad to find the connections that would lead him to his perfect line. The words were never written, never used, never recalled, until two years later, when *The Collected Poems of Camel Jeremy Eros* was released by New Directions and that line, that one perfect line, was the book's opening epigram.

49.

Meanwhile at the Pyramid.

Work progressed. They put another scene in the can.

Eric knew that soon, very soon, they would have to start shooting on location. He needed to talk to Jimbo, who had been conspicuously absent. He was, supposedly, scouting, scrounging, working on the little things necessary to their shooting outdoors. Eric was well aware of the misty rain falling and was worried that this might queer his schedule. Shooting on a low budget meant—Eric thought but wasn't sure—wrapping everything up in a timely fashion and shooting no matter the difficulties. If he had to film in the rain, would it work?

Sandy came to Eric late in the day. She looked weary, the circles around her eyes were like thumbprints.

"Did you like that? That last bit?"

She rarely seemed insecure about her writing.

"Yes, yes, I did very much. That was new—that line about the orrery."

Sandy looked nonplussed. That was rare.

"That was your hippie friend."

"Oh," Eric said. Should he apologize for singling out the one line she had not written? "Well, the whole thing really worked. It had a snap to it."

"It was also hot as hell. What was with Suze Everingham? She was like a cat in heat."

"I know. I don't know. Good chemistry, I guess. Perhaps they have hooked up."

"Of course they've hooked up," Sandy said with world-weary cool. "It's fucking Dan Yumont. Literally."

"Ah," Eric said. His powers of observation, never too sharp, were called before the court and humiliated.

"Anyway," Sandy said, waving a dismissive hand. "That's one that's good, I think. One scene."

Did she mean they were lucky to get one good scene shot? Perhaps Eric was feeling thin-skinned. This was Sandy, he told himself. He knew her.

"Should we consider this mission accomplished today? Give everyone an early reprieve?"

"You're the boss, Baby. Wasn't Hope supposed to shoot today?"

"Fuck," Eric said. "Yes. Lemme talk to her. I need the A.D.— what's his name?"

"Reuben. Wickring."

"Right, has he set up the shot?"

"He left."

"What do you mean, he left?"

"Quit, or was fired. It wasn't clear."

"Uh—"

"He said, ask Cash McCall."

"Who's Cash McCall?"

"That's what Reuben called Eden."

"Wonderful."

Eric, shame-faced, approached his star.

"Hope, you've been more than patient. We're supposed to shoot the living room scene, aren't we?"

"Yes. Is it too late?"

"No, no," Eric said. Did he have the juice to shoot more? He did. It was Hope Davis.

"Ok, I'm ready when you are."

"Yes. Let's shoot it. It is just you."

"It is just me."

"Yes."

Eric was stumbling like an amateur.

"I mean, yes," he said. "Of course. It's the scene where you are on the phone. Right. Right. Ok, let's get that set up."

Eric hustled about now. This will be a cakewalk, he thought. I can do this scene with my eyes closed. Five minutes of film. That's all they were looking at. Five good minutes.

Rica Sash, as if anticipating Eric's fumbling, had begun setting up the living room shot. Eric's heart rose. God, he's good, Eric thought. And the set looks beautiful. He never said, dress the set. He never had to—it was beautiful, naturally beautiful, as if it had grown there organically, like a garden. He must remember to send flowers to the set decorator. What the hell was her name?

Her name is Kay. Kay Tell. Can that be right?

At any rate, the set was a small masterpiece, a living room that looked ready for living, for the living. Then why, Eric stopped to wonder, was Eric's father sitting in the La-Z-Boy?

50.

Early evening. A rented house in Midtown Memphis.

Jimbo Cole is lying on the couch, his head in Sandy's lap. She is absentmindedly twisting his hair in her fingers. They seem to have spent their conversational energies.

When Eric enters Jimbo's eyes widen in mock alarm.

"Oh no, boss, we're caught!" he says.

Eric looks tired and offers no return of serve.

"Did you talk to Eden?" Sandy asks.

"I did not," Eric says.

"I think he might be going off on a new toot," she says.

"Great. What's his bug this time?"

"He's talking about replacing Dan."

"Fuck me. Dan is making this movie work."

"He wants Reliable Smith."

"Who's Reliable Smith? Sounds like a cowboy."

"You're thinking of Whispering Smith. You know Reliable. He was in De Palma's last film."

"Can't place him. What is he, the hot new actor this week?"

"Yes, I think so. As famous for firing his agent as for his work."

"He fired his agent."

"For not getting him the Wilson Pickett funeral."

"Wilson Pickett? I'm sorry, am I particularly dense today?"

"You remember the funeral was a who's who, a proof of insiderness, a badge of hipness. Well, Reliable got squeezed out when Prince called at the last minute and said he was coming."

"Well, hell."

"Oh, and also he wants you to see if we can get Lizabeth Scott. Apparently, Eden's just seen a movie called *Too Late for Tears* and he's gaga for her."

"For Christ's sake. Wait—is she still alive?"

"I can check."

"Do it."

"He also asked if I thought Sash was Jewish."

"Great," Eric says. "Just great. I'm blocking Eden's calls until he gets over this. His passions are notoriously short-lived. What are we doing tonight? What godawful meeting do we have lined up?"

"You're in a good mood," Jimbo says.

Eric looks at him without emotion. He suddenly cannot fathom who he is, what his connection to the movie, or his life is. Sandy he knows.

"Sandy, can I talk to you in the bedroom?" Eric says.

"Sorry," Jimbo says, sitting up. "I'll wait in the backyard. That's a terrific Japanese garden back there."

Is there, Eric thought, a Japanese garden in the back yard?

"What is it?" Sandy says when they're alone.

"I saw my father."

"Uh-huh."

"I mean it. I've seen him twice now. Is it twice? Or is it three times?"

"I'm sure I don't know. You mean, you've seen him, like in your dreams?"

"No."

"You've seen him walking around?"

"Sitting mostly. He just sits there, offering wisdom, counsel."

"Ok."

"I mean it, Sandy. Dammit."

"Ok, dear. And you want me to know this because?"

"Because you love me. Because you might be able to explain why I'm seeing ghosts."

"Plural."

"Well, yeah, Dad, you know . . . and . . . Elvis."

"You've seen Elvis!" Sandy squeals in ersatz delight.

"You know—in the photos."

"You're on board then. With Ricky Lime, I mean?"

"Shit. No. It's just that—something is slipping—it's beyond my grasp. And Dad, he was so solid—so empirical. He's here for a reason."

Sandy looked at Eric the way Claudette Colbert looked at Gable's hitchhiking instructions.

"I thought the shoot went well today. Are you concerned about the location shots—because—"

"No. No. I don't know. The location shoot—well, hell, it'll be ok. Rica's—God, where would I be without Rica Sash?"

"So, what's slipping?"

Eric looked at Sandy for a long time. He wasn't used to explaining things to her. You *know* no one, he thought. Suddenly, he doesn't know her either. You spend your whole life with a person and they remain a stranger who can, at any moment, do something you would have sworn was impossible for their character. At any moment the person next to you on the couch can turn into Mr. Hyde. Or worse. A Republican. A child molester. Someone who defends Bobby Knight. A stranger.

"Sandy," Eric said now, his voice a child's, "is it a movie? Do you think what we've shot is coherent, is—I don't know—building toward a story?"

"Biscuit, we've always flown this way, seat-of-pants. We've always worked without a net. It used to energize you, excite you. You always said, if they knew how we make these things they'd never believe in them. You said, nobody knows how to make a movie."

"I know. It's just, well, this movie—it's this or nothing, right? They're gonna take my toys away."

"Maybe. So what."

"Yeah," Eric said. "So what. What's one more washed-up director? The glittering highway is strewn with their talentless bodies."

"Untalented."

"Wordsmith."

"Come here, Biscuit. Put your two heads here."

And Eric did. He rested his face against Sandy's chest, a place still of comfort, a place unburnished by the ravages of time. He knew Sandy. She was the woman who loved him without reservation.

51.

Dan Yumont thought about his ménage-à-trois and he thought that it was good. He thought that it would last throughout the shoot and that it would stave off boredom. He hated the hours when he wasn't acting, the ones he had to fill with furious activity of some sort. If you believed the tabloids you would think just the opposite was true, that Dan Yumont existed only for the affair, the wild night, the dissolute nighttime.

He now sat across from Ray Verbely and watched her putting fried shrimp into her pretty mouth. The evening with her and Suze Everingham had made Ray Dan's odalisque. The debauchery had created a monster, one that was stuck to Dan with its suckered tentacles. She looked at him with misty eyes.

Dan's phone vibrated continuously against his thigh like another organ. He regretted giving Dudu the number.

Suze Everingham worked her way across the restaurant, signing autographs and smiling her beauty queen smile. In crowds it only took one recognition to set off a chain. Dan had already run the gauntlet and, with the restaurant owner's complicity, had been shunted to a darkened corner where he was protected by the wait staff. Now the other eaters only glanced shyly at his table. Ray Verbely made eye contact with them all. She winked and grinned as if the attention was for her.

"Helloo, Sweets," Suze said, bussing Dan's cheek.

"And you," Suze said, leaning over to press her lips against Ray's. Ray looked startled and tried to quickly reconfigure her face as if this sort of thing were common.

"What's good here?" she asked, sitting. "Do they have menus or do we just ask for anything and they bring it?"

Ray Verbely thought that perhaps that was how Hollywood restaurants work. These people were treated like kings and queens.

"Just order fried things," Dan said. "They fry everything here."

It was unclear whether he meant this eatery or the South in general.

"How 'bout that scene today?" Suze said. She looked like a pleased animal.

"Good stuff," Dan said.

"You were—you were phenomenal," she gushed.

"You also," Dan batted back.

"I mean—you took that thing to—to places I wasn't prepared to go. I was just hanging on, hoping I didn't tumble down the precipice."

"No, now. You more than held your own. It was pretty good stuff. Sandy's script—it has some surprising turns to it. I've been looking over some of the later scenes. I am—I am impressed."

This was quite a pronouncement from the word-stingy actor. The women were both goggle-eyed. A silence like worship fell over the table. A waiter came and went. More food was brought. Drinks. They all ate under that silence.

"Do you want to run some lines tonight?" Suze asked after a while. Liquor made her cheeks rosy.

"Or else what," Dan said.

"Right."

"We could go dancing instead," Ray said.

Discomfiture quickly flashed around the table like sheet lightning.

"Or we could go back to my place and fuck," Ray said, trying to recover. Her hole was getting deeper.

"Now that's an alternative I could go with," Dan said. He smiled at Ray. Now Ray's heart was about to burst.

"We can certainly do both," Suze Everingham said, with insouciance.

"We can," Dan said.

52.

Lorax slept in Camel's lap, curled up like a cat. Her whole body, a soft ring, fit on top of him. Camel was watching an episode of *Gunsmoke*. He was sure he'd seen it before but something was different about it. Then it occurred to him. It was shorter. Pieces were missing. Small pieces of time clipped off around the myriad commercials. It didn't matter. Camel liked the commercials as much as the show, though he fondly remembered when they were all one minute long, instead of the 15-second, bombastic brain-attack they were now. They came at you like a burst of fireworks. That they could get you in 15 seconds seemed frightening and it would have frightened Camel if he hadn't just lit up some Thai stick that he had been saving. It was powerfully mellow stuff and it was why Lorax slept so soundly in his lap.

Fido lay near the door, the better to watch the sheep. Except, now he was sleeping, too, his little legs jumping about, dreaming of things humans would never understand, of the Meadows of Cockaigne, where he ran free.

There was a gentle knock on the screen door. Even though the temperature outside was a crisp 55, the inner door stood open. Camel liked the chill. It reminded him that he was animal and that he was alive.

"Yep," he said in response to the knock.

"Camel?" the voice said softly from outside. Camel didn't know the voice and he couldn't see around the door jamb.

"Enter," Camel said.

Eric slipped inside. It took a moment for his eyes to adjust to the murk. During that time Camel sat, smiling like a child.

"Hey, man," Eric said. He'd never called anyone man before in his life, not that he recollected.

"Hey, sit down, sit down," Camel said, softly.

"She's asleep," Eric said. It wasn't his usual habit to state the obvious. Something about his surroundings upset his mental apple cart. This used to be his turf, this Midtown Memphis boho scene. Now it seemed—quaint, antiquated, as if he had time-traveled, as if he were in that *Twilight Zone* episode where the guy boards a train and gets off in his youth.

"Lorax," Camel said.

Then Eric recognized the pixie delivery girl.

"Oh!" he said. "She's real, real."

"Firmly," Camel said.

"I thought—Jesus, I thought she only materialized to bring your blues to me." He barked a quick laugh.

"She's part sprite," Camel said. "Only part."

"Huh," Eric said, as if this was making sense.

"What can I do for you?" Camel said.

"Oh, well, I was in the neighborhood. My driver—friend—my driver-friend Jimbo had to see somebody in the neighborhood. Some music writer. Maybe you know him. Anyway, I was near here and I thought I'd see if you had new pages for me. And," Eric quickly appended, "I just wanted to, you know, say hi."

Camel sat there smiling. Eric thought perhaps that soon Camel would begin to fade, leaving only his smile hanging in space. Hanging like a gibbous moon over the little sleeping fairy child.

"So," Eric said, sidling into a chair, "how are you?"

"The pages are on the stereo there," Camel said.

"Good, good," Eric said. He wondered if he was beginning to repeat phrases, à la Eden Forbes. "Listen, we're—that is, Sandy and I are very pleased with what you've done."

"Huh," Camel said.

"Yes, yes. It's really helping us along. Helping us to find these characters."

"Huh," Camel said.

Eric looked around. The sweet smoke hung in the air like London fog. The walls were peeling. Every surface was as dusty as the tombs of the Pharaohs.

Finally, he rose and picked up the pages. He fingered them briefly, saw a phrase here and there that sounded like Tristan Tzara writing Noel Coward. It wasn't his bailiwick, however. He knew Sandy could merge these warblings with her more concrete work. She was masterful. She was, he thought, the only reason his movies *worked*.

"Ok," he said. "I'm gonna find Jimbo."

Camel smiled.

"Ok," Eric repeated. "Thanks, Camel."

"Ok, bye," Camel said.

"Bye, Mr. Moviemaker," Lorax said, seemingly in her sleep.

"Goodbye, Craig," Camel said.

53.

And so it went for the next week or so. Shooting moved outdoors and back indoors and then back outdoors again. The movie, like most movies, was shot out of sequence. The only one who seemed to keep the story straight in his head was Rica Sash. Yet, there was a momentum created, one that Eric was only too happy to ride. His actors were pulling together, much like a basketball team during a playoff run. What just a week ago had seemed like disparate pieces, imaginary men and women walking around, bumping into each other, now seemed like a troupe, a *cast*.

Even the small role players were rising to the occasion. Even Kimberly Winks became part of the whole. She was a little too old to be an ingénue but that didn't keep her from growing a haughty élan that she exhibited around town on the arm of Ike Bana. And when it came to shooting her nude scene, a day Eric had been dreading like holy hell, she came through.

"I didn't think you meant like *all nude*," she said that morning when Reuben Wickring explained the shot to her.

"You didn't sign for this?" Reuben asked. Reuben was British and had once studied under the great Carol Reed. Nevertheless, he never seemed fazed by finding himself in Memphis, Tennessee, working on a film about which there was no buzz.

"I, I guess I did," Kimberly hedged. "I guess I thought when it came to it I wouldn't have to, you know, take all my clothes off."

"Uh-huh," Reuben said.

"I thought you could, um, what am I thinking of, you know, put it in digitally."

"Oh. Well, no, we can't do that."

"Oh. Well, can I talk to Ike for a minute?"

"Certainly."

The two conferred, nose to nose, for a few minutes and Kimberly returned with a smile on her face.

"Ok," she said.

They closed the set. Only Rica and Sandy and Eric (and, well, a dozen other people Kimberly wasn't told about) were on the set, a living room. Kimberly was to be seduced by Dan Yumont. She was to undress sitting in a wingback chair, a complex assignment even for a seasoned pro, supposedly daydreaming about a sexual tryst with Dan's character, and then Dan was to enter. On paper it had sounded like a soft porn scenario, except for Camel's left-field sex talk. Yet, Eric trusted Dan to raise the level.

"Ok," Eric said. "Let's try to nail this the first time, people. Kim doesn't wanna have to do this over and over."

He had actually said *people*. I'm only pretending to be a director, he thought, not for the first time.

He smiled tightly at Kimberly Winks. She seemed oblivious.

But when the camera began to roll her glazed-over expression was exactly what was called for. Her striptease while seated was just offbeat enough to be interesting, and the shot of her open legs Eric thought just might work for the film. Not the way Sharon Stone's did for *Basic Instinct*, but more the way Julianne Moore's did for *Short Cuts*.

And, seeing Kimberly Winks's lovely blonde crotch again, between her pale, strong, softball-player thighs, Eric time-traveled back to their time together. He was lost, staring at it, that hot center of her where he had drunk. She was still a lovely woman.

But the reverie was broken by Dan's entrance, buck naked, his flag already at half-mast. Kimberly gasped (as had many a younger actress before her) at the sight of him. He carried forth the banner handed down to him from Gary Cooper. Dan's thingum was long and dark like a mandrake root. Even Eric was impressed. And when the two actors came together on the floor in front of the chair, Kimberly Winks's acting seemed so unforced as to be engendered by real emotion and real heat. There was a moment when Eric thought he had lost control—were they actually *doing it*? he wondered, as Dan's crotch ground against Kim's—but by the end of the shot, done entirely in one take, due, in no small part to Rica's masterful camera movement, it was captured, like lightning in a bottle. Really, it rivaled *Rope* for the no-cut take. When the actors parted Kimberly held onto Dan's hand just a beat longer than necessary, her eyes wide like a schoolgirl's.

Reuben came over.

"I think they fucked," he said.

"I know," Eric answered. "Stay with the money."

"I mean it. I saw his schlong enter her. She looked like a mooncaught ghost. My God, what a poker he has."

"Yes. It's one of his many fine attributes," Eric said.

"Well, what are we gonna do about it? Should we reshoot? I don't really wanna give that bimbo another dose of that thing."

Eric snorted. "No. No reshoots. We'll edit it the best we can and the rest we'll put on the Director's Cut DVD." The Director's Cut DVD was secret code for anything outré, anything from mistakes to alternate endings to an extra 11 seconds of sex.

Memphis Movie had taken on a life of its own. And when asked about the shoot, as Eric was constantly in his peregrinations around his old town, he could actually lay down an articulate storyline, one that sounded compelling even as Eric told it. In other words, Eric himself began to believe in *Memphis Movie*.

Nights for Eric, when he wasn't feted by a host of different Memphians (everyone in Memphis was faking it around the film folks; no one really knew anything about movies here in the Bluff City, but their *enthusiasm* was palpable), or involved in a tricky night shoot, meant Mimsy Borogoves. Their relationship had grown warmer and closer, though there were still nights when Eric couldn't get in touch with her. There was something mysterious about these disappearances, though Eric was so grateful to have Mimsy when he could that he questioned little. And the fog he had been living in, the one in which dead people talked to him, had lifted, and Eric worked. He worked hard at his craft, even while falling in love. A new lightness came to him. He was floating.

Dan Yumont continued his drinking and fucking. Now, he was almost bored if he had only one partner. The threesomes excited him almost to the point at which he felt something. But the feeling was mostly concupiscence. Some nights, though, he reserved for his teen queen. Dudu wanted Dan to attend functions with her like school dances and football games but she settled for rutting in the back seat of a rented Beamer at the drive-in or the occasional visit to Dan's hotel room (she *loved* the porn movies on TV, had never seen anything like them before and often laughed with glee at their physical mummery). Dan, to his credit, didn't try to enlist Dudu in his geometric lovemaking. He didn't attempt to make a quadrilateral out of a triangle.

And Camel and Lorax kept their distance from the movie folks. Camel's part was all but done now; he had added his last fillip to the script. Even so, Eric stopped by sometimes, with gifts for him and for Lorax. He gave Camel a computer that sat in the corner of the room, about as useful as a rocket ship for a monkey. He brought Lorax food baskets and toys, like Slinkys and Silly Putty and vintage board games. She was particularly taken with the Addams Family Board Game. She said this to Eric, more than once: "Wow."

Camel spent all his time in his garden or in front of his TV. Some nights, while Lorax colored in her coloring books (she told him that was her art just as writing was his)—she said, really, Camel, all the original painting has been done, so all that's left is for the rest of us to color in the previously drawn lines, Camel even returned to poetry. He wrote some new poems.

Lorax, it seemed, had permanently moved into Camel's house and Camel's life. They shared the big bed most nights and she never talked again about hitching out west. California had been her destination when she first came to Camel, many weeks ago now, but it had become only something to talk about, a dream state, like a place in a storybook. And no one ever knew if Lorax had really come to Memphis to see a boyfriend. The boyfriend became another kind of ghost, one that leads you in and then disappears, ploink, like a daydream. Now, Lorax was learning to garden, learning to cook, learning that sex sometimes meant helping her partner reach the end with whatever means necessary and sometimes telling him the end is not the goal. Lorax, bless her, was learning how to be in love.

REEL THREE:
THE GUN GOES OFF

Always make the audience suffer as much as possible.

—**Alfred Hitchcock**

There is no terror in the bang, only in the anticipation of it.

—**Alfred Hitchcock**

54.

Dan Yumont lay in his luxurious hotel bed with the TV on and foodstuffs spread around him on the sheets. Dudu lay asleep across his thighs, her snores tickling Dan's little hairs. She had fallen asleep immediately after orally gratifying Dan. Her face seemed innocent in sleep, a drunken angel.

The basketball game Dan was watching broke for commercials. Dan was wide awake. He didn't need much sleep and preferred the long middle-of-the-night hours, when the rest of the world was gone. And so he loved the basketball games from the west coast, which trickled on into the early morning hours. Here the Nets were visiting the Kings. Now, abruptly, Dan's attention was drawn to the actress in a Lexus commercial. She was onscreen for maybe 10 seconds. Her face was puckish and as lovely as a September peach. Dan had never seen her before but his heart was stirred, if it was his heart that stirred when beautiful women crossed his ken.

He picked up the phone and called his agent.

"Roger," Dan said.

"What time is it, Dan?"

"I don't know. Roger. Look, you have to do something for me."

"Anything, Dan. You know . . . "

"I just saw a Lexus commercial. Maybe you've seen it. I think there was a forest. Or a mountain road. Something like that."

"Uh-huh."

"You've seen it?"

"I don't know. What do you want me to do?"

"There's an actress in the commercial."

"Ah."

"Find her. She's a brunette. Got a face like—what's her name in *Lost*, Lilly something. A face like a beautiful pixie. Dimples, Roger. She has dimples."

"Ok."

"Get her for me, Roger."

"Get her for you."

"Right. Find out who she is. And fly her to Memphis."

"Uh-huh."

"Uh-huh. You're on it?"

"Yes, Dan. I'm on it. I've written down what you said. I'll see what I can do. Should I promise her a part in the movie?"

"Yes. Get her here."

"Ok, Dan."

After he hung up Dan couldn't figure out how the Nets had blown a 12-point lead. Dudu stirred from her slumber.

"Who you talking to, Dan?"

"My agent, Baby."

"Oh." Dudu opened an eye. "Did I already blow you, Dan?" she asked.

"Yes, Baby. Go back to sleep."

"Ok, Dan."

55.

Eric and Mimsy were holding hands, walking along the river. It was just past sunset and the filming that day had broken early because the location they had planned on using called at the last minute to say there was some kind of flooding there, a toilet, a sink overflowing. The call came as Eric had just finally wrapped a scene in the Pyramid, the one in which Hope Davis, Deni Kohut and Suze Everingham first realized they were all in love with the same man. It was some of Sandy's finest writing, though its best line, perhaps, came from Camel: "Maybe your calm needed disrupting."

Now, Mimsy was prattling on about some ex-beau who had proven to be a major disappointment. Eric was barely listening, happy just to be near this woman, who was naturally so warm and convivial. He couldn't help but compare her to Sandy. Where Sandy was rough Mimsy was all succor and tenderness. Where Sandy made sex a sport Mimsy flowed like a bubbling stream. It was unfair to Sandy, this evaluation while strolling with Mimsy, but Eric couldn't help it. Mimsy Borogoves opened something in Eric that had been closed. Maybe his calm needed disrupting.

"And that's when I knew to walk, just walk away," Mimsy was finishing.

"Yes," Eric said and looked at her with earnest eyes.

Mimsy squinched her face into a quizzical grin. "Were you listening?" she asked.

"Not entirely," Eric said. "But I love to hear you talk. It comforts me somehow."

"Uh-huh."

"How long ago was this?" Eric feigned.

"Never mind," Mimsy said, but she was smiling. "Listen. Have you ever been to Mud Island?"

"Sure," Eric laughed. "When I was a young swain."

"Let's ride over. I love the tram."

"Sure," Eric said.

They boarded with a group of tourists who were speaking a language neither Eric nor Mimsy understood. They grinned at each other and shrugged.

"Elvis," one of them shouted suddenly.

The identifiable word was like a gunshot. Eric opened his eyes wide. The tourist who said Elvis seemed agitated. Others were gripping his arms.

"Elvis," he said again, this time softer, like a late echo. He was looking toward the island. His eyes seemed sad.

Eric followed his gaze. Someone was standing all alone near where the tram let out on Mud Island. A heavyset man in a long raincoat. It hadn't rained in days and the man seemed out of place somehow, as if he were waiting for someone who would never come. Eric squinted, trying to bring his face into focus.

"Whatever," Mimsy said, with a laugh.

Eric's attention was turned toward Mimsy.

"He's—" Eric started, and stopped himself. When he looked back toward the island the figure was gone and the tourists had moved away from them and were chatting amiably as if nothing had happened. Perhaps nothing had happened but Eric was rattled now.

"What is it?" Mimsy asked. Her brow wrinkled slightly.

"Nothing," Eric said. "I thought he—that is, I thought maybe he was seeing something."

"You ok?" Mimsy asked.

"Yes," Eric said, putting his arms around her. "I am," he said.

56.

With the movie people doing other things Camel and Lorax spent many evenings in quiet work, Camel at his new poems and Lorax with her coloring books.

This evening Camel was working on a poem commemorating the day Lorax came into his life. He saw it now as something peculiarly his, something blessed and uncommon. Tentatively the poem was called "Day of the Lorax." The TV was turned down so that a meaningless burble came from it, something sub-speech. *Gunsmoke* was on.

Camel looked at the wild gesticulations of Ken Curtis, whose emoting bothered Camel the way an Aunt Bee episode on *Andy Griffith* could ruin an otherwise lovely evening. Now, Camel let his eye wander to his roommate, who was on the floor coloring. She lay on her stomach like a child doing her homework. She was wearing only a pair of Camel's boxer shorts. At least he thought they were his. Perhaps they came from someplace else.

Her lovely golden back was something to behold, a bridge out of chaos. He started to add the line "a bridge out of chaos" to his poem but Lorax spoke to look at him and the words crumbled like a tower of sand.

"Doin'?" she asked. Her hair hung over her eyes. Her mouth was a bitten plum.

"Studying you," Camel said.

Lorax smiled. "Lovely Camel," she said.

"Lovely Lorax," Camel returned.

"What are you writing, Camel the Magnificent?"

"Poem," he answered her seriously. "About Lorax."

"Aw, Camel," Lorax said. "When can I see it?"

"When it's done. If it's done right."

"You can do it right, Camel."

"Yes, Baby. Sometimes."

"Camel, am I pretty?"

"Prettier than 20 other girls," Camel said. "Prettier than an oriole. Prettier than an Olympian deity."

"Camel," Lorax said.

"What is it, My Sweet?"

"Come here to me and kiss me on the lips."

"I'm not sure I can get down there, Sweet. Come up here to me."

Lorax did. Her warm body nestled into Camel's lap like a dream date. Camel placed his hoary old hand around one of her plump breasts. He could feel her heartbeat in it as if it were a separate life. They kissed for a while.

"You're stirring in your pants, Camel," Lorax said, blowing a hair out of her mouth.

"I am," Camel said, gravely.

"Do you want to go back to your poem?"

"It would probably be easier than, you know."

"Yes."

"Yes."

"Do you want to do the easy thing, Camel?"

"Not tonight," Camel said. And he pushed his legal pad to the floor. It settled at their feet like a dove. Later, the poem was finished and when Camel saw it he couldn't for the life of him remember penning those closing lines.

57.

The brunette actress from the Lexus commercial was named Sue (Lying Sue) Pine. She arrived in Memphis on an early morning flight, direct from Orlando, Florida. She had just come from shooting a commercial at Disneyworld. Her agent called her and said a movie being shot in Memphis had requested her and she took the first plane out. Barely 48 hours had passed since Dan Yumont had seen her on TV.

Hassle Cooley picked her up at the airport.

"Welcome to Memphis," Hassle said, once she was settled into the backseat.

"Thank you," Sue Pine said. "Am I supposed to go straight to the set?"

"That's what I'm told," Hassle said. He had an uncanny ability to drive his car and watch the backseat simultaneously.

"I don't know this director. What's his name again?" Sue Pine said. She had a cool, studied nonchalance to her speech, the product of good schools mixed with small dollops of dissipation.

"Eric Warberg. He's the real deal."

"Ah. Well, I hope my part is big enough to warrant this disruption of my life," Sue Pine said. Inside she was agog that she was about to appear in a real movie. The closest she had come previously was a walk-on in a Tim Burton movie. The day of the shoot Tim Burton was home sick with a case of food poisoning and, somehow, in the interim the scene was axed. She never even got to meet Burton, whom she idolized.

"There are no small parts," Hassle said with a grin.

"Right," Sue Pine said. She was already tired of her driver.

She was hustled onto the set as if without her the movie could not go on. The outside of the Pyramid goggled her. The inside was like a fairy tale. There were sets constructed with such detail that she thought people actually lived in them.

"Hi," a blonde woman with large hips said, rushing toward her and extending a hand. "You must be Sue Pine. I'm Mr. Warberg's assistant." Apparently she had no name, Sue thought.

"Yes," Sue Pine said.

"Welcome to Memphis. Right now, Mr. Warberg is shooting. So, if you would, I'd like you to come with me."

"Certainly," Sue said. There were people everywhere, people with many things to do. It was like an insect colony inside the Pyramid. Sue Pine thought that each and every person was more important than her. She also thought that given just one chance on the big screen she could be on her way to stardom. She had been schooled to believe this her entire life. Ambition bubbled in Sue like heady foam.

Sue was led to a dressing room. On the door was the name of an actor who, to Sue, was only a dream personage. Surely, someone as grand, as magisterial as Dan Yumont didn't actually exist in the flesh. Surely, he was created by the movies. *This is a Dan Yumont film*, she thought.

Sue hesitated outside the door.

"Go ahead," the blonde assistant said. "He's waiting for you."

Sue opened the door and looked back once, like Lot's wife. She entered a room that was like a set in *2001*. It was so white she thought she had gone blind. And there was no one inside. Only white furnishings, white walls, and a white rug so thick Sue wanted to sleep on it.

Sue turned back just as an inner door opened and she heard a voice. Or more precisely The Voice.

"Hello," Dan Yumont said. It was the voice from countless films that Sue esteemed. She stepped backward, a bit unsteady on her pins, and her eyes took in Dan Yumont, just coming out of the john, zipping up his fly.

"Sorry," he said. "Hello. I'm Dan Yumont."

"Sue Pine," she said.

Dan smiled. Then—he squinted. Sue Pine felt her heart drop a good half inch inside her chest.

"Is that your real name?" he asked.

"No," Sue Pine said. "Stage name. It means *morally lethargic.*"

"Does it?" Dan Yumont said. He was gesturing toward a couch. The couch was as white as a blank screen.

"Does that door lock?" Sue Pine said. She had no idea where that line came from. Her part was being written for her as she lived it.

58.

Dusk. A light drizzle through a Halloween light.

Camel and Lorax were at the Easy Way shopping for dinner. Easy Way was like an old-fashioned vegetable stand housed in a building the size of a gas station.

"Tell me again what you're making for dinner, Camel Dear," Lorax said. She was sleepy. She was sleepy a lot. Sleep was one thing that Lorax did really well. She was Past Master at Sleeping. She held a PhD in sleeping. She slept the way Jacques Cousteau sailed. She slept the way Marco Polo traveled. She slept the way Jimmy cracked corn. And she slept the way Meryl Streep acted: she put her heart and soul into it.

"Camel's Disambiguation Digestive Salmagundi," Camel said with a wry grin.

"Camel, can you do just about anything?"

"No, Sweet. Camel's ability to do things is very limited. I write an ok poem. I can sing like Dan Hicks if I've been drinking. And I can make a stew that opens your bowels and your pneuma at the same time."

"Good, good Camel," Lorax said. She picked up a pointed gourd. "What's this lovely thing, Camel?"

"Um, a parwal, I think. Also called green potato. A lovely vegetable indeed. But not intended to be part of Camel's stew."

"Do we need these big garlics?"

"Elephant garlic. Hmp. I was in Oregon once. I think it was Oregon. At an elephant garlic festival. I was with Kesey and he seemed to know everyone that day. That day he was cock of the walk, the sexy cynosure, and it was a pleasure just to walk around with him and witness how people were drawn to him as if he were the lodestone. Ken was a sweet man, a good man with a heart like a boar's. I use the past tense. Is Ken gone? I can't remember. That afternoon at the Elephant Garlic Festival, with Ken tripping and all smiles and pats on the back, was Magic Time, and it wasn't too long before we had female companionship, twins from Idaho, of all things, delicate, mink women. And they led us to their trailer and there they had some of the finest hash I have ever had the good fortune to smoke. And along with this hash they had a freezer full of garlic ice cream. Garlic ice cream. I couldn't make this up. They were there for the festival, see, and for a treat they had made garlic ice cream. High on hash, Kesey and I thought that ice cream was just about the closest thing to ambrosia we humans would ever be vouchsafed. That afternoon, in the trailer of the twins from Idaho, we saw a little of the godhead, just a glimpse, via the unlikely amalgamation of hash and garlic ice cream. What was the question?"

Lorax was standing in the narrow aisle of the Easy Way and there were tears in her eyes, little moist rims like dew on a flower.

"Camel, did you love one of those twins more than you love me?"

Camel considered the question seriously.

"No, Lorax. Now that I think about it, I did not. And the more I think about it the more I think, well, Lorax, I love you just about more than anyone ever in my life."

Camel paused and watched Lorax's round cheeks dry as if by abracadabra.

"Except for Allen," Lorax said.

"Yes, except for Allen," Camel allowed.

"I love you, Camel," Lorax said.

Camel put his big arms around the diminutive Lorax. They stood there like that for many minutes, as shoppers moved around them as if they were a natural part of the shopping experience at Easy Way.

"Camel," Lorax said, finally, pulling away a bit.

"Yes, dear."

"Is this a chestnut?" Lorax opened her small, sweaty palm and something rested there like an egg in a nest.

"Hm," Camel said. "I think that is a pignut. Yes, a pignut."

"Can we put it in the stew?"

"Yes, if you'd like."

"We should get a stew-bone for Fido."

"Yes, thoughtful you."

Lorax hummed a little tune and smiled. She looked around, seemingly aware of their surroundings for the first time.

"Oh, and Camel?"

"Yes, Sweet."

"Isn't that a movie star?"

Camel's attention was drawn to a woman shopping in the leafy vegetables. The woman was Hope Davis.

"I think so," Camel said. "I think she is a movie star."

"Ok," Lorax said. "Ok, Camel. Let's go home and make a stew and talk about movies and vegetables and poems and stuff. Ok?"

"Yes, Sweet."

"Oh, and Camel?"

"Yes."

"Let's not talk about the twins anymore."

59.

"So, suddenly there is this new actress on the set, some brunette goddess from Provo, Utah. Provo, Utah, for God's sake. Someone with no film experience whatsoever, keep in mind, who suddenly has a part in *my film*. How does this happen? This happens because Dan Yumont has an appetite like the jaws of a jail. Exactly like a jail, now that I think about it. So, now there is confusion on the set. Kimberly thinks this new woman—and get this, her name is Sue Pine, *Sue Pine*—Kimberly thinks she is going to get her part. Which, truthfully, if it were up to me she would, she would take Kimberly's part except that we already have so much of her in the can. The sex scene, well, Jesus, I don't wanna film that again."

Eric was sputtering like an overfilled kettle on the boil. Mimsy placed a cool palm against his temple.

"What are you going to do?" she asked.

"Well, that's it, isn't it? That's the question. That's what Joe LeRose asked today. What is Eric going to do now that his star has brought in talent that has no place? Suddenly it's Eric's problem."

"Well, it is, Baby. It is your problem. Who is Joe LeRose?"

Eric looked at Mimsy. Her face shown like rose petals.

"Yes," he said, after a minute. "Yes. It's my problem. I think Joe is an executive producer. Shit, I don't know. I think that's what he is. Maybe Sandy can write this bimbo a small part. Jesus. As if this film weren't confusing enough. Eden already thinks we have no plan, and he's constantly cooking up ones of his own. Which, well, it's the truth, but we don't tell Eden that. Eden's worrying me with who the releaser is gonna be. Christ, it's not my baili-wick. Call whatshisname—the tub thumper. I am the director. The movie. I am making *the movie*. But, just as it is starting to cohere, starting to look like there's a story behind all the smoke and mirrors, Dan throws me this curve."

"Did you ask Dan what he expected you to do?"

Eric hesitated.

"I did," he said. "I asked him how she came to be here and what I was supposed to do about it."

"And he said?"

"He said, 'Eric, she fucks like an alley cat.' No kidding. That was his answer."

"Good God."

"Right. Good God. What is Eric to do with his star's fuck buddy?"

It was around midnight. On the TV was one of those CNN screens with about 30 different messages showing at once. The sound was muted. Eric looked at it and he thought in the con-fused jumble of symbols he saw something, a mandala, a *signifi-cance*. He was fairly hypnotized by the screen. Mimsy lay beside him reading Marilynne Robinson's *Gilead*.

Eric and Mimsy were in a Peabody Hotel room. They had rented one for their trysts because Mimsy said her apartment was being redecorated. They were registered under the name Mimsy Borogoves to save Eric the anguish of speaking to wan-nabes. Room service had brought steak dinners about 15 minutes ago. The steaks sat on a table next to the bed. They were a task to be accomplished sometime soon, before the fat coagulated, before the potatoes cooled.

"Are you hungry yet?" Mimsy said, absently, turning a page.

Eric was drawn back from the edge of enlightenment. The room took shape and color around him.

"I guess I am," he said.

"I guess I am, too," Mimsy said.

"Let's eat in the bed," Eric said.

"Let's," Mimsy said. "Let housekeeping worry about the grease."

"Right."

"First let's find something worth watching," Mimsy said, pulling her plate onto her lap.

They agreed on *The Laughing Policeman*, a Walter Matthau police picture.

"Never heard of it," Mimsy said.

"It's pretty good. Matthau. And Anthony Zerbe. What ever became of Anthony Zerbe? Well, I imagine he's dead now. It's based on a Dutch thriller, I think. Bruce Dern, too. You know, I asked for Bruce Dern on this picture."

"Is that Cathy Lee Crosby?"

"Um, yes, yes, it is."

"Hm."

They ate in silence for a few minutes. Eric seemed to be watching the movie keenly.

"You know if they can make Cathy Lee Crosby look good I can make Sue Pine look like a Barrymore."

"That's the spirit."

"Really. I'll throw her in there. I'll ask Sandy to give her a nice, nutty, tough little speech and we'll just throw her in. No, wait, wait—"

There was urgency suddenly in his voice.

"I'll get Camel to write her one of his surrealistic little monologues!"

Mimsy's smile threatened to erupt into laughter.

"It's perfect! It might be just what the damn picture needs. I mean it's left-field enough already—but to introduce a new star—see, see—in the credits *And introducing Sue Pine.* See? We go all-out. Rather than hide her, we give her a star-making turn."

Now Mimsy did laugh.

"No good?" Eric asked, but he was smiling, already way gone into his fancy.

"It's brilliant," Mimsy said.

"Yes," Eric said. "It is. It's brilliant."

60.

Dan Yumont took Sue Pine to dinner that night down by the river. The restaurant was cool and dark and there were few rubberneckers or fans. Still, Dan and Sue were given a semi-private room, off the main floor. There they sat at a table with a white tablecloth and Dan squinted into the middle distance and Sue Pine kept pulling on his fingers as if milking them, her eyes nearly vacant. She felt as if she had been swept into a tidal wave from which she would be late coming down.

Dan's other women, while this was occurring, were chewing on their separate disappointments. But only one of them was a cauldron of boiling rage, a toxic impulse arising in her like bile. Only one, this time.

"I can't believe I'm here," Sue Pine said, as if she had just landed in the Emerald City.

"Movie magic," Dan said.

"You have powers."

"Yes. Because I have money. Because I am famous," Dan stated baldly.

"And a reputation," Sue Pine said.

"Yes, that."

"Why the bad rep? From what I've seen you're a—a stand-up Jack."

"A reputation is built slowly, brickbat by brickbat."

"Yours is womanizer-bred."

"Yes."

"You don't seem dangerous."

Dan only squinted.

"It's funny, I was just reading about you in the gossip columns while I was in Orlando. Something about being mistaken for a terrorist on your arrival in Memphis."

"I lit a match on the airplane."

"Why would you do that?"

"To hide the smell of my fart."

"Hm. How do you like Memphis?" Sue Pine asked. "I've never been here."

"How would I know?" Dan said.

After they ate Dan and Sue walked a bit. This part of downtown, from which you could still see FedEx Forum, was as yet not entirely developed. There were still dark pockets of empty buildings and broken alleys. Through one of these alleys Sue espied the river.

"Oh, Dan, let's go through here. Look at that river. It—it—"

"Just flows on," Dan suggested.

"Yes, exactly," Sue Pine said.

Halfway through the darkened passage Sue Pine pushed Dan against the damp, dank wall and pushed herself against him, grinding her pubic bone on the front of Dan's jeans. She kissed him hungrily.

She spoke into his mouth, "It's been hours," she said.

Dan's eyes were open. On the wall just opposite them was graffiti. The yellow paint read GODISALIVEMAGICISAFOOT. Dan smiled.

"She's got a great ass," came a voice from down the shadowy corridor.

Dan turned his head slowly. Sue Pine pressed herself harder against him.

There were three of them. A black kid, a Hispanic kid and a guy who looked Asian, possibly Vietnamese. Behind them, in the light at the end of the alley, a young woman stood, shifting herself uncertainly from one foot to the other, chewing a fingernail. She appeared to be as white as Sue Pine. Their aggregate age couldn't have been 65.

Goddamn, Dan thought. I'm about to be mugged by the Rainbow Coalition.

"I said, she's got a great ass," the black kid said.

"I heard you," Dan said.

The teens were stopped short. They looked at each other apprehensively. It was the voice. There was something familiar about it, something dangerous, something challenging.

"You might wanna share a woman as fine as that," the kid suggested.

"I might," Dan said.

Again the nervous eyes.

Sue Pine now turned her eyes toward the gang. She was scared shitless but they were kids. This did not seem comforting. Their mouths were vicious.

"Move away from her, Big Man," the leader now commanded.

"She not enough for you?" Dan asked, motioning with his chin toward the doll at the end of the alley.

The gang didn't like this questioning of them. They were dead sure they wanted to be in charge.

"She's too much for you, white boy," the Hispanic kid offered. The thread of the conversation was hanging loose.

"What did you have in mind, guys?" Dan asked.

"Oh, maybe your money first, smart ass. And then your woman."

"Uh-huh."

"So—uh, you just move her aside and we'll, uh, show you what we mean."

Dan peeled Sue Pine off him, gently.

"Show them your legs," Dan said.

"Dan," Sue Pine said, her voice a jerrybuilt construction.

"Show them what they want," Dan said. He was looking at the leader of the gang, who was smirking now. He thought he was on the brink of getting what he wanted.

Sue Pine was wearing a shin-length black dress that clung to her like silk. She kept one steadying hand on Dan's chest and with the other inched the dress slowly up her legs. Every eye, save Dan's, was on her.

When the dress was about four inches above the knee Dan spoke.

"That's enough," he said.

Only then did they see the pistol in Dan's hand. It was the size of a holiday ham.

"Fuck," the black kid said.

"Not tonight," Dan answered him.

"Fuck," the guy repeated. He looked at his compatriots.

"Jesse, let's get out of here," the girl squeaked.

"Don't use my name, dammit," the kid snapped. He turned on his heel and jogged back to her. Everyone stood still. The air was prickly with assault.

When he reached her he placed a palm against her cheek.

"We go now," he said. And with that they were gone.

"Jesus God," Sue Pine said. "Is Memphis always this way?"

"How would I know?" Dan Yumont said.

61.

In the middle of the night Sue Pine woke up, her head full of bees. She couldn't fathom where she was. The last 48 hours had been more than a whirlwind. It had changed her life irrevocably. The light was middle-of-the-night hotel light, a strange diffusion through thick drapes. She was in a hotel room sleeping next to Dan Yumont. Could it be true? Yes, it was. She could make out his face in the murk, a whiskered handsomeness known the world over.

Sue Pine carefully got out of bed. She didn't know she didn't have to be careful. Dan Yumont slept the sleep of the just. He was never bothered by bad dreams, never tossed and turned, had never known the cacodemon Insomnia. Sue turned back to look at his face. She knelt next to the bed and put her face up close to his. She wanted to lick his cheek and lips. She knew the lips would taste of herself. Or a heady mix of her own juice and tobacco and alcohol. It made her dizzy just contemplating it. Her tongue was already tasting him.

Sue Pine stood back up.

She let her eyes adjust to the dimness. Naked, she walked around the room, went into the bathroom. There she removed her diaphragm and while doing so thought about her new life as a movie star. They had told her that sometime in the coming week she would get her own scene. It was being written now. They were going to make her a star.

After ablutions she reentered the hotel room. She could just make out the chair over which Dan had slung his clothes. She quietly went there and began going through the pockets of Dan's clothing. She took out his wallet, removed a hundred-dollar bill. She fingered his change, his pocketknife, his keys.

Then she found what she was looking for, in the inside pocket of his jacket. She calmly took the gun from there and weighed it in her hand. It was surprisingly smooth; the silver matte metal she found almost soft. She didn't know a gun could be so beautiful. And its barrel was as long as Dan's dick.

She took the Raging Bull and the money and moved them into her purse. After snapping the purse shut and putting it under her own clothing she slid back into the bed. Once there she moved Dan's limbs and torso a bit so she could fit in against it, spoon-style. Her ass felt good against his prick, which stirred a bit, though Dan Yumont did not wake. Dan Yumont continued sleeping the sleep of the just.

And, a few moments later, after taking time to smile and reflect once more, Sue Pine joined him.

62.

Exterior. Riverside. A fructiferous light, lemon, lime, tangerine.

The next few days called for outdoor shoots. Eric relished the sweet fall air, temperatures in the mid-60s. And the crew and cast seemed to soak up the ambience and give it back as inspiration. This was, perhaps, the Memphis Mojo, so-called. Eric, at times, regretted going elsewhere to make his mark, leaving behind a city that some found culturally bereft, a backwater burg that would forever lag behind more sophisticated spots on the American map. But a city that had an electric undercurrent, a vibe, though he hated that word, that resonated musically, artistically. Someday perhaps he would capture it on film, a valentine to the city of his birth. Perhaps someday he would tell the story of Sun, of Stax, of Big Star. Of Elvis, Otis, Rufus, Carla, Jim and Sid. He could do it. Today he felt, he could do it.

The outdoor shoots, though posing problems in logistics and transportation, gave Eric breathing room. It worked literally and metaphorically, the outdoors, the expansiveness of it. The Pyramid was beginning to feel like the tomb it resembled.

Even Sandy, whose veins ran with pure big-city cynicism, seemed to enjoy the Memphis air. And, again, Eric began to wonder where Sandy went when they were not together. Not that it mattered in the big picture, since he had Mimsy to occupy his heart and body. Eventually, he and Sandy would sever their ties to each other. Perhaps that time was drawing nigh, as Eric began to think about Mimsy in new ways, ways he thought he had buried.

One day, during a break for lunch, he and Sandy sat under a tree with box lunches that had been prepared for them by one of the downtown eateries. Sandy was concerned with this new starlet, what her scene would be like, what they would get from Camel. Not that she was throwing up any roadblocks; this was just the way she worked. She talked it out. And she always had been expert at working on the fly, adapting, taking new ideas in and making them work. This was just one more opportunity for her to tackle a bit of a sticky wicket. She believed in the idiom of empiricism, whereas Eric did not.

"How do you see it, this new scene? I mean, sure Camel can do his thing, his, what to call it, Lewis Carroll thing, but that leaves me to shoehorn it in. If that's not mixing metaphors," Sandy was saying. She held a catfish po' boy in one hand, gesturing with it as if it were a baton.

"I don't know," Eric said. He was distracted. Someone had handed him one of the West Coast papers. In it there was a story about the movie, Eric's Memphis movie.

The article was written by Luke Apenail, a critic who had been a burr under Eric's saddle for years. He hadn't liked anything since *After You I Almost Disappeared*. Luke Apenail had made his name in the 1980s with a series of critiques basically bemoaning the state of American filmmaking after the golden age of the 1970s, though, perhaps he was most famous for his essay expounding the theory that *Citizen Kane* was really the work of Everett Sloane. He had called *Spondulicks* "chin dribble." Eric partly blamed Apenail for the critical tidal wave that ruined him, that sent him back to Memphis.

Now Apenail was expounding on the quagmire, as he called it, in which Eric found himself in Memphis. He likened the shoot to the notorious by-the-seat-of-the-pants hijinks of *Beat the Devil*, without the talent involved. He proclaimed himself a fan of Dan's work, and of Hope's, and wondered in print about this career move for them, working with a has-been in a town whose downtown was "like Dresden after the war." And he was particularly hard on the rest of the cast, pointing out the B list, as he called it, from which Ike Bana, Suze Everingham and Elena Musick had been plucked. Not to mention the "hometown nobody, Kimberly Rinks [sic] apparently an old girlfriend of the director, who was playing a key romantic role."

But, the oddest part of the article was the part questioning Eric himself. Apenail wrote that Eric "hadn't made a significant contribution to cinema since he was 30 and, now in Memphis, he was floundering with a script that was being written on the set, doctored by a hippie burnout, and, what's worse, he was seeing visions of the dead, perhaps representing his career, which now seemed moribund beyond reclamation."

Eric was shocked. Not so much at Luke Apenail's tone or attacks—he had come to expect nothing else from him—but by his knowledge of things that Eric thought were private. Whom was he talking to? Apenail knew way too much about the Memphis shoot, about the confidential plights of the picture. No one knew the extent of Eric's struggles, at least not spiritually. These "visions" were private. They were Eric's secret theomachy.

63.

"What's that, Camel, My Inamorato?"

Camel smiled at the use of the term he had given her. Lorax wanted to call him something besides boyfriend. Or lover.

"New work," he said.

"Movie work?"

"Yes."

"I thought you were through. And I thought you hated it, this movie."

"I thought I was through too. Eric called and asked for one more scene. A love scene."

"Mm."

"And I don't hate the movie, Cubbybear. If they want to throw those kinds of dollars Camel's way, Camel will give them his choicest words."

"You're a good man, My Inamorato."

"Not really, Sweet."

"You can write a love scene with your eyes closed. Perhaps that would be the best way to write a love scene."

"Ha. Yes."

"By love scene do they mean a dirty dirty?"

"I suppose so," Camel said. "They told me I could wing it. As a matter of fact, they specifically wanted me to wing it, to make it whatever I wanted. They have a new ingénue. This is for her."

"Oh."

"Why so interested today?"

"Dunno. Nothing to do."

"Want to help me write it?"

Lorax's round face lit up like dawn beyond the tomb.

"Can I? Can we do it together?"

"Let's," Camel said and he couldn't help but smile.

Lorax nestled next to him on the couch. Camel had his legal pad on his lap. He was still in his pajamas, a housecoat loose and open, spread out around him like a cape. Lorax wore only one of Camel's T-shirts.

"How do we start?" she asked, eyes bright.

"Well, we're gonna have a conversation that will lead to a speech. They want a speech for their ingénue."

"Ok," Lorax said. "Camel? What's an ingénue?"

"Sorry, their new actress, a young actress looking to make a name for herself. A starlet."

"Ok."

"So. Let's say where they are first."

"The bedroom."

"Hm. No, not the bedroom. No." Camel tapped his temple with his pen.

"The bathroom?" Lorax said.

"Better. Better. He's in the bath. She's a visitor in the house, a guest. He's tired, slightly drunk. She's just come from Europe, where she was using a Europass to explore the continent and her own inner geography. She has returned to the States because she discovered in herself something horrific, or at least she finds it horrific, an un-expiated guilt, and she imagines that other people will as well. She imagines that people can see the monster inside her and she has returned to the States and is visiting her college friend, in whose house our hero is bathing and unwinding after a long day, a day in which he was briefly arrested on a drug charge."

"Wow. Do we say all that?"

"No. That's just for us to know."

"Oh."

"So she enters the bathroom."

"Gulp."

"Ha. Ok. The first line is yours."

"Gulp."

"Go for it, Sweet. Talk in her voice. There's no wrong response."

"Um, ok. Um. 'Sorry,' she says," Lorax said.

"Come in."

"I have to pee. Didn't know there was anyone in here."

"Go ahead. Pee. I'm nothing. I am less than zero. I am ghostly."

"Wow."

"Stay in character."

"Yes. Um. I didn't know anyone else was staying at Angela's."

"Not staying. Only cleansing myself. Attempting to cleanse my soul through ancient wudu."

"I can find another toilet."

"Nonsense, sit."

"Thanks, I—I guess I drank too much beer."

"Tell me things. Tell me how high the moon. Tell me how low the sun, how crepuscular the crepuscule. Tell me how you came to rest in this sudatorium."

"You talk funny. And you're drunk."

"And you're peeing like a cow pissing on a flat rock."

"Wow, I am. Ah, yes. That feels good."

"Nothing like it."

"Um. I'm Nicolette."

Camel smiled.

"Hello, Nicolette."

"How do you know Angela?"

"Days gone by. Nights gone forever."

"Are you the boyfriend?"

"No. Never that."

"Who needs it, right?"

"Exactly."

"You are naked. I am sitting here talking to a naked man. And a naked man with a semi-stiffy."

"And I am talking to a woman who uses words like *stiffy*. And one who is in no hurry to pull her pants back up."

"Yes. I mean no. I will now pull them back up."

"Don't."

"Oh my."

"Don't. I mean, I am a lonely man. A man who longs for love and finds only recalcitrance and storm clouds. And you are the last woman. The one of whom the oracles spoke. The one predicted in my life story, back and back. The woman who brought the night, the breeze, succor. A womanly wind-tee."

"All that?"

"Yes. Take your pants off. Kick them aside."

"You are bold, sir."

"Yet you do as I ask. You have lovely legs, legs the knowledge of which could drive a man corybantic."

"I don't understand but I like your salute."

"Bathe with me."

"I want to. Why do I want to?"

"Because there is balm in Gilead. Because a second summer returns to blind the phantom fall of snow."

"Wow. Here then."

"You are now naked also. An Atalanta come for my golden apples."

"How shall I enter?"

"Here. Enter here where dragons await. How shall *I* enter? Spread your legs and shimmy down over me."

"Camel?"

"Yes, Dear."

"I want to fuck now."

"Do you, My Sweet? The writing is going swimmingly. You are inspiration, pure-dee."

"Camel, I don't want to write anymore. I want you to talk to *me* about golden apples and stuff. I want you to open your pajamas and give me your stiffy."

"It's not—"

"Shh, Camel. Don't say not. Shh, come here."

64.

"Dan, they're supposed to be sending over my pages today. They said today. I'm nervous as hell about this. Tell me it's gonna go well," Sue Pine said as she and Dan were being driven to the Pyramid.

"It's gonna go well."

"It's only one scene, right?"

"Yes. It's your start. Careers have been launched by one scene."

"Truly? Tell me truly that that is truly true."

"You are nervous. Take an Ativan."

"I think I've taken too many already. I think I've taken my daily dose already and it's not 8 a.m."

"Take another."

"Right."

"You the new actress?" Hassle Cooley asked.

Sue Pine's face went through some dramatic contortions. First, snobbery that *the driver* should feel he could talk to her. Second, annoyance that he knew about her already. (Oh, fuck, she should have said to herself, this is *that* driver, but she did not recall that he had picked her up at the airport, because at that time she was so distracted.) And, finally, with one quick twist of readjustment, pride that she was recognized for the first time. She was, suddenly, a movie star.

"Yes," she said, flatly.

"Good luck," Hassle Cooley said.

Sue Pine turned back toward Dan. His eyes were closed. Sue Pine imagined that this was his way of psyching himself up before acting, a sort of pre-game ritual. She felt ashamed that she had no ritual, and what was worse, no idea how to act. She assumed her scene would be with Dan and that he would lead her, he would make her do things *the right way*.

Inside the Pyramid the panorama seemed akin to one of those biblical epics with workers running everywhere, pushing giant granite blocks, one man with a whip yelling imprecations, activity seemingly random and without purpose. It also vaguely seemed like Bosch's depiction of hell.

Sue Pine's pretty, dark face was a tight mask of inscrutability.

"Hello," Eric said, approaching her. "I'm so happy you could make it."

Sue Pine draped her hand over Eric's palm.

"Dan," Eric nodded.

"Her scene really today?" Dan asked.

"Yes. That is, I hope so. We're waiting for Camel's blues."

"How fast grind the wheels of art," Dan said.

"Have to, Dan. Money is breathing down my neck about how close we are to the finishing line," Eric said. Quickly, he added, "Of course, that's not your concern. At any rate, yes, we're gonna try to nail her scene right away."

"Works for me," Dan said. "I'll be in my dressing room."

"I'll be in his dressing room, too," Sue Pine said.

"Wait," Eric said. "Here's the little pixie now."

Standing in the doorway, backlit as if Spielberg were hovering, Lorax stood. Her gossamer dress was invisible in the light. Her small, round body seemed to shine like ambergris through it.

"Jesus," Dan said.

"I know," Eric said, scuttling over to her.

"Hello," he said, approaching her with a hand outreached as if she were a shy doe.

"Good morning," Lorax said.

"You have our pages," Eric said, smiling.

"I do," Lorax said. "I helped Camel write this one. It's very groovy, very sexy."

Eric swallowed hard. This was gonna be a mess. Where was Sandy? He was suddenly sure she would have to rewrite it.

"Heh, heh, can't give you screen credit, of course," Eric said, taking the pages from her dainty little hand.

Lorax smiled. Her face seemed to curl upward like the Cheshire Cat's.

"After we wrote this we made love until dawn," Lorax said. "I gotta go home and get some sleep."

"Ok," Eric said. He turned back toward the bustling sets. "You want some breakfast?"

When he turned back she was gone.

"Did you—" Eric started as he walked back toward Dan and Sue. "Did you see her?"

"Yes," Dan said. "A petite parcel of unearthly sensuality." He squinted.

"But—" Eric didn't know what he wanted to say. "Anyway. Let's see what they've done to us. We may need Sandy to—"

Eric studied the pages, his eyes scanning downward. The dialogue was crisp enough, witty in places. He skipped back to the final pages. The speech Camel had written for Sue Pine was three pages of thick, unbroken prose, a block that would intimidate an old pro. Eric felt he couldn't throw this at Sue Pine this early. Yet—there was something there—something almost transgressive, something so outré it just might turn an unknown into a known. Damn, he thought, this is an amazing speech.

"What is it?" Sue Pine said. "You look as if it were written in Egyptian."

"You don't know Camel," Eric said.

"It's good," Dan said. He made it a statement and he accompanied his words with a buss to the cheek of Sue Pine.

"It is—it is good," Eric said.

"Wonderful," Sue Pine said.

"Hm," Eric said. "Hm, hm."

"What is it?"

"How do you feel about nudity?"

Sue Pine looked temporarily nonplussed. It seemed a silly question.

"I love nudity," she fairly sang.

Eric smiled. Dan smiled.

"For art, of course," she said.

"Of course," Dan and Eric said.

65.

Lorax returned home to find Camel asleep. She toddled into the kitchen, humming a Lovin' Spoonful tune, something Camel had played last night while they were entangled. Something about "Six o'clock, hm, hm, hm, at six o'clock."

She thought she would make herself a smoothie in Camel's ancient blender. She couldn't remember what they had blended last but there were marijuana seeds stuck to the sides of the blender with what looked like strawberry sauce.

Now, what did she want to drink? She eyed the bananas warily.

In the fridge she found some yogurt, some wrinkled grapes, some fresh mint (when had they bought fresh mint?), some fat-free milk and some carob powder. With these she concocted her morning meal. She turned the blender on and while it whirled she herself whirled around the kitchen, her short skirt a whirly.

"My Polymnia," Camel said.

"Oh," Lorax stopped dancing. "My Sweet. The blender woke you!"

"It's alright," Camel said.

"I'm sorry, My . . . Ignaramo."

Camel's laugh was quick and hearty. It really woke him up and startled Lorax.

"Wrong," she said.

Camel took her in his large arms and held her as one might one's most cherished thing. The morning began with love, a conjuring as old as old Sol himself.

They split the blenderful of muck into two mugs and repaired to the couch. Camel loved early morning TV, which seemed as sleepy-headed as its audience. Many shows seemed to be slow in waking, their participants walking around, bumping around, drowsy but pleasant, smiles half-written on their handsome faces. He found a talk show where the guest was a young actress whose beauty was like Atlantis sinking. She was talking about Meher Baba and macrobiotics and why the president seemed constipated.

Lorax heard none of it. She sat, lotus-style, her drink in her lap, bobbing her head to a melody only she heard.

Camel was half-listening, his attention partly on his teenage love. She made Camel smile deep down.

"Camel," Lorax said, her eyes still closed, her head loose as a puppet's.

"Yes, my dear Lorax," Camel said.

"Aw, you never say my name."

"Lorax."

"Camel."

"Yes."

"Do you love my name, Camel?"

"I do, Lorax. Because it signifies. It signifies you."

"Doodley do, Camel. What's in a name? Doodley do. I love your name, my Camel."

"Ok."

"Camel."

"Yes, Dear?"

"Don't mess with the movie people anymore."

"Ok, Dear."

"I mean it."

"Ok. Why the concern?"

Lorax opened her eyes. They were steely grey.

"Something bad is happening out there. Something I cannot fix or pinpoint. I have tried but I can't."

"Ok, Baby. It's a bad scene. Money does that."

"It's more than that, Camel."

"Is it?"

"Yes. Bad juju. There's bad juju in the Pyramid. I got a very bad vibe there this time."

"I'm through anyway, Sweet."

"Ok, then."

"Ok, then."

"Mean it this time."

"I do, Dear."

"Ok, Camel. This smoothie tastes like bacon."

"It's not very good, no."

"Can we get sinkers and Joe?"

"Yes." Camel smiled at the strange phrase.

"Can we get sinkers and Joe from Otherlands?"

"Yes. Yes we can."

"Good. Good Camel."

66.

Eric and Mimsy were eating on the deck of Central Barbecue that evening. The weather had turned unexpectedly balmy, the kind of day that reminds Memphians why they live in the South.

Eric was trying to describe his new actress, this nobody thrust into their midst at the worst possible time. He had used the word *sinuous*.

"This the gal Dan said fucked like a jungle cat or some such?" Mimsy asked, her cheeks comically streaked with sauce.

"Yes," Eric said. "You are a carnivore."

"Save the sexy talk for later."

"Can't tell you about the shoot today then."

"Eric, another sex scene? Isn't the audience going to tire of the endless coupling?"

"It's germane," Eric said, a small stinger in his chest.

"Sure. So you saw the new actress naked."

"Do you want to hear?"

"Of course. Sorry. Tell me how the shoot went today."

"Camel wrote this scene. Well, Camel and his Ariel."

"His Ariel?"

"I can't begin to—forget it. Camel's girlfriend contributed, apparently. Anyway. This scene he—they—wrote takes place in a bathroom, for God's sake. The bathroom on the set, well, I can't see how Camel or the little pixie knew, but it was perfectly suited for the scene. Setting up the scene took longer than the whole shot, which we did in one amazing take. If this girlie makes it as a star it will be partly because she can deliver the goods with almost no preamble. She was given the blues and three hours later we were setting up the shoot and, damn, she knew every line—but, wait, I've gotten ahead of myself.

"She enters this bathroom where Dan's character is bathing. Dan is resplendent in the bathwater, which had to be boiling hot, per his instruction. And, naturally, Dan will go nude at the drop of a hat, so to speak. And, well—how to say this? Have you seen Dan's willie?"

"An absurd question."

"Sorry, yes. Anyway, it is, uh, sizable."

"Good for Dan."

"Yes, and good for Sue Pine, apparently. Anyway, they do this tap dance first. They've just met, he's naked, she's peeing. They do this thing. It's pretty good. The lines are pretty good and coming out of Dan's mouth, well, hell, they sounded like Mamet. And this Sue Pine is holding her own. When it comes to her dropping her clothing onto Dan's and entering his bath she did it like a pro. Obviously the scalding water was a surprise but she added it to the scene, ad-libbed a humorous little dance over Dan, a water sprite bobbing, and then lowered herself over him in the bathtub."

"Not another live fuck for your film?" Mimsy said.

"No, I don't think so. Anyway, no, I don't think so. So they're in the water and they get amorous and Dan says something about home, something something something. And then comes this speech, which this unknown actress, with the unlikely name of Sue Pine, nails in one take. An amazing speech, a free-flowing eruption of emotion and anger and an underlying pain that, if feigned, was the performance of the film. After she did it—in one fucking take—there was a moment of silence and then everyone, crew and cast, applauded. Everyone except Suze Everingham who, inexplicably, has disappeared. It was the arrival of a star. I'm telling you. And this Sue Pine took it as her due, as if she knew all along that this was her fate. She kissed Dan long and hard and they both stood up, dripping and naked, and bowed to a renewed round of applause."

"Wow."

"I know. It was a wow."

"So, she really is in the film then."

"Oh, Baby, she is in the film. This scene might be the making of the film."

"Baby?"

"Sorry. Too Hollywood?"

"By half."

"Sorry. Anyway, besides being out-of-this-world gorgeous, this gal is so talented it is only a wonder that no one else has discovered her. If nothing else happens in this film they will credit me with discovering Sue Pine."

"Huh."

"Yeah. And then Dan's other girlfriend showed up."

67.

"Hello, Eden."

"Hello, Eric. How's Memphis, eh? How's the old hometown?"

"Not seeing much of it, Eden. Not many of the old stomps anyway."

"Good, good. How's the timetable? We on schedule? You can't go over, you know, not if you want to hang onto the scraps of your reputation. Ha, right?"

"Right, Eden. Ha. We're on schedule. That is, if you want us to finish the thing."

"What do you mean?"

"Joke. Just a joke, Eden."

"Oh. Ha. Ha ha. Listen, who's the new starlet? Do I know her? Is she single?"

"Friend of Dan's. Sue—something. Did damn good work yesterday. I am very impressed with her."

"Ah, good, good. Long as it's not the Angel of Death, right?"

"The angel of death, Eden?"

Eric's heart hurt suddenly. Mortality with its small awl.

"Sue Aside, they called her. The Angel of Death, they called her. She couldn't get work in the movies because everyone was afraid of her. Born under a caul. Black arts her calling card. Real name—no, can't think of it. Who was her agent? Anyway—"

"This is some actress from a commercial. Dan wanted her."

"And Dan gets what he wants."

"Yes. Yes, he does."

"Good. Good, Eric. Wish I had that power, eh? What am I saying? I have that power. It's why I wanted to make a fucking movie. Right?"

"I suppose so."

"Listen. As long as we're adding cast. How about this Capucine? You know her? I'd love to meet her. Can you write her in? I'm sure Sandy can do it. Eh? Can you get Capucine?"

"I don't know. Time constraints now, you know."

"I guess so. Still. She's quite lovely, isn't she?"

"Yes, Eden."

"Prettier than this new Sue, I'll bet you."

"You're going to like her, Eden. Her scene, well, it might be the best film I've gotten so far. She shows up. She shines like a damn jack-o'-lantern."

"Right, then. You know best. Love to Sandy."

"Goodbye, Eden."

68.

When Dan realized his gun was missing he assumed it had been lifted by the hotel staff. Damn nosy maids, going through his things. Not the first time. One of the casualties of stardom, nothing private. They'll root through your damn trash cans.

Meanwhile, he had to contend with a ferocious teenager and her broken heart. Dudu had shown up on set, a wild gleam in her eye, an eye like a lynx. She made a beeline for Sue Pine and had security not restrained her God knows what she would have done.

"You had a part for me!" she kept screaming. Dan let the security guards drag her out. He didn't even turn to look. Not the first time he'd had two women go after each other in his presence. Still, he didn't relish it.

And what about Suze Everingham, who didn't report to work? Perhaps it had been a bad idea to bring Sue Pine to Memphis. He could have waited for the next movie. No, no he couldn't. One thing about overpowering desire is its immediacy. It couldn't wait. He was hungry for her instantly and he made her appear. His personal magic. His own genie-conjuring.

And wasn't he surprised when she turned out to be such a powerful actress? He swore she read through that scene no more than once and then delivered her whole scene-stealing speech dead solid perfect. How did she do that? What was that kind of memory called? She read it once. Very impressive.

The evening after that momentous shoot Dan took his new canary out to dinner at Chez Philippe in the Peabody Hotel. There they dined in a private corner on pheasant and champagne. She deserved it. What was this new feeling stirring in Dan? Surely not love. It was something else. He had been in love before and it didn't feel like this. This was—necromantic. Necromantic instead of romantic.

"You were magnificent today," he found himself saying, raising his glass.

"I followed. That's all. You're like a powerful magnet. I was drawn along in your wake."

"Kindly put," Dan said.

"It's true. I loved the scene they wrote for us."

"Yes."

There was a pause. Dan thought the muzak was Dylan played by a klezmer band.

"Do you think you could get them to do another for us?"

There it was.

"I don't know. We're awfully close to wrapping. I think Eric is under the gun. You know, on a short leash, especially money-wise, time-wise."

"Right."

"I think this one scene is going to be the making of you."

"Do you? Really?"

"Yes. I've known careers started with less. You were—*electric*."

"Hm."

"And, you know, it doesn't hurt that naked you look like a goddess. Audiences won't just remember you—they will seek you out. Your private life is probably over."

"Hm."

"At any rate, there is reason to celebrate. Today, you were reborn."

"Yes."

"My Streep."

"Was I that good?"

"Yes, you really were."

"Then you can get them to write another scene for me."

69.

Sandy found herself alone at the house, alone as the sun set, and she found herself, for whatever reason, missing Eric. She and Eric, well, this had been going on forever. From the start they had understood each other's private proclivities and it was not much discussed, the desire to keep the relationship open. *Open*, with its stink of 1970s pop-psychology.

She also was thinking that her part of the picture was over. She had finished the script, and barring any unforeseen changes, she wasn't really needed on set. Which left her feeling somewhat deflated and disheartened. While Eric was humming along, gaga over his new actress, proud of how Dan's part had coalesced into a thing of power and importance, and seemingly in love with someone new, Sandy was planning her return flight to L.A. The Memphis part of her life was over. Was it over for Eric? Would it be soon? Would it ever be? Had he rediscovered home? These thoughts troubled Sandy.

She decided to watch TV to try and take her mind off things. She also didn't want to think about her new paramour, the man who had suddenly appeared to take up space in her already over-crowded heart. She didn't want to analyze that. She didn't want to think about him and how it reflected on Eric. She knew it was betrayal. Betrayal beyond what their loosely structured relationship allowed. Because of who it was.

On TV there were men and women talking about the movies. Quick snippets of interviews that lasted about 15 seconds each. Sandy hated this, this new way of presenting things to an audience whose attention span was shrinking daily. Everything moved too fast; nothing was absorbed, or it was, but not digested. Everything was absorbed because the human mind is a sponge and it cannot filter things too quickly, so pulses of light and sound enter and take up residence, like cancer. TV works this way. MTV, CNN, VH1, all the initials, sent their information to their audience in scraps, explosive little scraps of sound and fury, each blast no longer than the initials by which they are known. Humans no longer had time or patience for anything that took longer than 15 seconds to develop. Would anyone still sit still for Bergman or Tarkovsky? Sandy doubted it.

Then, there he was on screen, the man she was seeing secretly. There he was, one more talking head.

And what was he talking about? About Eric Warberg and his mire down in Memphis. Eric Warberg, rudderless by the Mississippi. Sandy squirmed. She knew that at least part of his information came from her, little secret confessional whisperings in bed, little winks between two lovers. Now she felt ill.

"And the question remains," he was saying, "can Eric Warberg pull it together and make a coherent film again? Or was this another *Spondulicks*? The skinny out of Memphis is that he is flying by the seat of his pants, that this film will not come together at all, and that the money behind it, mogul Eden Forbes, was nervous. Moviegoers: Eric Warberg has not made an important film in decades. There is reason to believe he is not capable of it even now. The word I have is that he is allowing Dan Yumont to run wild, that he is constantly off on his own, disappearing at night with no explanation, and that he is relying on his girlfriend, Sandy Shoars, and his cinematographer, the estimable Rica Sash, to pull this errant project together. It's the old story, a man losing touch with his muse, wandering around in a town he used to call home, but one that now is only a city of ghosts for him. Literally, a city of ghosts."

Sandy allowed herself a good cry. She felt horrible. She only hoped Eric hadn't seen the broadcast. Fucker, Sandy thought. Fucking Luke Apenail. He wouldn't return to her warm embrace anytime soon. And, dammit, he was set to return to Memphis to see her the next day. What would she say to him? That he betrayed her even as she was betraying Eric? That he referred to her as Eric's "girlfriend" in such a demeaning way that she felt humiliated and relegated to the sidelines while the film she was working on was dismissed before it was even finished? Sandy was hopping mad.

"What's wrong?" Eric was saying. Sandy didn't even want to open her eyes. She hadn't heard him come in and now he was kneeling next to her while she wept.

"What is it, Ducks?"

Sandy opened her eyes. Eric's face was all loving concern.

Jimbo Cole stood in the shadows, studiously gazing elsewhere.

"I—I—Oh, Eric, tell me the movie is going to be great. Tell me we've made something here," Sandy blurted.

"Of course, we have, Love. Of course we have."

Sandy looked around. She returned her eyes to Eric's.

"Ok, Biscuit. Ok. I trust you."

"And I trust you," Eric said. "Now, get dressed. We've got the meet-the-media shindig tonight."

"Oh, fuck, I forgot."

"Eric says the press loves you," Jimbo said from the shadows.

Sandy began to cry again in earnest.

70.

"Camel, is this one ready?" Lorax was proffering a dirty carrot.

"Well, if not its life is through anyway." Camel narrowed his eyes looking at her, the sun behind her like a halo. She was kneeling in the dirt of his yard-sized garden, surrounded by abundance.

Fido was rooting around in the flowers, seemingly in search of something precious. The Treasure of the Knights Templar, perhaps.

"Ha, hm," Lorax said. She looked at the carrot seriously. "You're ready," she concluded.

Camel, himself on his knees, was concentrating on his lettuce, which was coming up with streaks of purple in its delicate leaves. He had never seen that before and he was studying it as if it were a knotty poser in a Pound canto.

"Hm, hm," Lorax said, pulling up another little carrot and adding it to her basket.

"Aunt Lettuce, I want to peek under your skirt," Camel sang, softly.

"What's that, my parasol?" Lorax asked.

"Poem, Sweet."

"Is it one of yours, my parasol?"

"No, dear. Wonderful poet named Charles Simic."

"Oh. Was he a friend of Richard's?" Lorax often asked about Richard Brautigan because she knew it made Camel happy to talk about him. It kept him alive for Camel.

"No, no, I don't think so. And not the past tense. Mr. Simic is alive and well. I think."

"Do you know him, Camel?"

"No, Sweet, I do not. Wait. Do I know him? Charles Simic. No, no. I only know his poems, his books."

"A good enough way to know someone, isn't it?"

"It is, My Love."

"Do you love Lorax, Camel?"

"I do. I do love Lorax."

"Can we have carrots for dinner?"

"Yes, of course."

"Camel, I am thinking seriously about becoming an artist. A real artist, not a coloring book one."

Camel set down his spade and sat in the dirt. He looked earnestly at his love, this creature who came into his life like a benison for his waning years.

"Ok," he said. "Ok, Lorax. Talk to me about that."

"Well, I was thinking. First I was thinking that there was enough art in the world. Enough writers, painters, musicians. Enough books, paintings, songs. That they basically drowned each other out, you know? There were too many artists and not enough appreciators. That was Thought One. Then it occurred to me that there are people out there picking up a book for the first time. Hearing a poem for the first time. Looking at a Jackson Pollock for the first time. And, my second thought was, there will always be artists and there will always be art appreciators, even if their ranks shrink and swell with the fortunes of the, you know, tides of time. And my third thought, Thought Number Three, Camel Dear, was that I wanted to be part of that special family, no matter its fortunes or lack thereof. I want to add to the world, Camel."

Camel looked at his catechumen, his wonder child, with doting, awestruck eyes.

"A noble thought, a good thought."

"Thank you, Camel. Do you think I can?"

"Yes, I do. I think you can. What, um, medium would you like to work in?"

"Hm, hm," Lorax began to sing again to herself some. "I don't know. I thought, you know, that when we wrote that scene that perhaps I could be a writer."

"Uh-huh. You did good help."

"Thank you, Camel. But, you know, the movies, well, I think they might be—not evil, certainly not evil—but, but—"

"Corrupted."

"Yes!" Lorax was gleeful that Camel understood. "Yes. I was worried when you were party to their corruption."

"Yes, dear. Filmdom is not for us."

"Film. Dumb."

"Ha. Yes."

"So, you know, then I thought maybe I could paint."

"Uh-huh."

"Do you mean, uh-huh, you could try, or uh-huh, that sounds harebrained."

"My Sweet. I have nothing but love and encouragement for you. I believe that if you wanted to paint that you could open your heart on canvas and the world would sit up on its hind legs and pay close attention. I believe, My Sweet, that you can do anything."

"My Camel."

"Yes, Lorax. Your Camel. I am tired now. I don't think I can garden anymore."

"Do we have lemonade, Camel?"

"We do."

"Come inside and I will get us lemonade and we can watch *Gunsmoke.*"

"That would be heaven," Camel said.

71.

Another night transpired during which Eric could not get ahold of Mimsy Borogoves. When he was alone at the house in Midtown Eric's mind began to feed on itself. He knew better than to spend such hours alone, hours of heartquake and ghosts.

Ghosts.

Sandy had left in a whirl of anger and flying clothing. She was a dervish of incoherent sputtering. Eric sat in the large den with only the TV to illuminate his solitude. On IFC they were showing one of Dan's most recent films, *Paths of Pain*. Eric tried to concentrate on the story but somewhere early on he lost the thread and it was not to be found again. Instead he studied Dan's method, though Dan was not, strictly speaking, a *method actor*. *Paths of Pain* was directed by Ulysses Pandour, a friend, and a man who knew his way around a script. It was said of him, more than once, that he could direct Danielle Steel and make it Shakespeare. No one said that of Eric. Not anymore.

Dan's squint. Was it just a gesture, one used when he had no other idea, similar perhaps to Renee Zellweger's moue, or Robin Williams's bag of shticks, or any of Jim Carrey's chucklehead antics? No, that was too harsh. Just because it was well-known, almost expected, didn't detract from how appealing it was, how sexy really. Eric could understand that. And he was happy to make use of it in *Memphis Movie*. He was happy Dan was aboard.

As he was that a pro like Hope Davis was aboard. Perhaps he could call Hope, find out what she was doing for the evening. The talk was that she stayed in every night and worked, prepared herself for the next day, went to sleep early so as to be fresh. Her performance certainly could be evidence of that. She was dead-on, every time. When the camera rolled she was Gayla Spring, her character.

The desk at the Peabody informed Eric that Ms. Davis was receiving no calls. Eric couldn't remember Hope's anonym. He explained who he was, asked for David, the concierge, the name he had been given. David was off for the night. Just as well, Eric thought.

He set the phone back down and began flipping channels. His restlessness found its correspondent in the fast flickering of color and light.

He was stopped short by another familiar face. It was Deni Kohut, his own Isabel Pettigoat in the movie, her darkly beautiful face and apple cheeks, her eyes as wide as summer. And her Rubenesque body was—oh my!—clad in a Harlequin's outfit. Behind her bright colors swirled, a background seemingly born of an LSD fantasia. What channel was this? One of the children's channels. Eric hit the info button: a children's show called *Uranium for Your Cranium*. He had to smile. It was not the kind of credit actresses put in their résumés.

Suddenly the satellite reception was lost, though the night was as clear as righteousness. The screen was a shower of grey sparks, a nothingness that was troubling somehow. Some deep Neanderthal fear gripped Eric.

Then Eric was made aware of another presence in the dimly lit den. He was almost afraid to turn his head.

"Eric," his father spoke from the shadows.

"Dad, I, I thought our colloquy was through."

"Did you, Son?"

Eric now turned. His father, dressed in the clothes in which he had been buried, was sitting in a wingback chair, the murk almost swallowing his rough-hewn features.

"I did. I thought we had—we had finished."

"The dialogue between a father and son is never finished, never finished."

Eric marveled that the ghost spoke like a specter out of Poe.

"Eric, tell me what's going on. Tell me you're not still floundering."

"No, Dad. It's ok. The movie is coming together. There's a real sense of purpose here now."

"Eric, is there? Is there a sense of purpose? That would be comforting to me."

"Yes." Eric hesitated. Did he mean that the story was drawing to a close and that therefore he had a better understanding of the project, of its merits, of himself?

"There are no second acts in America, Eric. Relish yours."

"There are few first acts, Dad."

"Sandy. Is she happy with it?"

"Dad. What difference does that make? Don't you trust my assessment? I'm telling you, this is happening. I'm telling you I'm happy."

Eric's father's silence felt severe, a judgment. Eric found himself straining to see, thinking perhaps that the ghost had left him *in media res*.

"Dad?"

"There are factors you have not considered. There are doings about which you know nothing."

"I don't understand."

"That's what I'm saying."

"You always looked out for me. I miss that. Occasionally, I need that again."

"Yes."

"I dream about you. In the dream I am so happy you have returned from the dead and there is a sense that you have come to straighten me out. Once more."

"Dreams—" Eric's father waved an airy hand about.

"You're trying to protect me now."

"Yes."

"Why?"

It was then that Jimbo Cole turned the lights on. It was a blast of illumination which staggered Eric and obliterated the dream-stuff of his father.

"Why you in the dark, Cowboy?"

Eric swallowed his anger.

"How did you get in?"

"Door was unlocked. Did you not hear me knocking?"

"I didn't. I'm sorry."

Suddenly Jimbo Cole, an irritant at times, was a life preserver. Eric grabbed for it.

"Jimbo, what are you doing tonight?" he asked.

"Free for the asking, Pal."

"Ok, then. Have you eaten?"

"No, no, I haven't."

"I tell you what I need first. First a quick shower. Then some coffee. Is there a coffee shop nearby where we can get some before dinner?"

Jimbo looked at Eric with a smirk, a well-traveled smirk, which, between them, spoke volumes.

"Right," Eric said. "Coffee on every corner. When did that happen?"

"Modernity, Chum. It happened while we slept. There's a great place, independent and boho, on Madison. Called Java the Hut."

"Perfect," Eric said. "Lemme shower."

"Okeydoke," Jimbo said. "Hey, Eric, man. Who were you talking to when I came in?"

72.

Dan had to turn his cell phone off. The other women were after him like disenfranchised harpies. Of course it was a bad situation of his own making and it was not the first time he'd found himself in such a tangle. The difference, he told himself, was that he thought he was really falling for Sue Pine. His lust was only engaged for her and that was a curious feeling in and of itself. Is only wanting one woman *love*? Dan pondered.

The disappearance of Suze Everingham was troubling, if only because Eric was now thinking he had to find a replacement quickly and reshoot her scenes. This affected everyone, including Dan, who didn't want to spend more time in Memphis than necessary.

The last he had heard from Suze Everingham was an elliptical message on his cell phone. There were long, unnatural pauses between the words.

It said:

"Dan.

Please call me.

Please, Dan.

Call me.

Where are you?

When. You. Get. This. Please. Call. Me.

Please.

Dan.

Call me.

Oh . . . oh . . . oh . . . "

Dan listened to it but his heart heard it not.

Dan was already making plans in his head to take Sue to his ranch in Montana where, alone together for a few weeks, they could see what would occur, a mad alchemy or a thunderstorm collision. Either one excited Dan, who loved his emotions raw and edgy. This Sue Pine provided. There was a danger to her that was partly inexplicable and partly the danger of the newborn star. He'd seen it before, that first adrenaline rush of attention and a monster is born.

Dudu had been calling every half hour or so. Crying into the phone. Threatening him and Sue Pine. She was going to bring all 16 years of her terribleness to bear. It made Dan laugh for a while and then he had to cut her off. And Ray—Dan felt a little bad at how quickly Ray let go. She called a few times, ran herself down to Dan, said the threesome had killed the love, blamed herself for agreeing to that "perversion," cried a bit, hung up on him twice. Dan gave her little encouragement other than a half-hearted apology. He told her she was "sweet" and promised to keep in touch. Even Ray didn't believe *that*.

Now, in Dan's deluxe suite, he had spread a vast picnic out on the floor. Food from various downtown eateries, handpicked by someone named Jimbo Cole, a runner for the movie apparently, were spread out like pirate's treasure. There were chicken wings from Gus's World Famous Fried Chicken, fried green beans from Friday's, hummus from the Arcade, Wild Turkey sandwiches from Café Francisco, pickle-flavored popcorn from the Flying Saucer Draught Emporium, Isaac Hayes's Famous French Fries, ribs from the Rendezvous, some other fried veggies from someplace called Marmalade, and other foodstuffs untagged. Dan had gotten the hotel staff to set the picnic area up on the floor on a large white sheet, laid over the thick, teal carpet of the room. It was as big as a parson's barn and there was enough food for ten people. To one side of the picnic sat a large-screen TV with pornographic movies playing. This Dan did not ask the staff to do; he did it himself.

"Well, this is formidable," Sue Pine said. "I hope I'm hungry. Oh boy, movies!" She watched for a moment. "Is this one of yours?" she asked.

"Yes," Dan said. "You are hungry."

"I believe I am, yes."

"Only one stipulation. Gotta eat naked."

Sue Pine smiled her sinuous smile. Dan dropped his robe. He was wearing nothing else.

Sue looked at Dan's handsome body, some scars, a few extra pounds well placed, a nice thin scattering of body hair, and that cock. My God, that cock, she thought. Even flaccid it was a thing of great beauty, like a long sausage, thickly corded and the color of loam.

"Join me," Dan said.

Sue Pine did a slow striptease. She was wearing a dress that clung to her body like a snake's superfluous skin. Coming out of that was a delicious thing to watch. Her underwear seemed to be made from butterfly wings. Dan watched her seriously, bringing his artistic concentration to bear. When Sue shed her last covering Dan asked her to just stand there a bit, legs akimbo. He loved the long line of her, the dark snaky outline of her elongated but perfectly proportioned torso. It really was a work of art.

"My," he said, succinctly.

"You, too," Sue returned the compliment.

"I want to eat you," Dan said.

"Your gun is cocked, or your cock is gunned," Sue said with a smile.

"Yes," Dan said. "Oh—speaking of guns. Mine is missing. I think the maid took it but how do I accuse someone of taking something I have illegally?" he asked as he surveyed her pubic patch.

"Your gun?" Sue Pine asked.

"Yes, my sleek, mean gun."

"Hm," Sue Pine said. "Do you want to talk firearms or—"

"Eat," Dan said.

"The spread here?"

"Maybe the spread there first," Dan said, moving toward her and placing his gnarled hand over her pubic hair. "I'm glad you're hairy," he said. "Not a big fan of the shave, or the wax. I don't know how that started but it's out of hand."

"You've seen many," Sue said, even as she grew lubricious.

"I have," Dan said, his finger finding a wet groove.

"Ah-ah," Sue Pine said.

Soon, they were both spread out on the picnic, feeding each other bits from here and there. Their faces grew slick with juices, their fingers sticky with sauces and grease. They touched each other often, between bites, and they rolled around on the floor with no regard to the waste of eatables. At one point, Sue, with fingers oily from fried chicken, wrapped her hand around Dan's pizzle.

"Oh, how big you are," she said, stating the obvious perhaps, but how many of us compose sonnets during moments of passion?

"How good that feels," Dan countered.

"Jesus, you just got bigger. I bet you taste like chicken now."

"That's—huh—what the cannibals say."

Sue Pine laughed but continued to minister to his engorgement.

"I think I shall eat you now," Sue Pine said. She spread herself over Dan, kneeling over him so that her ass and crotch were over his mouth, and lowered her buttery maw over Dan's great length of meat. Dan was careful not to push too far in. And he was grateful for the view.

He pulled her ass downward so he could employ his own oral action.

He paused for breath once to say, "Did I tell you I was Cancer, that my sign is 69?"

Sue used her laugh as an opportunity to remove the large undertaking from her mouth.

"Shut up and make me come," she said, smiling.

Later, they went to sleep in the bed. The food lay on the floor congealing and stinking. Small creatures made their way toward such bounty. Dan slept immediately upon placing his head on the pillow, his snores a soft concatenation. Sue Pine lay beside him, replaying their lovemaking, and thinking about her newfound attention. She had been interviewed that day by someone named Beiffuss from the Memphis paper. Sue Pine recognized, there in the dim Peabody suite, with food rotting around her, that her life had taken a sudden turn toward the marvelous.

There was only one dark cloud that endeavored to edge into Sue's blue sky. Sue had lost the Raging Bull.

73.

When Sandy agreed to meet Luke Apenail "one more time," she knew her defenses were crumbling. What was it about the creep that drew her, that hung her up like a summer dress on the line? He was sexy, in a sleek, water rat kind of way. He still dressed and combed his hair like Pat Riley. Of course, Pat Riley still dressed and combed his hair like Pat Riley. Sandy hated those kinds of men, normally. The cocky, snake-oil salesmen.

Yet, when Luke called and smoothly attempted to calm her ruffled feathers, promising that if she would just see him he could make her feel less like Judas, Sandy folded like a pup tent. She did want to see him again—she told herself so she could tell him to his face what a skunk he was, perhaps publicly humiliate him—but, really, in her vitals she felt the pulse of lust and desire. She desired him. No man had done that to her since Eric.

They met at Huey's as usual. He was already seated.

She pushed through the throng and sat without looking at him. She turned her face to the ceiling where toothpicks hung like petite stars.

"You not even gonna look at me?" Apenail said.

"I'm not," Sandy said. Some of us are in the gutter . . . she thought.

"Sandy, look, it's not that big—let's eat first," he said as a waiter came near.

"Turkey burger," Sandy said, her head still upturned. At this rate she was going to have one helluva crick in the neck.

"Same," Luke Apenail said. "Side of onion rings. Scotch."

"Scotch," Sandy said, as if mocking him. It was a poor gambit and she immediately knew it. She slowly lowered her eyes until they met his.

"Sandy, what upsets you so much about this? That you are involved in a doomed enterprise or that you passed on inside information?"

Sandy hated his lawyerly ways. She hated him.

"Either," she said. "Both."

"Ok," Luke Apenail said, as if that had decided something.

Sandy felt herself softening. What she really wanted was a roll in the hay with this man, whom she had just decided she hated. She really wanted him to hold her and tell her she should be adapting Ionesco for the screen. She wanted to hear herself praised even if it meant Eric was damned. And she hated herself for this, too. But, why? she asked herself. Why do I need right now to hear I am a better writer than this film will show? It was a bedeviling question. It bedeviled her.

Now Luke Apenail took her hand. Now he smiled his soft smile. Now he relaxed his mouth, which seemed so desirable, wet like a dewy leaf.

Now she was putting her hand in his, her Judas hand.

And now they were talking of other things, the current monkey in the White House, the newest lawsuit concerning plagiarism, Julia Roberts's baby, Brittany Spears's baby, Angelina Jolie's babies.

And Luke Apenail asked, "What's the latest on Dan? Tell me how many women he has in this port."

It is to Sandy's discredit, perhaps, that she thought this innocuous enough.

74.

Evening, an eggplant sky seen through an open screen door.
Interior of Camel's home.

Camel is working on a new poem. He has one line so far but it's
a good line.

Fido is lying in front of the door, watching for wolves. His
attention is focused. His ability to concentrate highly regarded.

And Lorax is in the bedroom painting. She and Camel had
gone to the Art Center on Union and there Camel had spread
his arms wide and said, all this, all this. Whatever inspires you
we will buy. Lorax, though overwhelmed, made her choices with
respect and serenity and prescience and insight.

The stereo is playing a shaky version of "Cowgirl in the Sand."

Camel is vaguely aware of Lorax singing along to the song.
Her lyrics are her own and only occasionally do they tangentially
touch on Neil Young's. Camel smiles and his heart expands. His
poem wiggles about like mercury on glass. He watches it crawl
around on the page. He tries to spear the one good line with the
end of his pen but it evades him. He is not rushed; he is not pan-
icked by the words' recalcitrant orneriness.

Camel's heart expands and he can feel it. Lately, he has been
feeling his heart inside his chest as if it had just been born, as

if it were beating for the first time, a ragged tattoo. The truth is somewhat more prosaic though. Camel's heart is running on fumes. He does not have too many more days on this contaminated spaceship. Can he know, can he recognize his own mortality? He can.

Lorax, while vaguely aware of Camel's frailty, believes that he is immortal. She believes that her love makes him so. He cannot leave her. Not now that she has discovered her muse. They cannot be parted, not by this world's rickety designs. She puts paint to the canvas with the confidence of an old master. Her colors are muted, like the sky at sunset or sunrise, before it wakes to its own strength. Lorax paints as if Nature itself held the brush. Her canvas takes shape; an image begins to emerge and it almost startles her. She did not know she was heading in that direction. Yet she sees that it is germane, that it is just. Her painting is a reflection of something that has entered her life, something not exactly transgressive but transformative. It has to do with Camel and it has to do with—she cannot bring herself to see it clearly—something to do with that damned movie, that awful, corrupt, soul-killing movie.

But she faces her truth bravely. The movie is the shadow. She recognizes the shadow. And she does not turn away. Instead she decides to dance with it. The shadow, at first reluctant because it believes it is being trifled with, begins a slow dance, circling its partner, matching her faerie gigue, step by sparkling step. The shadow is *intrigued*.

Something in the house of Camel and Lorax stirs. Something formerly hidden, something that belongs to the realm of, we can say it, magick. There it is. Art. Magick. The whole dance of existence, if that's not overstating it.

Lorax puts her brush down because she thinks she hears Camel calling her. She stops and listens.

Camel's pen is the contrapuntal sound to the record spinning, the needle stuck in its final silent black groove. Camel's pen is the only sound as he writes line after line.

75.

Monday morning, on set.

There is a noisy reverence to the bustle as sets are being dressed, actors readying or late, grips gripping what grips grip, cameras being checked, craft services keeping their almost religious silence over their tables, juicers juicing the juice, someone rattling in the scene dock, call sheets lost and found again. Sandy thought there was a negative energy to the set that morning. She didn't say it to anyone though.

She was arguing with one of the techs, something about continuity, something about the call sheets. She was doing someone else's job—she didn't know whose.

Eric sat by himself, studying the scene he was about to shoot. On the page it seemed so right. Yet, every time they rehearsed it everyone groaned. It just felt flat. Even Dan, working Dan's magic, couldn't find his way. Eric was about to excise the damn thing except that Sandy said it was key to working toward the denouement. Yes, they were close enough to use the D word. Dan's answer, whenever the shooting was going poorly was, "Don't worry about it. We'll put it on the DVD."

Sue Pine lay languidly on a couch, her naked feet propped up. She was a new princess already measuring her new kingdom, the one that would be hers once the Queen died. For once Dan was nowhere near her. He seemed to be lodging an inordinate amount of time in his dressing room.

Another problem with today's scene: it was supposed to feature Suze Everingham, who had simply gone missing. No one had talked to her. No one knew anything. Eric was contemplating using Sue Pine for the scene, though it would require some extra shooting. ("No golden time," Eden Forbes had said on a number of occasions.) Actually, Eric was contemplating asking Sandy what she thought about rewriting the movie to put Sue Pine in this scene. Sandy had no use for Sue Pine, so that was prickly.

"Are we talking?" Sandy asked, sidling up to Eric.

Eric didn't stir for a moment. He was lost in his reverie. Sleepless and spaced-out, he was barely there. He turned his head, slowly.

"Yes, always," he said.

"We've got a problem," Sandy said.

Good old Sandy, Eric thought. She has been cogitating on this herself and already working on the solution. Good old empirical Sandy.

"I know," Eric said.

"You know?"

"Yes, well . . . I mean, last night, I was—"

"Eden called you, then."

"Eden? No, no, I didn't talk to Eden."

"He's on his way to Memphis."

"Fuck."

"I know. The word is he's not happy. That article—"

"Fuck."

"Ok. Calm down. Nothing's decided, I am sure. We can finesse this. You can handle Eden. You've been doing it all along."

"I haven't though. I've been avoiding Eden, half-listening to his inane suggestions. You wanna hear the last one? Ferlin Husky. He wanted Ferlin Husky to do the fucking score."

"Is Ferlin Husky alive?"

"Who knows? That's not the—"

"I know, I know. Eden's, well, he's harmless, mostly, don't you think?"

"Except that he's the money behind the whole damn thing. So he has the power to simply destroy my life. Other than that he doesn't bother me much."

"Destroy your life. Cabbage, what would destroy your life? Losing this movie? Nah, c'mon. This is a way station only. Another on the road. We've been through rougher times."

The use of "we" woke Eric fully.

"Have we, Sweetcakes? Have we? And is it still gonna be *we* after Memphis?"

Sandy's face twisted into a configuration that Eric would swear he'd never seen before. It spelled Doom, he was sure. They didn't ask each other such direct questions. It was part of their unspoken trust, now apparently breached.

"We'll talk about that later," she said.

Eric's heart, already dyspeptic, sputtered.

He was about to offer some kind of supplication, some kind of whiny bridge-repair to Sandy when he saw the gun. The gun was as big as a wolf's foreleg and as shiny as death itself. And in Suze Everingham's hand, at the end of Suze Everingham's shaky, spindly arm, it looked like something straight out of hell, by way of Smith and Wesson. She held it out in front of her like a flashlight. She strode forward with the determination of one of Haiti's walking dead. Her face, set and unwavering, was a frightening thing to behold.

"Su—" was all Eric got out.

The report from the gun sounded like a cannon. It echoed off the walls of the cavernous space seemingly for many minutes. No one had even turned around to see Suze Everingham's resolute entrance. Hence the gunshot sent many to the floor. At first, Eric thought she had hit everyone. Then he thought she had hit no one.

Then he saw the bright blossom of blood on Sue Pine's upper chest. Her shoulder had exploded and she seemed as dead as earth. Her eyes were rolled upward, a horrifying visage.

And, now Suze Everingham was spinning in a circle, the deadly firearm still ramrod straight in front of her. It was a mad, deadly dance. Eric dove to the floor himself. So, not even he saw the final shot, the one Suze turned on herself. It wasn't quite as loud, muffled by the inside of Suze Everingham's once-lovely head.

76.

Eden Forbes stepped off the plane in Memphis and sounded a sour note right away.

"It's goddamn hot here for this time of year," he said. A toady answered something.

Sandy stood at the end of the velvet ropes, her face grim and lined. She managed a tight, counterfeit smile.

"Sandy, good to see you," Eden said, bussing quickly past her cheek.

"Eden," Sandy said.

"Can we get a drink here?" Eden said, already hustling toward a bar.

Once seated Eden's rosacea glowed as if his face were strung with Christmas lights. Neither spoke until the bourbon began to course through his system. The background of the airport terminal resembled a movie set. The people scurrying about could be grips and gofers and juicers and assistants to the assistant director. Sandy saw it as a scene almost ready to exist, a wavy premonition of future reality. The kind of reality she and Eric created.

Eden spoke: "So, what the hell are we gonna do?"

Sandy considered her answer carefully.

"Shut down shooting for a week. We're so close to being finished."

"Out of the question," Eden said, signaling the bartender for a second.

"Eden," Sandy said. "A cast member is dead."

Eden looked at Sandy as if she were the robot crew member in *Alien*.

"No one is gonna die, Sandy. We just need to change horses."

Now it was Sandy's turn to look quizzical.

"Eden, you don't know."

"Of course I don't know," he fairly spat. "I'm only the money. But, goddammit, when things aren't right I act. That's what I do. Ask anyone. Ask my shareholders. Ask the goddamn government investigations committees. I act. Sometimes I go off on a toot, but when the money starts to go down a hole, it's Eden Forbes Time."

"No," Sandy said, which gave Eden Forbes pause. He didn't hear "no" very often. "No, literally, a cast member is dead. Suze Everingham. She shot herself on set. After shooting our new ingénue, Sue Pine."

"Jesus God," Eden exploded. "Sue Pine is dead. She's the future. She's the thing that could save this sinking ship." He was already reaching for his cell phone to call Eric.

Sandy wondered briefly at Eden's ability to exaggerate with so little knowledge.

"Sue Pine didn't die. She is in surgery and will be fine. She has a shattered shoulder, or collarbone, or something."

"What the hell is happening?"

"I don't know. A love triangle, I think. Or perhaps a love hexagon, if I know Dan."

"What's Dan got to do with it?" Eden exploded one more time. "Tell me Dan can go on."

"Dan's fine. Dan's in clover."

"Good, good."

"Eden, your message. What did it mean? Why have you come?"

"Sandy, I want you to take over the movie. I'm firing Eric. He's washed up."

Sandy's sour stomach went sourer.

"Eden, I don't know—"

"You gotta do it, Sweetheart. No one else can save this mess."

"What—what are you basing this on?"

"I read, Sandy. I keep my nose to the ground."

"Your ear."

"Yes, I keep my ear to the ground. I know what I know."

"I'm sorry now for everything I've said. I am sorry I am dragging this picture down. It's not Eric's fault. It's mine. I am death to the picture."

"Nonsense. Eric came back to Memphis with his tail between his legs. He was chased out of Hollywood because he couldn't do it anymore. And when he was given this small project, he fucked it up, too. So—we move on. We finish the film under your name."

Sandy felt as if she had been kicked in the stomach. Kicked by Francis the mule. Kicked in the stomach in a low comedy, in a farce, and left in charge by the Mindless Whirlwind from the Absurd. She suddenly felt so alone. Luke Apenail became vapor in her cosmos, became a phantom. She wasn't a writer; she was a ghost writer. And she certainly wasn't a director.

Then, in her mind, her restless mind, her peripatetic mind, she began to block out the final scene. The one she was proud of writing, where *Memphis Movie* became what it was meant to become. Where it became *her* film. It could work *this way*, her head told her. You can do it.

77.

That night Eric found himself alone in the vast house in Midtown Memphis. He could not get Mimsy on her cell phone. It seemed to pick up but there was never anyone there. He spoke to the silence.

What had happened today? he asked himself. Bad karma. It followed him like a stink. This movie had been doomed from the outset, the whole project ill-conceived.

Now, Eric was at loose ends. He felt suddenly friendless, cold, alone. He even tried Jimbo—Jimbo who was hired to be at his beck and call. But Jimbo had a date. Imagine that. Someone he met on set. Movies initiated more adultery than half a dozen harems. Eric thought the whole damn company had betrayed him with their concupiscence and their amoral lifestyles.

But, no. It wasn't literally true. There was Hope. He laughed to himself. There is always Hope. She seemed to float above it all. She was so pure, so professional, so truly an artist, that Eric felt honored just to know her. Should he call her tonight? No. She had left the Pyramid today nearly in tears. She glanced once toward Eric, Lot's wife's stolen peek. Her expression said it all: we tried to build art on a dunghill. Or that's how Eric read it.

Eric felt near the end of something. Not just the movie, which part of him—that stone hard, cold part of him that did things, that *created*—knew could still be finished, could even be made great. Eric felt the end was near, as if Charon awaited outside instead of some lackey driver named Hassle Cooley. What had happened to Hassle Cooley? What was the last conversation he had had with the nutty driver? Cooley was explaining to him that in the complete Zapruder film—which he had *seen*—Kennedy lives. Now, like JFK, Hassle had disappeared also.

And, in thinking about disappearances, Eric's mind conjured another vision: a young sprite, barefoot and fey, dancing in the rainbow mist of the sunrise. Where had he seen that recently? That Ridley Scott film with Tom Cruise? No, it wasn't on TV, was it? Eric sat on the edge of his bed and held his head in his hands. His mind wouldn't cohere. Then he saw her whole: Camel's amanuensis. If that's what she was. Camel's sylph. She danced on light.

And then—and Eric knew it before it occurred—his father sat across from him, studying his son's despair with the cool of the dead. His face, craggy and beautiful, seemed to hang in the room like another light. Like a secondary image caused by signal interference. Eric could only raise his head and meet its eye—a cold eye, Yeats's cold eye.

"Eric," his father said. The voice was less distinct. Perhaps he was at the end of his haunting.

"Father," Eric said back. He felt weary, too weary to even parlay with his dead father.

"You feel a failure. You feel that you have reached the end."

"The end . . . " Eric said. He was losing steam.

"When God closes a door he opens a window."

"Right, so you can jump out of it," Eric said.

Eric's father's ghost chuckled.

"That's good," he said. "That's very good."

Now Eric had to smile. He made the ghoul laugh. Making the Ghoul Laugh. That's not a bad title.

"Eric, listen to me now. I don't have much time left."

"Ok, Dad."

"When you were young, son, you had such ambition. Such raw ambition. It frightened your mother and me somewhat. You were so driven. You wanted to read the right books, know the right art, see the right movies. You fell into existentialism as if it were a calling, like Mormonism or being a butcher. And you saw the world as an absurd place, a place run by morons. And you made Sartre's nausea your nausea. You see? You see what, as a parent, I was forced to confront. Refute Sartre? No, I couldn't. I could only hope that out of that pool of nausea you would rise and do something significant. And, for a while, you did. Your ambition held your nausea in check, and you added something to the old workaday world. You made films. Now, I like your films, Eric. I always have. If I never said so, well, chalk it up to an old man's reticence, the reticence of my whole generation. But, now, Eric, the old nausea is back. You are finding the world strange and unwelcoming. Eric, it *is* an absurd world, full of alien objects and strange people who will always be strangers. Still, why should we find this nauseating? Have you asked yourself that? If it's a given that the world we inhabit we will never fully understand, isn't that cause for celebration? The artist must tackle that strangeness, without letting it rub off on him, without being consumed by the *bêtise.*"

Eric's father's ghost rested. His eyes seemed rheumy and lifeless.

Why was he lecturing me about Sartre here at the end? Eric thought. Was this speech left over from his time on Earth, something he had always wanted to say but could not?

"Eric, I am your father," the ghost now said, faintly. "That's all I came back to tell you. I am your father and that never goes away, is not diminished even by death's darkling cloud. Be brave, son. It's all we have left . . . "

The voice was even weaker now. Eric leaned in.

"All . . . we . . . have . . . Eric . . . "

The room was so dim Eric was not sure the specter was still there. He was about to reach out his hand when it spoke again.

"And, Eric. Love those women. Love them, son."

And he was gone. The room seemed brighter suddenly.

Still Eric felt alone. He lay back on the pillow, his hands behind his head. He did feel nauseated. Was that only suggested by the ghost? Eric thought about dying. He thought about the work he was leaving behind, his legacy. He saw that some of it was good; he was happy some of it would go on without him.

Then he sat up. If he was to die, here, now, in this rented house in Midtown Memphis, who would speak for him? Who would write his obituary?

And, instinctively, he reached for his nightstand book. It was not there. Someone had taken his Samuel Beckett. In its place was a book entitled *We Are Their Heaven: Why the Dead Never Leave Us*.

"Sandy," he whispered into the space around him. And then a moment later, "Oh, Mimsy."

78.

Interior. Camel's bedroom. Crepuscular desinence.

As Camel's life leaked out of him, he began composing a poem in his head. The poem would spin out like gossamer or like the indurate substance with which caterpillars cocoon themselves. The poem would be his eternal shroud.

Lorax sat on the bed next to her Camel. She was as naked as Eve. Her face was so lovely that Camel avoided looking at it lest it break his poem apart like so much dreamstuff.

When the poem was finished Camel was not sure whether he would find the strength to write it down. Lorax had surrounded him with flowers from their garden, virtually stripping it bare. It was now a field of stalks. The vegetables had all been harvested and distributed around the neighborhood. In the coming weeks they would be consumed in households as far away as the Evergreen Historical District and the Cooper-Young Historical District. Folks, portly and gaunt, happy and morose, jaunty and earthbound, would spear a bit of squash or zucchini or banana pepper, and chew it with newfound thoughtfulness. There would be words burning and bubbling in heads formerly unpoetic. There would be linguistic splendor sprouting on tongues formerly tame. And there would be gastric tempestuousness born that would remind many Memphians that they were alive and animal and walking around in a flesh suit that worked 85 percent of the time and that was a damn lovely thing. Such was the magick of Camel's gardening.

Now, Camel turned his kindly face toward Lorax, his salvation and the joy of his last days. He smiled their secret smile and Lorax let a tear fall, one tear as crystalline as a glint from an icicle.

"Is this the final time, Camel?" she asked, holding his heavy, hoary hand in hers.

"Yes, Sweet Lorax."

"Are we to be sad?"

"No, I don't think so, Sweet."

"Did the movie do this, my Camel?"

"How do you mean, Dear?"

"Did it enter us and taint us and turn our insides sickly?"

"No, I don't think so. This is nature, the Earth's recycling. That's all."

"Yes, Smart Camel."

"The wind that bowed our sails is abating."

"Yes, Camel."

"Did you ever see *Little Big Man*, Lorax?"

"A movie?"

"Yes, a wonderful movie from a wonderful book."

"No, Camel."

"I guess there will not be a time for us to watch it together." He had lost the thread of why he was asking about *Little Big Man*.

"Who can say, Camel?"

"True. Now who is wise, my Sweet?"

"Am I, Camel? I am. I am smarter for having known you. And richer. I paint now."

"Yes, you do. You paint beautiful things."

"Thank you, Camel."

"Lorax?"

"Yes, My Parasail."

"I didn't know death would be so loud. It's deafening."

"Yes, Camel."

"Here we go," Camel said.

And Camel opened his eyes wide, for the last time.

Lorax put her hand to Camel's cheek. It was as warm as Summer. Then she undressed his beautiful body, gently removing all clothing and folding it neatly and putting it on a chair. She looked around the room one more time and smiled at the space that had become hers and she its. She wanted to remember every bit, which was made difficult by the profusion.

Then Lorax climbed onto the bed made catafalque. She positioned her body over Camel's like a winding sheet, belly to belly, arms to arms, legs to legs. And as Camel's soul lifted upward, all 21 grams of it, it passed through Lorax and Lorax evanesced like dew. She was never seen again.

She was never seen again. Eric, after Camel's funeral, made a concerted effort to find the fey lover of the dead poet, but no one knew what had happened to her. One day she arrived and one day she was gone. There was a woman at Camel's funeral, someone named Carla Binnage, someone Eric was sure he was supposed to remember. Carla smiled at Eric. Was it a smile that said, I know something you need to know? Or was it just that recognition thing—yet another fan or critic who knew Eric only from his work?

Camel's house became a shrine of sorts. The garden continued to feed many souls though no one tended it and the house, especially on warm summer evenings, when the cockshut came later and later, was alive with ghosts, if you can accept that awkward wording. Often music was heard coming from it. Some said it was *Déjà Vu*. Some said it was a simple dulcimer tune, "Bonaparte's Retreat," perhaps.

And when they removed Lorax's large canvases from the house and moved them to David Lusk Gallery, some said they shimmered and changed like a flickering TV reception. Some say those pictures, to this day, continue to change, to roll, to mutate. The gallery won't sell them, though they have been offered the riches of kings.

79.

Dan Yumont didn't care who was helming the picture. He worked well with almost everyone. His talent was rich and deep and he could call it up at any time, for anyone. When he met with Sandy he was all professionalism and passion. Of course he would finish the picture with her. Of course she could do it, he reassured her, though she wasn't seeking reassurance.

She was, however, thinking about Dan's sex scenes, how good he looked for his age, how strong he looked—his body a burnished nut-brown—and how dedicated he was to the craft. She also thought about his magnificent penis. And she began to craft another sex scene in her head . . . .she began to form it as if from clay. How fast it took shape, how right it was for the end of the movie. She could see it all whole. And, perhaps wrongly—who can say?—she began to lay it out for Dan right there in the office.

"I'm just now shaping this," Sandy told Dan.

"Mm," Dan said.

"I'm just now seeing it whole, large as life, you know?"

"I do," Dan said.

"It's growing in my mind, in my hand . . . " Sandy said.

As a rule, Dan lived by no rules, as far as his infamous concupiscence was concerned. He did, however, very rarely fuck his director or producer, though there had been many opportunities.

This time Dan felt it was meet and right. He felt that it was the least he could do for his fledgling megger.

Sandy locked the door to the office.

"On the couch, of course," she said.

"Of course," Dan said.

80.

After Eric was fired from *Memphis Movie* he thought he would leave Memphis immediately and for good. But he could not. For one thing, at about the same time he was being told he was axed, a message arrived that Camel Eros had died. He had to stick around at least long enough to see his old pal buried, if they were going to bury him instead of burn him upon a pyre like the old Indian in *Little Big Man*. What made me think that? Eric wondered briefly.

Also, there was Mimsy Borogoves. He had not been able to talk to her for days and now, now that he had been disgraced, finally and irrevocably, he needed her. He needed her wisdom and calm, which seemed to exist in her like some deep, warm spring. She was preternatural, he thought. And he needed her prescience, her ability to see tomorrow as if it were already whole and full of possibility. God, how he needed that now. Her cell phone number was out-of-order. There was no answer at her apartment. He drove by at night and there was no light from the window that he imagined was hers.

So, he moped around inside the spacious Midtown Memphis home the movie company had rented for him. Sandy had cleared out. Eden had told him she was taking over the movie and that seemed right to Eric. He could not feel rancor toward her. He had called her immediately upon finding out.

"So, for you, this is good," he said.

"Oh, Cabbage, I am sorry. For you it's hell, I think."

"Yes, thanks," Eric said.

"What can I do for you? I almost threw this right back in Eden's face. I want you to know that."

"Of course. But you didn't. And you shouldn't. Breaks come and they should be honored. Gifts from the gods. You deserve this."

"You're a kind Cabbage."

"I'm not, not really. I am beaten down. I am an ex-director."

"You are most decidedly not. You know how these things work. Second chances, rebirths. It's Hollywood's special magic."

"Not this time. This was my last second chance. I was made to see that."

"I don't believe that."

"Well, whatever. For you, Sweetheart, I only wish good things. Finish this movie. It was yours anyway, made mostly of your smart and bright words."

"I will, Cabbage. I will finish it for you."

"For yourself," Eric shot back, perhaps too sharply.

"Yes," Sandy said. "That too."

"Only one thing still rankles."

"Only one?"

"Ok, not only one, but one in particular. I'd like to find out who leaked our inner secrets to that fucker Apenail. That's what started this unfavorable denouement."

Sandy swallowed. "Yes," she managed.

"What's the difference, right? It's over for me. Rightly so. It was a mess from the beginning. I am a mess. I have no idea how to direct a picture."

There was silence, silence from Sandy, his biggest supporter, his love.

"Eric, listen, sorry, I've got another call and I have to take it," she said finally. Her distraction was like a hot knife.

"Right," he said, but she had already disconnected.

So, he haunted the big house by himself, Sandy gone, Mimsy missing, his father finally, ultimately, for the last time gone gone gone.

After a few days, after Camel's funeral, Eric grew desperate to find Mimsy. He had to wait through a long weekend to call Linn Sitler's office.

"Hi, it's Eric Warberg," he said.

Did he imagine a hesitation, as if the receptionist had been warned he might call?

"Mimsy Borogoves, please," he said, quickly.

The woman laughed. "That's very funny, Mr. Warberg. Um, look, Linn isn't here."

"No, seriously, this is not about the movie. I don't need Linn. I mean, tell her I love her and thank her, but, really, I need to talk to Mimsy."

"Is this a riff, some kind of movieland joke?"

"I'm not sure I follow you," Eric said. "Mimsy Borogoves. I know it's an absurd name. But it is her name and I know she works for Linn."

"There's no one here by that name," the receptionist said. She managed to keep some sunshine in her voice, almost blotted out by a now creeping concern.

"Mimsy," Eric said. "There's no Mimsy there."

"N-no, sorry."

Eric didn't know where to go with this. Hadn't Mimsy told him she worked for Linn Sitler? Now Eric wasn't sure.

"Then lemme talk to Linn, I guess."

"She—she's busy, I'm afraid. She's had Spike Lee on the phone all morning. Can you imagine? We think he's gonna do a film about Dr. King."

Eric could imagine. He could imagine anything about the movies. Their capacity to conjure magic was unchecked and boundless. What he could not imagine was why they were hiding Mimsy Borogoves from him. He hung up.

To whom could he turn to find Mimsy? Who knew her? Who saw them together?

This last construction gave him great pause. Who saw them together? Wait. He was not honestly thinking that she was a child of snow, a fever-dream? He knew her, her creamy skin, her pale eyes, her laugh. Her laugh was a thing of rare production. Her laugh could turn him inside out.

He went to her apartment building. He went to her floor and knocked on the door. He pounded on the door. He found the super of the building.

"Hi, sorry," Eric said, hustling over to the busy man. "I needed to find Mimsy, Mimsy Borogoves. She lives in 738."

The man looked him up and down. He recognized a non-Memphian, Eric was sure. The clothes were a giveaway.

"No one in 738. Haven't rented it in a year."

"W-why?" Eric said. It wasn't really what he wanted to ask.

"Accident in there. Still a mess."

"What kind of accident?" Eric said.

The man now was growing suspicious. He shook his head and tried to move away.

"Wait, please," Eric said, grabbing the man's arm. "When—when was the accident?"

"Year ago, I think." he said. He looked at Eric's hand on his arm and Eric removed it. "Gotta get back to work now, Pal. No one in there, ok?"

"Ok," Eric said, weakly.

Eric called numerous people from the movie. Jimbo Cole—his

old running buddy, the ludicrous Jimbo Cole—wouldn't take his call. He found a number in his book in a woman's handwriting for someone named Bandy Lyle Most. This Bandy Lyle Most informed Eric that he had just gotten a deal with Dreamworks for his first film and didn't really have time to talk.

Eric made a damn fool of himself quizzing each and every cast member about his lost love. Hassle Cooley—even Hassle Cooley denied all knowledge of her. He did take the opportunity, Hassle did, to tell Eric of one more project he was sure Eric would be interested in—to be called *It's a Horrible Life*—about a guy who is given a glimpse of the world without him and discovers that it's a much better place. The devil shows him it would be a better place without him.

He called Rica, good Rica. What he got from him was a theory of metaphysics.

"Here's what I think happened, " Rica said. "Here, in Memphis, perhaps through us, perhaps through our coming here, for whatever reason, there has occurred a breach into the otherworld. The thin membrane that separates life from—whatever else is not life—has ruptured, oh so slightly, right here, where we are working. Now, we can ask why, we can wonder at the wonder of finding ourselves up to our third eyes in otherness, but that's fruitless. Instead, we need to listen, to pay attention, to let the dreamspace inhabit us or let ourselves inhabit it. Does that make sense to you? That it's ours, this rupture, this bleeding through, it is somehow *ours*?"

No one had seen her. No one knew anyone named Mimsy Borogoves. He called Hope. Surely Hope would not desert him now.

"Hello, Eric, dear," she said.

"Hope, thank God," Eric said. Even to himself he sounded reckless. He took a deep breath. "Hope, you remember Mimsy

Borogoves, don't you? Beautiful woman who worked for Linn Sitler's office. She and I—" He didn't finish the thought.

"I'm sorry, Eric," Hope said. Her voice was honey. "I don't recall meeting her."

"Yes," Eric said. "I see. I see now."

In his distraction, he even called Dan's women. Sue Pine hung up on him. Somehow he found a number he didn't know he had. A young woman named Dudu Orr. He thought Dan had given him the number, had promised her a part.

"Hi!" Dudu said, brightly. Easily the most friendly response Eric had gotten.

"Hi, listen," Eric said. This woman sounded like a child. She probably was a child. "I am no longer working on the movie."

"Oh," Dudu said. Her disappointment was palpable. "Me neither," she said.

"Right. Listen. Do you remember a woman whom I was seen with occasionally, pale skin, beautiful eyes—oh damn, wait. This is impossible. Her name was Mimsy. Mimsy Borogoves."

"Sure, I know Mimsy," Dudu said.

Good God. Eric hesitated. He felt closer now.

"You do?" he said, warily.

"Of course. Beautiful chick."

"Yes!" Eric said.

"Why do you want her?" The child's voice had a sharpie's inflection to it.

"I need to see her. I will be leaving soon, going back to California. I need to let her know where I'll be."

"Back to Hollywood, huh?"

"Yes."

"What's it worth to you, this Mimsy's whereabouts?"

What was this, some kind of negotiation?

"Worth to me?"

"What is in it for Dudu? I want to go to Hollywood."

Eric was up against it.

"Of course you do," he said.

"You'll take me with you?"

"Of course," Eric said. "Please—just tell me where she is."

"You remember me, right? You know I'm one beautiful chick. I'm prettier than Mimsy even. I've got a body men love. Dan Yumont said I had tits like Marilyn Monroe. I could be a movie star."

"You could," Eric said.

Now there was silence. He wasn't playing her right. He'd forgotten how to do these things.

"You're not taking me to Hollywood," Dudu said.

"I would do what I can, really," Eric said. "My power is limited, of course—"

"Right," Dudu said. He had lost her.

"Dudu—please, Mimsy. Tell me, please."

"I've never heard of no fucking Mimsy Merigrove," she said. And ended the call.

Eric had one last chance. He called Dan.

"Hey, man," Dan said. "First of all, before you say anything, you got a raw deal, Buddy. When I get back to the coast I'm gonna see about it. Of course I've got one more shoot after this, so, it might be a while."

"Thanks, Dan. You're good people. Listen," Eric took a deep breath. "Do you remember a woman named Mimsy Borogoves, a lovely pale-skinned brunette I was seeing during the shoot? She worked with Linn Sitler."

"You were seeing someone during the shoot?"

"Yes," Eric said. He could see it crumbling. His hope.

"You were cheating on Sandy?"

It was ridiculous, of course. He almost sounded disapproving.

"Yes, in a sense. Do you remember her?"

"No, Buddy, sorry. I don't know her."

"Ok," Eric said.

Why was Dan's ignorance the final stroke? Eric turned off all the lights. The house in Midtown Memphis, which would soon pass out of his hands, was dark. In the dark Eric saw shapes he didn't want to see. Cast members past, characters from his early movies, they all passed in judgment of him. But, unlike his father's ghost, they did not speak to him. They passed silently by, a once-glittering entourage, now reduced to shadows.

What had he lost? Everything. What had he not lost? Mimsy Borogoves. He had not lost her. He never had her. Not in the old sense of a bird that he kept caged but in the sense that he never had her because she did not exist. She was a product of his *Memphis Movie* endgame. She was special effects, the kind of high-gloss, Spielbergian faker that he eschewed in his films, the kind of Hollywood humbuggery he hated. She was broken pieces of mirror that simulated water.

And where was he to go now? Hollywood, that expensive set, that wasteland, did not welcome him. He had come to Memphis to die, he now realized. Like poor Suze Everingham. Like Camel. He would lie down and die. He would welcome the closing of the light, the shutting down of the movie of his life. The dressed set undressed, the hot set cooling and ticking in its abandonment. He saw a sign clearly: filming winds today. His final credits would roll and he would not be there to see them.

But then he remembered that his Beckett was gone and he thought, I cannot die. Tonight I cannot die. And the dark rolled on like the waves of celluloid, dreamed and procreated.

Yes, in the dark, Eric saw much that he did not want to see. But he saw one thing that was comforting to him and this one thing saved his life. Eric didn't want to die. He didn't really think his life was over because his career was over. This one thing made Eric sit up and take stock. He turned on a light. Its glow was weak, a yellow glim in the fusc. But, in that glow, he saw it clearly.

It was not one picture but a montage, something film excelled at, the melding of images, the sexy slide show. Like a trailer—the best bits illumined by polish and fairy light. There, in that rented house, in a home that was no one's, Eric saw this: he saw Cary Grant's dimple; he saw the Ferris wheel in *The Third Man*; he saw the light in Tuesday Weld's hair, McCabe dying in the snow, the child Napoleon's snowball fight, Chaplin's "Smile" fadeout. He saw Annie Hall's tennis game, *Blow-Up's* feigned tennis game, Bibi Andersson's luminous close-ups; he saw the sweat run down the nun's face in *Black Narcissus*. He saw Virginia Woolf writing *Mrs. Dalloway*. He saw Monica Vitti's smile, the solar eclipses of Anna Karina's eyes, Lee Marvin's silver nose. He saw Dr. Strangelove, the poet Morant, George Bailey, Aguirre, Amelie, Kane, Sally Bowles. He saw Baptiste, the mime; he saw Mabuse, the dacoit. He saw HAL's murderous red eye. He saw Marilyn playing the ukulele, Marcello Mastroianni floating upward on a tether, the Who exploding at Woodstock, Pamela Franklin's perfect fundament, George and Martha exploding in their living room, Monty Clift decking the Duke, Christina Ricci chained to a radiator. He saw King Arthur's coconut shell horses, Astaire and his firecrackers, Peter Sellers's unctuous Quilty, Jack Lemmon waiting for Shirley MacLaine outside the theater, Barbara Stanwyck's ankle bracelet. And he saw the Beatles explode into manic anarchy, their beautiful young faces caught for all time, frozen at a moment when the world was their own.

He saw it all and saw, not that it was good or meet or right or even inspiring. He saw that it was absurd. And as Camus said, the absurd is the first truth.

It made him laugh, the absurdity, the incongruous, somehow paranormal absurdity. Flickering images, that's all they are, that's what his life has been up to this point. Flickering images. Grainy photographs made of waves and particles, in the same way the world around us is not continuous but grainy. It made him laugh.

And it gave him rest. Just for now, it gave Eric some peace.

Epilogue

Q: So, Sandy, welcome. *Memphis Movie* is a wrap, isn't that right?

A: Yes, Donald, that's right. We have finished the film and most of us have moved on now to other projects.

Q: Well, we appreciate you staying behind long enough to answer a few questions.

A: My pleasure.

Q: First, for all those who don't know, you were not the director when the film began shooting in Memphis.

A: That's right. This film is really Eric Warberg's film. We finished it in honor of him.

Q: And why was Eric unable to finish the film?

A: It's complicated.

Q: Give us a simple version.

A: Well, there is no simple version. Eric is from Memphis. This became a burden to him as shooting went on. He was unable to create the necessary distance from the material an artist must master. Memphis became the subject of the film for Eric. And, for Eric, the subject of Memphis is, in a way, overwhelming. He became overwhelmed.

Q: I don't quite understand.

A: I told you it was complicated.

Q: Where is Eric now?

A: I don't know. I haven't talked to him in a week or so.

Q: Will he be directing again?

A; I have heard a rumor that he's already picked up another gig.

Q: Can you tell us about that?

A: Just a rumor, mind you, but talk is he was offered the new Dennis Quaid, Meg Ryan comedy, *If This Is Heaven Then I Must Be Dead.*

Q: Isn't that a remake of—

A: Yes, *Here Comes Mr. Jordan.*

Q: I've heard it's been turned down by every A-list—

A: No.

Q: Ok. Ok. Let's see. How are you with working with actors? I have a quote here from you about a certain leading lady. You were quoted as saying, "She's a waste of good shampoo."

A: Ha-ha—no, no, that was certainly taken out of context.

Q: So actors.

A: Unlike Hitchcock I see them as collaborators, cohorts, cohabitants, coconspirators. There's probably a few more co's I'm missing.

Q: This leading lady—

A: Can we talk about *Memphis Movie?*

Q: Of course. Tell me how you want this movie to be perceived. Tell me your vision of the movie, or for the movie.

A: My vision? I don't know. It's a good picture. It's a story made of words, really, which, as you know, is a sticky wicket in film, it being an almost totally visual medium. What I wanted for the ending—at first—was this backward montage at double speed—triple speed—showing the story rewinding all the way back, scene by scene, backward—denouement to beginning, so the characters *undevelop*, back through to the opening scene, to the opening credits, and, finally, back through that to the director in his—uh, her—chair, through the set, outside the set, zooming through the tunnel of the unconscious, and ending with the writer putting down his pen."

Q: Wow.

A: But that didn't pan out, so to speak. I rewrote that.

Q: You are a writer, correct? You also wrote the movie.

A: Yes, I wrote it.

Q: So, naturally, you are a word person.

A: Unnaturally, perhaps. (She laughs.)

Q: Tell us the storyline.

A: Oh, a recounting of the storyline only bores. I'll leave it to the trailer people to capture it.

Q: Rumors have it that the film is all about sex. That its sex scenes will surpass all previous sex scenes. This is hyperbole, I imagine.

A: I sense a question in there. The sex in *Memphis Movie*? It's real, not in the sense that the actors engaged in actual intercourse on film, but in the sense that it is true.

Q: And there is a lot of it?

A: I don't know what a lot is. Listen. It is all about sex, filmmaking I mean. Hollywood breathes in sex and exhales sex. Every scene in every damn movie is about sex, about seduction, about man wanting woman and woman wanting man or man to man, woman to woman. Every scene. You get me? *E. T.* Watch it closely, it's about sex, desire. *Raiders of the Lost Ark, Romancing the Stone.* What are they in actual fact looking for? The old in-out. Consummation. *Bambi. Godzilla.* Sex is all Hollywood knows. Or, what's the biggest damn movie of the past decade, *Titanic.* Jesus, sex sex sex. *Ram that iceberg!* Hell, it may be an accurate representation of the world. Maybe sex is the only question and the only answer. In Hollywood everyone sits around watching themselves. You see?

Q: Well, that's certainly a provocative statement.

A: I was not aiming at provocation.

Q: Well, quickly, Sandy, before we have to end, can you give me a plot summary, *something*, a reason you finished the movie and Eric could not, something in the writing? Something in Eric Warberg's character and the movie's premise? What about *Memphis Movie* drove Eric away and brought you onboard?

A: (After a long pause) I'm sure I don't know what you're getting at. *Memphis Movie*, which may be renamed—they are now playing with titles—*Ralph Meeker's Blues* is one, *Bananas on Bananas* another, and there was a cryptic message left on my voice mail—a young girl's voice—with I believe another suggestion, *Boo Enema*, imagine that, *Boo Enema*—or my choice, which is *Regicide*—but this movie exists because of Eric Warberg. It is Eric's movie. And I will tell you this last thing—maybe it's important; maybe it's only another soap bubble. Here is the tagline they will use to sell this movie. Ok?

Q: Yes, please.

A: "In Memphis he went searching for soul. Unfortunately, he lost his."

Q: That's it?

A: That's it.

DELETED SCENES

Eric and the Ghost of Sergei Eisenstein

Eric had grown frustrated with the day's shooting. They only had the one scene scheduled but everyone seemed to be off their game. He had repeatedly told Kim not to block the key. Even after explaining to her what that meant she continued her histrionic movements. He wanted to shackle her.

He headed to the men's room during a break. There he splashed his face with cold water and stood long before the mirror. The face in the mirror was his and not his. He didn't know how long the little man had been sitting there before he noticed him. He was suddenly in the mirror as if his portrait had just developed.

Eric turned to face him. He looked familiar. The nose, the strong jaw . . .

"Hello, Eric," the man said.

"Do I know you?" Eric rightly asked.

"You do," he said.

"I'm sorry—I—"

"I am Sergei Eisenstein," the man said. Even his smile looked grim.

"Another ghost then," Eric said.

"Yes, if you like."

"Whether I like it or not. Apparently, the line between the dead and the living has become smudged."

"Other specters, then," Eisenstein said.

"Yes—my father repeatedly."

"One's father is omnipresent. Death does not diminish that."

"Yes. I see."

"How's the shoot?"

"Frustrating."

"Always, always. Do you know how many times I shot that damn baby carriage?"

"No, that is, I have read . . . somewhere."

"At any rate. Stay with it. You are the visionary. Everything else is just—lunch."

"Yes," Eric said, uncertainly.

"Watch some of the master's work, Eric. Study your predecessors. I had no such luxury."

"You—you were like God. You practically invented the language of film."

"Ach, nice of you to say. We did what we could. I was an architect, in a way, an engineer. We were working in a new medium. The field was wide open. A liberating feeling at times. At times overwhelming."

"I can see that."

"Go home and watch *Nevsky*. Watch *Sunrise*. *Pandora's Box*. Any Chaplin. Chaplin worked those fields as if he were alone. And perhaps he was, alone on the mountain. Watch *Napoleon*. Gance, goddammit, he was so *ferocious*. Pay attention to where his camera stops."

"Yes, thank you. I've seen all the films you mentioned. *Sunrise*—what a masterpiece!"

"Don't just *see* the films, Eric. Study them. Inspect."

"Yes, sir." Eric felt as if he were in school. Or heaven.

"Oh, and Eric."

"Yes—"

"*Snow White and the Seven Dwarfs*. It's the finest film ever made. I still believe that."

And his image flickered and was gone.

Sandy and Jimbo after the fight

"He said to me, 'You're a stoop.' So I hit him."

"But—"

"He called me a stoop!"

"No, dear, he said astute. You're astute."

"What's a stoot?"

"Astute. One word."

"There is such a word?"

"Yes. There is."

"What does it mean?"

Eric and Sandy in the morning

"Did I wake you?"

"I didn't know I was asleep."

"So I woke you?"

"I didn't know I was asleep until I wasn't."

"Uh-huh."

"There's a metaphor there but I need coffee first."

"Who needs metaphors?"

"Ortega y Gasset said something or other about the metaphor."

"Uh-huh."

"Can I just have coffee before we continue?"

"Is this to be continued?"

"Coffee?"

More Sue Pine

Sue Pine took the last flight out of Memphis on a damp, dark Memphis evening. She found her aisle seat and watched as the flight attendants moved up and down the plane with their synthetic smiles. One attendant, a burly male who could have played tight end in college, stopped in front of her seat.

"Sorry," he said, his blond hair like styled flower petals. "I know you . . . "

"I don't think so," Sue Pine said.

"Are you on TV?"

"Are you supposed to chat up female passengers?" Sue asked with a feline smile.

"No," he said, quickly. "I am not. I really am not."

His apprehension made Sue repentant.

"I'm sorry. I won't narc on you. My name is Sue, Sue Pine."

"Willie. Waugh." He shook her beautifully manicured hand.

"You may have seen me. I'm an actress. I just finished shooting the Eric Warberg picture."

"Oh, Jesus. With Dan Yumont?"

"Yes, that's right."

The poor swain was speechless. He was also handsome as mountain snow.

"You wanna be in pictures?" Sue asked. She retook his hand and tickled his palm as if it were his foreskin.

Willie Waugh's beam spread across his face like mercury on glass.

"I think maybe you are a dangerous woman," he said, still smiling.

"You have no idea," Sue Pine said.

On Babel

Camel took his time answering when Lorax asked him if he would critique her newest painting. He rubbed the stubble on his chin, thoughtfully.

"I'm not sure a critique is what you want from me," he said finally. It still sounded wrong.

Lorax's face went through a few contortions.

"But, Camel, dear, what do I want? I want you to see it," she said.

"Yes," Camel said. "It's just—never mind. Let's look at it."

"And you'll tell me what you really think," she added.

"Yes, of course," Camel said.

They walked the 20 feet to the next room as if they had been called by forces beyond their own control. Lorax held Camel's hand.

Camel wangled his way in front of the canvas. The room was small and chaotic. He felt sorry he could not have offered her a better space.

Camel felt as if his eyes were blurring. He blinked many times. What was he seeing?

"I wanna call it 'On Babel,'" Lorax said.

The painting was of the Tower of Babel but it was a modern view, so far from Brueghel's as to be in a different medium. Camel was sure that Lorax had never seen the Brueghel. She was painting from ignorance, and from that *other place*.

"Sweetheart," Camel said, moving slowing forward and slowly back, "I am momentarily stunned into silence."

Lorax stood patiently by. She was not sure what her Camel meant. She began to feel dread in her chest, a painful little thrum.

"It's magnificent, of course," Camel said. "It's beyond magnificent. It's marvelous, as in full of marvels."

"You like it?" Lorax sang. She executed a little dance in what space was there. She may as well have been a brownie on a toadstool. Camel laughed, his great face crinkling with pleasure.

"I do. I like it very much, Lorax," he said.

"You said my name," she said, stopping her twirl.

"Yes. Is that ok?"

"You have never said, have you?"

"I'm not sure," Camel said. He watched her young face wrinkle.

"I'd rather call you My Paramour," he said, quickly.

"Yes, that's it," she said. But neither of them knew what she meant.

"My Paramour," Camel said. "Your painting. It seems to grow beyond the canvas. It seems to occupy a liminal space outside the physical world, outside of time."

"Wow," Lorax said. "They are trying to reach Heaven."

"Yes."

"Yes."

"These figures toiling, climbing, moving toward their false goal, their false gods . . . I recognize some faces, don't I?"

"I think so," Lorax said.

"They're—movie people."

"Yes, some of them are," she said.

"Hm," Camel said. He put his face nearly flush against the canvas.

"They're climbing, climbing . . . " Lorax sang.

"Yes. It's quite a struggle for them, isn't it? A meaningless struggle, you might say, except that all struggles have meaning."

"You say nice things, Camel," Lorax said.

"You paint wonders," he answered.

"Camel. My Parapet."

"Yes, dear."

"Do you want to know my real name?"

ACKNOWLEDGMENTS

A portion of this novel appeared in *Southern Gothic*, edited by Jeff Crook, and another in *Alice Blue*, and another in *A cappella Zoo*, and another in *The Prague Revue*.

Special thanks to my readers Terry Bazes, Peter Coyote, Chris Ellis, Nicki Newburger, and Joel Rose.

SELECTED BIBLIOGRAPHY

"The Chronosynclastic Filmmaking of Eric Warberg." Stanley Kauffmann. *The New Republic*, August 1990.

"But No One Wants to Be Eric Warberg." Aleah Sato. *The Sum Times*, January 1994.

"Eric Warberg: The Director Interview." Chris Agee. *Filmmaker Magazine*, November 1994.

"Eric Warberg and the Culture of Dissolution." Creole Myers. *Film Forum*, January 1995.

"*Sunset Striptease*: What Eric Warberg isn't Telling Us." Jojo Self. *Premiere*, August 1995.

"Kiss Kiss Wink Wink: Eric Warberg's *When I See Beverly*." Andrew Sarris. *The Village Voice*, September 1997.

"Sandy Shoars and Eric Warberg: A Marriage Made in Stop-Motion." Creole Myers. *Premiere*, February 2000.

"Eric Warberg: From *Shlomo Stern* to *Spondulicks*: Can Anybody Here Direct a Movie?" Jay Cocks. *Time*, April 2005.

The Films of Eric Warberg. Stefan Kanfer, ed. New York: Grove Press, 2005.

"Stuck Inside of Memphis with the Eric Warberg Blues." Luke Apenail. *Newsweek*, September 2007.

BOOKS BY COREY MESLER

POETRY

For Toby, Everything for Toby (1997), Wing & the Wheel Press.
Ten Poets (1999), editor only, Wing & the Wheel Press.
Piecework (2000), Wing & the Wheel Press.
Chin-Chin in Eden (2003), Still Waters Press.
Dark on Purpose (2004), Little Poem Press.
The Agoraphobe's Pandiculations (2006), Little Poem Press.
The Hole in Sleep (2006), Wood Works Press.
The Lita Conversation (2006), Southern Hum.
The Chloe Poems (2007), Maverick Duck Press.
Some Identity Problems (2007), Foothills Publishing.
Pictures from Lang and Follini (2007), Sheltering Pines Press.
Grit (2008), Amsterdam Press.
The Tense Past (2010), Flutter Press.
Before the Great Troubling (2011), Unbound Content.
The Heart Is Open (2011), Right Hand Pointing.
To Writing You (2012), Origami Poetry Project.
Mitmensch (2013), Folded Word.
Our Locust Years (2013), Unbound Content.
My Father Is Still Dying (2013), Flutter Press.
Body (2013), Chapbook Journal.
The Catastrophe of my Personality (2014), Blue Hour Press.
The Sky Needs More Work (2014), Upper Rubber Boot Books.
The Medicament Predicament (2014), Redneck Press.
Stone (2015), Origami Poems (chapbook).

PROSE

Talk: A Novel in Dialogue (2002), Livingston Press.
We Are Billion-Year-Old Carbon (2005), Livingston Press.
Short Story and Other Short Stories (2006), Parallel Press.
Following Richard Brautigan (chapbook, 2006), Plan B Press.
Publisher (2007), Writers Write Journal Press.
Listen: 29 Short Conversations (2009), Brown Paper Press.
The Ballad of the Two Tom Mores (2010), Bronx River Press.
Following Richard Brautigan (full-length novel, 2010), Livingston Press.
Notes Toward the Story and Other Stories (2011), Aqueous Books.
I'll Give You Something to Cry About (2011), Queens Ferry Press.
Diddy-Wah-Diddy: A Beale Street Suite (2013), Ampersand Books.
As a Child: Stories (2014), MadHat Press.